| AUTHOR | CLASS |
|--------|-------|
| POLAND, M | F   G |
| TITLE   Train to | No |
| Doringbult | G 02328693 |

# TRAIN TO DORINGBULT

# TRAIN TO DORINGBULT

# Marguerite Poland

THE BODLEY HEAD
LONDON

British Library Cataloguing in Publication Data
Poland, Marguerite
Train to Doringbult.
I. Title
823 [F] PR 9369.3.P

ISBN 0 370 31051 9

Printed in Great Britain for
The Bodley Head Ltd
32 Bedford Square London W C I B 3 EL

by The Bath Press, Avon

A glossary of Afrikaans and Xhosa words
appears at the back of the book

## ACKNOWLEDGEMENTS

Many people gave their support while I was writing this book; family, friends and those who, in themselves, were an inspiration to me.

For the help and encouragement as well as for the laughs, frustrations, triumphs, journeys and good times so generously shared by all in their different ways — my love and my deepest thanks.

Marguerite Poland
DURBAN 1986

FOR MARTIN

The light, just rising cobra-coloured up above the *bult*, was fading out to green, to white. Still the ridge was dark, shadowed with euphorbias, with *gwarri* and *karee* and a cold wind was washing in across the lands and down towards the Rooikloof where thickets, clustered at the *krantz*'s lip, loomed like huddled cattle, branches white as horn.

Near the house a pair of *dikkops* ran back and forth across the lawn and Elsa, standing alone in the darkness of the kitchen window (she had not lit the lamp) watched them circle in towards their nest beneath the hedge.

She was still absorbed, the unfilled kettle in her hand, when Jan came in. 'Coffee will be ready in a moment,' Elsa said without looking round. She had known that it was Jan; he had descended the stairs silently, missing the fourth which creaked. Only those that had lived long in the old house knew how to move without sound. There—Adrian, the snap of a footfall: he had forgotten.

'Morning! Morning! Morning!'—affable Adrian rubbing his hands together. He put his arm round Elsa and said, 'Jan's a lucky chap! I wish my wife would make me coffee in the morning. She'll be burrowed in that bed till ten if you don't throw her out. Farm girls are worth their weight in gold— not so, *kleinboet*?'

But Jan had already gone outside, down the path between the sweet-thorns to the workers' houses to call up the beaters.

Elsa hooked her pale hair behind her ear and said lightly, 'A lot of good I'd be with all that entertaining and socializing you do in Grahamstown.'

Adrian laughed, his belly pouched neatly above his belt, his round face bluish in the gloom, his teeth spaced apart, oddly predatory.

9

Elsa lit the lamp and set the kettle on the stove. Adrian went to the window and glanced out. 'What do you want for your larder, Elsa?'

'Anything. A guineafowl or two would be nice.' She pushed a rucksack over to him. 'I've made some sandwiches. There are rusks and *biltong* and a can to boil water. The coffee and sugar are in those jars and there's salt for Jan.'

'Still puts salt in his coffee? He's just like Pa.' He did not hide the condescension.

Elsa said nothing. Instead she turned to the lamp and adjusted the wick, steadying the flame.

Jan's elder brother Adrian de Villiers only came to the farm to hunt. At other times he rarely bothered to drive up from Grahamstown to see them. But now he had arrived for a long weekend—August and the season running late—and brought his wife Elizabeth and their pretty children: daughters with their dolls' prams glossy with plastic upholstery, a small son, clean-faced, curly-haired, who chased sheep and threw stones underhand into the dam.

Jan took his brother on a customary inspection. They walked around the yard and outbuildings.

'Why's the gutter hanging?'

'Time. Money.' Jan shrugged.

The gutters had always sagged, heavy with the leaves of the pepper trees. That was not important. Not as important as the goats and the sheep, their lambing, their shearing, their dipping or banking eroded gullies and keeping machinery repaired.

Jan laughed and fobbed him off.

Elsa felt a familiar irritation. Adrian arrived from Grahamstown full of big talk. What did he know of the sharp winter mornings when Jan, raw-fingered, struggled with the tractor or the pump? What did he know of the long hours soothing a cow through labour or walking a horse with colic in the night, Petrus taking turns to keep it moving? He only saw the balance sheets at the end of the quarter, assessed his share in the profits of Blackheath and filed them away.

When they were boys Jan and Adrian had explored the lands together, fished the dam, shot birds in the orchard.

But now Adrian only saw what *kleinboet* had failed to do. Always '*kleinboet*', and so it seemed when he sat at table imprisoned in his jacket and tie, his straight dark hair obedient, wetted flat against his skull. But out there in the lands Adrian trailed behind him, sweating and irritable and Jan would go ahead with a quiet satisfaction.

Jan returned, blowing his nose loudly. 'It's cold. You ready to face the frost?' He turned to the window and glanced out. A truck was making its way up the farm road. 'Here's Kobie,' said Jan. 'Make him some coffee, Els.'

Big Kobie blustered through the flyscreen across the kitchen door. 'Hello people! Adrian!' He thrust out his hand. 'How's it, Jan?' He turned to Elsa. 'Hello Elsie.' He kissed her. The bristles of his moustache were rough against her skin.

'Good to see you again, Kobie. How are you?' said Adrian.

'Ag man, no complaints, hey Jan? Except that we're going to have a hell of a drought. *Yirra* it's tough being a farmer! Good for you guys in the law though. With everyone going bankrupt you'll make a killing, hey Jan?'

'I've got an interest in this farm too you know,' said Adrian. 'When things are bad on Blackheath they're bad for me.'

'Here Kobie, have a rusk,' interrupted Elsa. She offered the tin around.

'Thanks Elsie,' he said, sending her a wink. 'Annatjie says she'll be over with the kids before lunch.' He turned to Adrian. 'So, what's it to be today Adrian? *Rhebok?* Guineafowl?'

'Everything! It's a long time since I had a rifle in my hands.'

'Right,' said Jan. 'I'm ready when you are.' He put his arm around Elsa's shoulders and kissed her on the top of the head. 'Stay well, love.'

'Take care of yourself, Jannie,' she replied softly.

They went out, Adrian striding ahead. They climbed into Jan's truck. The beaters boarded at the back, hoisting each other over the tailboard. Elsa knew them all: Chrissie's elder son Bongani, the herder's nephew, old Nontinti's grandsons Abedingo and his younger brother Sipho, smaller children tagging behind.

Their voices, their laughter, were sharp in the winter

11

morning. Abedingo got up last. The tallest, he stood legs astride, holding onto the roof-bar, his balaclava pulled over his face, his younger brother Sipho huddled at his feet. He looked down at Elsa standing in the doorway and she raised her hand. He had often done odd jobs in the garden, washed cars, fetched milk from the dairy. A small intense young man, he kept to himself except that Sipho always followed him, carried his tools, pushed the barrow for him or simply walked beside him, his wire car jingling as it rattled over the lawn.

The dawn was quiet after they had gone. A *bulbul* alighted in the birdbath, fluttering its wings. It flicked its tail and flew over the quince hedge into the orchard.

Soon the shadows would be gone. The long lingering slant of the outbuildings across the yard would retreat in the bright winter morning and the time would go slowly from tea to lunch to tea with the sounds of the shots echoing across the lands.

Jan glanced up at the sky. The willows down by the *vlei* stood bare in the stubble of the earth. He stooped to pull burrs from his socks. Adrian and Kobie were sweating, striding out beside him. The beaters—small tattered creatures in shorts, and skippers, or long-sleeved tee-shirts, here, there, a holey balaclava, an old black blazer—drifted along effortlessly.

Jan directed them with a word, a gesture, a whistle. They knew the routine well. Already a pile of birds with blood-congealed feathers lay under a bush, tended by a child.

Jan sat down at the edge of the gulley and waited. Adrian and Kobie stood with their guns, impatient for the beaters to send the guineafowl in their direction.

'There don't seem to be many birds around here anymore,' said Kobie. 'Same on my place.'

'There used to be thousands,' remarked Adrian. 'Those bloody *kwedinis* have been poaching again. You must do something about it Jan.'

Jan shrugged. 'Of course they poach. They only get a few.'

'Leaving the poor bloody bird to strangle in a noose.'

'Any better than blasting them out of their roosts like you did last time?'

12

He slid down into the *donga* and Adrian and Kobie crept ahead, raising their heads every now and then to listen for the beaters.

Jan looked out across the stubble. A flock of guineafowl ran diagonally towards them. Run, listen, contact, with the small creaking sound of a gate opening: necks outstretched, men and flock converging. The men bobbed up. The birds stopped to chutter among themselves. Adrian had his shotgun against his shoulder. The birds turned and ran, wide-haunched, casques bouncing.

'Shit!' muttered Adrian.

Jan laughed.

Elsa took the teacake out of the oven. Nella peered into the tin. 'Can we have some now, Mummy? Do you want cake?' she asked her cousins, dragging at the arm of the smallest.

'Smells divine,' murmured Elizabeth de Villiers, Adrian's wife. She perched on the kitchen table and crossed her long legs. She gazed at her reflection in the window pane, stretched her neck to see herself better. 'I've spent a fortune at that hairdresser and he's made me look like a tart,' she said.

'Don't be silly, Liz. Your hair is always lovely.'

'But when it grows—you should see the roots!' she exclaimed. 'I always put on so much weight here,' she complained. 'Cellulite! It's like cottage cheese forced into a sausage skin.'

'You make me sick Lizabeth!' said Annatjie de Jager who had arrived with a carload of daughters and a nanny in attendance. She plumped up her short, bleached hair and lit a cigarette. 'You're the only one we ever knew who was a Rag Queen.'

'I was thin then.'

'Man,' said Annatjie. 'I got so fat with my kids!'

'That's no excuse,' said Elizabeth. 'You have to work at it to keep your figure.' She stretched, shook her hair back. Wheat-pale and thick, it hung to her shoulders.

Annatjie glanced down at her own stout thighs and said impatiently. 'I don't know why you complain. You make me and Elsie look like a pair of porkers!'

13

'Whose fault is that?' retorted Elizabeth. 'I can tell a farmer's wife a mile away! It always amazes me that you people have so little individuality. I'd really like to take Elsa on a shopping spree.' She giggled. 'Can you imagine Jan's face when I present him with the bill. But really Els, it's your own fault if Jan's mean about a clothes allowance . . .'

'Who said Jan was mean?' said Elsa.

'Well then, next time you come to town let's take the day off and go to Port Elizabeth together.'

Elsa did not reply. She eased the cake from the tin and the children clustered round. Nella sucked a finger singed from trying to pry a cherry from the crust.

'Shall we walk to the dam after tea?' said Elsa.

'I'll show them *Thekwane*'s nest up in the tree.'

'What's that?' asked Elizabeth's small son.

'A bird.'

'My Dad's going to shoot all the birds and bring them home. He's got a huge big gun. Pow! Pow! Pow!' He ran outside followed by the others. He found a stick. 'Pow! Pow! Pow!' he cried, jerking it to his shoulder.

'You can't shoot *Thekwane*,' cried Nella in alarm. 'Nontinti says you'll die in a *donga* and the crows will pick out your eyes.'

'Nella only has a weird imagination, Elsa!' said Annatjie. She scooped her daughter from the floor and wiped her face which was sludged with rusk. 'Come,' she said tenderly, 'Mommy will make you clean.'


Abedingo slung the guineafowl across his shoulder. He tossed another to Sipho and backed down the ditch where a fence straddled it. There, in a runnel in the grass, he checked his bird snare. It was empty. He glanced about. The men with their guns were sitting near the *spruit* boiling water in a tin. Abedingo thrust the guineafowl he was carrying into the grass. He would fetch it later.

'What about a bushbuck, Kobie?' said Adrian.

'Why not? Let's try Rooikloof,' suggested Kobie.

Jan said, 'I haven't seen any bushbuck for a long time. I'd rather we left them alone.'

'The place used to be lousy with them.'

Jan said nothing. The farm was Adrian's as much as his. He emptied his cup. 'Come on then.'

He walked across the lands, following the *spruit*. He branched off towards the Rooikloof. He turned to the beaters. 'Abedingo,' he gestured down into the *poort*. '*Nkonka!* Bushbuck.'

Abedingo nodded reluctantly.

'Go home,' he said to the other beaters. 'Take the birds to the house.' They stood uncertainly, disappointed, the guineafowl hanging limply in their hands. '*Godukani!*' he repeated.

Kobie and Adrian were loading their rifles. They laid their shotguns under a bush. Jan propped his rifle against a branch. He would never hunt the Rooikloof.

Abedingo hitched up his shorts and said something softly to his brother Sipho. The boy sniffed and looked down the slope. He picked his ear thoughtfully, then nodded. Abedingo started along the path with Jan, skirted him and went ahead. They disappeared into the undergrowth. Kobie and Adrian followed. The beaters turned back across the *veld*, the birds divided between them.

The boy Sipho stood on the lip of the *krantz*. Already the white men were far down the slope, Abedingo leading them away from the snare set in the game path where the contours of the gorge converged. Sipho hurried along the edge of the ravine, going carefully towards the snare to see if anything had been trapped.

A *hamerkop* lumbered up. Jan watched its wing shadow jigsaw on fragments of stone, steady small and swift across a *krantz*. It turned ponderously, sank down among the trees. He felt a slight unease as he followed the pattern of its flight. He knew *Thekwane*, the gaunt-winged *hamerkop*, relic of a pterodactyl, an ancient bird that wades in *vleis* and sees the destinies of men reflected from the sky. There—a star streams: someone's heart has fallen over. *Thekwane*, seeing it, dedicates another of its feathers to the dead. Jan looked away irritated. He was absorbing Elsa's own strange cosmology, full of birds and stars, creatures and beliefs taken from her father Norman Southey and from old Nontinti.

15

A small stone arched and skidded in the sand at his feet. He looked up. Abedingo crouched above him on a rock, gesturing with his head. The men ascended the slope quietly.

Sipho inspected the trap. It was empty. He peered through the bush. He wondered where the white men were, wondered if he should go down further to the other snare set near the stream. He looked again. There was no movement, no sound. Then a shot rang out, a flat, dull crack. Birds rose from unseen places, flew round and settled again as the echoes died.

'Not the best shot Kobie!' Adrian laughed.

Kobie looked sour. 'Anyway, it was only a *duiker*.'

'Where are the bushbuck?' said Adrian to Abedingo.

'*Icashile!*' It is hiding. Abedingo grinned and moved his shoulders as though forcing his way through thickets.

Adrian pointed back up the *kloof*. 'Let's try the waterfall end.'

'Right.' Kobie checked the breach of his rifle.

Abedingo shuffled. '*Hayi!*' He shook his head.

'We won't find it here in the open places,' remarked Adrian impatiently.

Abedingo did not look at him. He scanned the slope. Nothing stirred. He followed behind the men.

Elsa went out into the afternoon. The children ran ahead. Elizabeth's boy still carried his stick gun. 'Pow! Pow! Pow!' he cried, aiming at a startled dove. Elizabeth and Annatjie wandered down the path. Elizabeth walked, arms folded, hugging herself against the cold wind. Elsa breathed in the dust of the cart track. She could smell the dryness of the bush, the pungency of dung and urine near the water trough where the earth was churned into mud.

She heard the shot. She turned her head. It had come from Rooikloof. She must be mistaken. Jan would never hunt there: not since the time when they had picnicked at the stream, five, six years before. Elsa had been pregnant with Nella and Jan had guided her down the slope with that strange unsolicited tenderness of his. They had seen a pair of bushbuck under the trees in half-light. The buck returned their gaze

16

with the same watchful stillness. They had been there many times since then—on Sundays: just Jan and Nella and herself, the dogs left behind so that nothing could disturb the silence of the *poort*.

Elizabeth was elaborating on the trials of her sister's labour. Annatjie interrupted with a story of her own. Annatjie's confinements were legendary in the district. Elizabeth had no choice but to listen once again. The children ran ahead, down to the dam.

Sipho crept under the bigger trees. The warmth of the upper slopes that had lain in the thin, flat sunlight was gone. The cold of the late afternoon pushed up through the soles of his feet.

The trap was close. It had been made from a strand of wire stripped from a fence right off on the border of the farm. He crouched down and wriggled his way along the trail. Sipho grinned. A bushbuck lay on the ground, its neck in the noose. There would be meat again today, tomorrow, longer.

The buck was alive. Its eyes were hooded, its legs limp, its breathing so shallow, Sipho wondered if it breathed at all. Then it moved an ear. Flies and grubs and mites had gathered there, sucking the ooze of nostrils. Sipho had no knife to cut its throat. He feared the small strong horns. He crept closer to the animal. It hardly moved. He slipped his fingers down the wire, tightening it. The buck jerked convulsively, the beetles scattered, the flies rose angrily from its nose. Sipho jerked the wire again. The buck kicked once, its hooves thrashing at the undergrowth.

Sipho looked up, startled by another movement. The buck was heaving and choking. A shot exploded through the leaves. A deep silence, after-shock of shots, fell across the *kloof*. And then the flies were back, frenzied predators of blood.

Elsa heard the second shot, a counter-note to the sound of stones plopping into the dam which the children were tossing from the bank. Egrets flying home across the pale sky seemed to check in flight, re-form and head on towards the

17

roosting trees in Rooikloof. She looked at her watch. Four-thirty. The sun was low above the *bult*.

'We'd better go,' she said.

'Why?' cried Nella.

'It's not late,' said Annatjie. 'Jan and them won't be back for ages.'

'Let's go,' she said again, finding no explanation for her need.

Crows squabbled in the lands. Elsa turned from their loud ungainly capering. The dark crept up the Rooikloof, the stubble of the fallow land stretched to the edge of the *krantz*, netting the earth with its small withered death.

'Christ! It's a coon!' shouted Kobie. 'Adrian, you shot a coon, you bloody fool! I told you not to shoot!'

Adrian and Jan ripped apart the branches of the bush. Abedingo stood behind them, ashen. Crumpled across the body of a bushbuck lay a boy. Abedingo did not look further than the small calloused feet that curled against each other. The wind lifted the edge of the old black blazer.

'Who is he?' whispered Adrian, his teeth clenched against the vomit in his throat.

Jan stooped to the body. 'Sipho,' he said.

'Is he dead?'

'Of course he's bloody dead,' said Kobie. 'You blew his head apart.'

Jan squatted by the boy, eyes averted, only the small feet and the dirt-grey knees within the range of vision. A horsefly waded in the blood, wing-trapped in the ooze. Sipho lay, his arms flung out, his fingers limp, the small swimming hands of a newly-emerged frog, seemingly boneless.

Jan looked around for Abedingo. He called. His voice rang flat against the *krantzes*. There—the *hamerkop* again. It rose, dragging up its wings.

'Abedingo!'

There was no reply.

Abedingo walked away with the silence learnt in setting many snares. He climbed the slope to the lip of the *kloof*. He paused at the place where the white men's guns rested against the bush. He reached out for Jan's rifle and wrapped it in his jacket. Then he took the bag of ammunition. He went alone across the fallow land, through a fence and along the road that carved a path around the *koppie*'s edge.

Abedingo Ngubane crossed the grid and passed—a fugitive—the old stone gates of the farm called Blackheath.

It was Elsa who stayed with the boy while Jan and Adrian, hunched against the cold, went down to the workers' houses to speak to old Nontinti, the boy's grandmother. Quietly she slipped into the shed where the body lay in the back of the truck, covered with a sack.

As she pulled open the shed door her foot touched something soft. It moved like shored dust, retreating under pressure, light against the leather of her shoe. She looked down and saw the pile of guineafowl left by the children. Stiff, dark-spotted feathers curved to back and breast, heads intertwined in death: pale blue skin, glutinous casques, eyes closed with a scale of membrane, bodies punctured by the small, hard searing grains of shot.

She took a blanket for the child and covered him. She turned from his face. She looked no further than the khaki shorts. They had been bought at the farm store some days before. She had taken them from the wholesaler's box in their stiff plastic wrapper, unpinned the starched creases and shaken them out for Nontinti's inspection. Nontinti had brought the boy forward and measured the shorts against him, smoothing them with her hand. The child had watched, his eyes darting every now and then to the sweet box behind the packets of instant beer mix.

Nontinti had considered a long time, holding the shorts and feeling their newness. She had paid for them and slipped them into the folds of her shawl.

Elsa tucked the blanket round the boy, remembering Nontinti's careful fingers smoothing the hem above his knee. Lambs, goats, sacks, pump equipment would all be carried in that truck in time. But on the floor, for her, would always be, traced out on the ribbing, the small figure of the child who had gone to check a snare: Sipho Ngubane in his khaki shorts.

Elsa returned to the house. She could hear Adrian speaking on the telephone, his voice urgent. 'If you could just go to the police station, Uncle Cedric. No, I can't talk on the phone. Will you do that?'

She pushed past him and went into the living room where Jan stood by the fireplace. Kobie, Annatjie and Elizabeth sat around silently.

'What are we going to do Jan?' she said.

'We'll take the body to the police station,' he replied hoarsely.

'Nontinti?'

'Chrissie's with her now. And Petrus.'

Adrian came in. 'Uncle Cedric will meet us in town. Let's go.'

'I'll be off then,' said Kobie. 'Let me know if I can do anything, hey?' He drained his glass of brandy. 'Get the kids, Annatjie,' he said. He put his hand on Jan's shoulder as he hurried from the room. 'See you,' he said.

The air was cold and star-bright with wind. The branches of the pepper trees surged above the roof of the shed. Adrian held open the doors as Jan backed the truck.

Jan drove along the farm road. Adrian fumbled for a cigarette and flicked the match out into the gloom.

'What the hell am I going to tell the police?' he said.

'You're the Advocate, not me,' said Jan.

'Jesus!' Adrian held the cigarette to his mouth. His fingers shook. 'Where do you think that coon's gone with the gun?'

'I don't know.'

'We could say he did it—fooling around with the rifle and it went off by mistake and he ran away in panic?'

'Don't be an arse, Adrian. You can't use Abedingo as a scapegoat.'

'Why not? Christ Jan—what about the inquest! Do you want me to end up in court for culpable homicide?'

'No—of course not. But what about Abedingo?'

'Indirectly, it was his fault.'

'Crap!' Jan snorted. 'How can you blame him?'

'The publicity would bloody ruin my practice.' Adrian

ground out his cigarette on the floor. 'Uncle Cedric better make a good case for me with Captain Olivier.'

Jan said nothing. He gazed out at the night. Like a film which has come loose from its sprockets, the landscape jiggered past the windscreen.

Adrian reached for another cigarette. His face was sweating and he breathed heavily through his nose. In the dark the road peeled back before the headlights. They drove on in silence towards the town.

Cedric de Villiers' big car was parked outside the police station.

'Thank God he's here!' said Adrian.

He got out and hurried to Uncle Cedric waiting in the doorway. Uncle Cedric, taller than Adrian, stooped in his loose tweed jacket, put his arm briefly round his nephew's shoulders and guided him into the building. Jan went round to the back of the truck and adjusted the blanket over the boy, pushing it in under him with reluctant fingers. Then he followed Adrian inside.

A black constable was leaning desultorily against the counter. He nodded at Jan and indicated a closed door to his left. Jan knocked and went in.

Cedric de Villiers had taken charge. With his hands behind his back, he walked about the room as Adrian spoke, smoking a cigarette and chewing at his false teeth in concentration. The Station Commander, Captain Olivier, sat at his desk, leaning back in his chair, a pencil balanced between his fingers. Adrian addressed them both as he might address the court, authoritative in mitigation for what he'd done. No one spoke to Jan.

'What d'you think, Koos? What d'you say?' Uncle Cedric interrupted every now and then, glancing over at Captain Olivier. 'What if there's an inquest?' He turned to Adrian. 'We'll sort things out, you mark my words Adrian. Koos here can turn his mind to anything.'

Captain Olivier enjoyed the seat of power. His small mouth opened and closed, opened and closed beneath the stencilled moustache. He wrote out the forms and necessary documents. 'I'll be speaking to the Magistrate,' he said. 'He's a good friend of mine. He'll hold the inquest in chambers. Private, you know.' He waved his hand expansively. 'You don't have to worry. It was an accident, after all. The story won't get out. It's a simple matter.'

He folded the affadavit that Adrian had signed, put it in a drawer. Sipho Ngubane's life was filed away—the manner of his death.

Captain Olivier stood, at that moment as affable as Adrian. And yet, the edge of obsequiousness was there, the deference for people as wealthy and as powerful as the de Villiers. Jan could imagine him—at a police *braai* perhaps—saying 'Yes, I'm a personal friend of Advocate de Villiers—know him well. I did him a favour once.' His expression would be smug, but closed to prying. 'He won't forget Koos Olivier in a hurry. That I can tell you for free!' And the sergeants and the new lieutenants would be impressed.

Captain Olivier hitched up his pants. He ran his thumbs around the inside of his belt. He held out his hand to Cedric. 'Mr de Villiers, it's been a pleasure!' To Adrian, 'Advocate.' At last he came to Jan, smiling. Jan took his hand briefly, giving no further acknowledgement. He could not share in the general satisfaction.

'We'll find the boy with the gun, Advocate,' the Captain said to Adrian. 'We'll bring him back.'

'No charge for him,' said Adrian magnanimously. 'He's a young fellow and he got a fright. I'm certain he'll be home in a day or two. We can only hope he will.'

Jan turned to the window with distaste. Adrian had been ready to use Abedingo as a scapegoat. He would have done it, without question, if Captain Olivier had been unsympathetic, if he hadn't arranged the papers and put them in the drawer and said gravely, 'Well, Advocate, I think we can say the matter is settled. The inquest will pass—shall we say, unnoticed or postponed, or whatever seems to be best.'

Jan leant tiredly on the windowsill. He could see his truck parked out in the open lot, the hump of the boy's body in the back, so small and abandoned where it lay.

Away from his seat behind his desk Koos Olivier became the middle-ranking policeman once again and Adrian, imperceptibly, resumed his tone of gracious condescension. He said to Jan, 'I'll go on with Uncle Cedric if you don't mind Jan. Liz was very upset and I'd like to get home. You'll follow, will you, once the Captain's disposed—you know . . .'

He turned back to Captain Olivier, 'Thank you again,' he said. 'You've been a great help. I'll say a word to the Commissioner, you can be sure. We need men like you in the force.' On and on.

Cedric clapped Koos Olivier on the shoulder, shook his hand vigorously and steered Adrian towards the car. They drove away. The big lights arched smoothly across the yard. Then they were gone and Jan stood in the darkness with Captain Olivier.

'Right,' said the policeman. 'Where's the corpse? I'll get someone to bring it in. Djantjes!' he shouted.

The black constable appeared at the window.

'No,' said Jan. 'I'll take him, if you don't mind. And I'll want him for burial as soon as the post mortem's done.'

He lifted Sipho Ngubane. The blanket was wet with dew and blood. He carried him inside and laid him out where he was told. A small thin arm dangled down at the edge of the table and Jan took it gently and concealed it beneath the covering.

'You want the blanket back?' said Captain Olivier.

Jan shook his head and went outside. As he climbed into the *bakkie* he could hear Captain Olivier shouting from his office, 'Djantjes! Put the corpse in the fridge and where's my bloody coffee?'—a strident whine—'Move your black arse!'

Nontinti appeared at the house in the morning. She crossed the *spruit*, walking upright in the track, her long skirt tilting with the movement of her feet. Nontinti, her turban green with age, coiled wide on her head, an old striped towel secured with a pin around her chest; Nontinti, matriarch of vagabonds, walked into the yard of Blackheath house, squatted on the step and waited. There was no need to knock. Someone would come. Then she would speak.

Elsa found her. She had wandered since first light in the orchard, going from garden to kitchen and back again, unable

23

to sleep. The sounds of the morning were the same as they had always been; fowls scratched, the man with the milk cans clanked in the dairy, the goats jostled in the road—except that now Nontinti waited on the steps, silent and inscrutable.

'Greetings Grandmother,' said Elsa softly.

'*Molo*,' returned Nontinti. She did not rise. She took the long pipe from her pocket and lit it. 'The wind is cold,' she said. 'Indeed there are no children in my house to tend the fire.'

'I will make you coffee.'

'I wish to speak to *Nkosana*.'

'I will call him.'

Elsa went inside and slid the heavy kettle onto the hotplate of the stove. She climbed the stairs and crept into the bedroom. 'Jan,' she whispered.

He jerked upright, rattling the iron bedhead against the wall. 'What is it?'

'Nontinti's here. She wants to talk to you.'

Elsa returned to the kitchen. She cut a hunk of bread and made Nontinti coffee. The old woman had not moved. Nor did she look up when Elsa placed the mug and bread on the step.

Jan came heavily down the stairs, pulling on his jersey. He went out to Nontinti and closed the door behind him. Elsa could hear Nontinti's voice, slow and halting. She turned away, going through the front to the garden beyond.

The grass was brittle. Only the sentinel palm, its head shaking high above, was dusty green, the colour of Nontinti's turban. The window of the guest room, up in the gable of the house, was still curtained. Adrian was asleep.

Later, when she went round to the back, the cup of coffee, scummed with clots of milk, and the slice of bread, were untouched on the step. Jan stood alone in the yard and Nontinti was walking down the road beside the *vlei*. The sky was wide and empty where the hill swept down towards the deep and sudden cleft of Rooikloof.

'What did you say to her?' Elsa asked Jan.

'We arranged the funeral.'

'And Abedingo?'

'There's nothing I can do about Abedingo.'

'We'll have to find him, Jan.'

'He'll come back himself.'

'How can you be so sure?'

'I'm not—but we don't know where the hell he is. We'll have to wait for him to make a move.'

'It's no good being complacent about Abedingo. Someone's got to carry the can, and it certainly won't be Adrian! He'll get up, have breakfast, go home in his fat car and think no more about it—I know him! And you and I will be left with a corpse, Nontinti to worry about and Abedingo somewhere out there with a gun.'

'I know that,' said Jan. 'I told him what I thought last night, but he doesn't give a stuff. The matter's at an end as far as he's concerned.'

'Well it's not for me!' She went up the back steps and banged the flyscreen closed behind her.

They buried Sipho Ngubane below the *bult* where others, before him, lay in the shade of bush willows. It was a small grave heaped with stones. From the house Elsa watched the procession wind across the hill, stopping sometimes to rest, the thin sound of song rising as they proceeded once again.

'Why'd he die?' asked Nella. 'Why'd they put him in a box? Nontinti says the ancestors will sit on her shoulders and make her bent. Why bent Mama? What are ancestors? How can they sit on her?'

Tough hardy weeds grew across the grave in time and thorn bushes dropped their pollen balls to wilt. Others lay there too: Piet Zingaphi, Joseph Witbooi and the child that died at birth. It was an abandoned place where laughing doves foraged among the stones or sat crouched on the hot sand, wings fanned out to warm, heads tucked in against their breasts.

25

# 2

Elsa stood at Nella's window gazing out across the yard. The moon was rising behind the pepper trees. She watched it awhile and then she said, 'The stars are dim tonight Nella. But there,' pointing, 'I can see the old Bushman star that Grandpa talked about.'

She had often told Nella the legend of the star and the hare that lived in the sky.

Nella looked at her, a scar on her nose where a thorn sprig had brushed it. 'How did Grandpa know about the hare in the sky?'

'Because he loved the stars and knew all their stories.'

'Why did he die?'

'Because he was old.'

'When will you be old?'

Elsa laughed. 'Not for a long time Nellie. Now, go to sleep.'

'Tell me?'

'No—it's late.'

Elsa reached for the light cord and pulled it. Nella made a small frightened sound. 'Where's the lamp?'

'In the passage.' She bent and kissed her.

Going downstairs, for they were steep, Elsa held the bannister, sliding her hand down the worn wood. So many hands had touched it in weariness or children pressed their faces to the bars.

She herself had often sat there as a small girl when she had come across from Kleinfontein to stay the night with her best friend Jannie de Villiers and searched for the light seeping under the kitchen door. They had crouched in the stairwell side by side in their pyjamas, Jannie with his dark, spikey hair sticking up on the crown of his head, she in maroon felt slippers with rainbow-coloured pompoms. They had listened to the wind and Jannie, with carefully suppressed glee, had told her of the tramp who had called at the farm years before in his Grandma's time.

'He was old and thin and'—Jannie considered a moment —'stinking like a jackal. He was locked in the shed for the night in case he stole anything.'

He looked at her until she curled her hot fingers into his. 'No Jannie, no more!'

'And,' he'd continued in a whisper, 'in the morning when Grandma went to look, he was dead!'

'No Jannie! You make me scared.'

'Sometimes,' Jannie with relish, 'they say he scratches at the windows and opens the doors . . .'

'No Jannie!'

When she was asleep he had climbed onto the windowsill and tapped at the panes and moaned until she woke.

How she'd screamed! Jannie's father, Dick de Villiers, had come down the passage and shouted at him. Jan stopped laughing then and went to bed contrite.


Elsa leant on the balustrade. She could hear Chrissie in the kitchen filling the kettle. She was singing that song again: *bayeza kusasa, bayeza*—tomorrow, tomorrow they come. In a truck? On a cart? Strangers walking in the red dust road? Only labourers walked, herding goats along the steeply cambered track. Dark, slant-eyed men, paler on the cheekbones and finger tips, the mark of other ancestors. Flutter-handed children, vivid still. Slower women, moving with grace, with balance.

Elsa stood undecided in the hall, the stairs going up, twisted like a trunk. She hesitated between the kitchen—Chrissie, the warm coal stove, cats, dogs—and the living room where Jan relaxed with the newspaper, slack-limbed, feet on the fender.

She stayed in the hall. She drew the curtains aside. Small slats of moonlight fell across the floor. She pressed her face against the pane to see the stars.

27

Long ago, Nontinti had said to her, 'Look at the sky. There —the last star that shines is the lamp of the man that milks the cows. It will fade when he is gone and the milk will be sweet with its light.'

The dimensions of Nontinti's world, the dimensions of Elsa's, met in beliefs about the stars. The Lord of the Sky, *Mvelangqangi*, had his herds way, way above.

'See,' the Milky Way, 'that is the pathway to the cattle *kraal*, for the cows have walked the sky bare and their hooves have pushed through the roof of the world.'

If, Elsa thought, she could peep through the star hole, she would find herself a midnight sun always shining where *Mvelangqangi* lived. And cattle, red and gold and gleaming.

But now Nontinti no longer spoke about the stars. She did not seem to speak at all. Each day she raked under the poplar trees, to what purpose no one could imagine for the pile of bruised weeds was always small and dead. She would sometimes stop, hand on her hip, the other supported by the top of the hoe, and gaze round slowly. Elsa would hurry away then. She could not look at Nontinti for Nontinti watched her, her mouth pursed, her eyes intent, waiting.

Sipho had been dead six months, Abedingo had not returned, Nontinti's house was empty. Elsa could not change it, but it seemed, unwittingly, that all her life Elsa had taken from Nontinti and now, when Nontinti asked in return, she did not know how to give or what to say and she cursed Adrian for what had happened.

The wind was rising. It surged in the pepper trees, flaying their branches. The *bult* curved away from the *mealie* lands. Elsa closed the curtains again, dragging rusty rings across the rails. She did not wish to be alone in the big house without Jan, Rooikloof dark below the *bult*.

Soon—a week, a little more—Jan would be gone, north to the new damsite with Kobie de Jager, and Andrew Fraser to work as a foreman.

He had said it over and over, more to himself than to her, 'Blackheath's finished, Els. We can't go on in this drought. Kobie heard that they need foremen at the new dam they're building up on the Orange. At least if I went there for a bit I could pay off some of the debts and buy feed for the winter. Don't you think Els? Don't you think?' He needed her support.

It was not his going that disturbed her. It was being on Blackheath alone: just she and Nella. Chrissie in the kitchen, Nontinti in the garden, gathering the leaves she had raked into a sack.

'I don't want to work on the site,' Jan had said. 'But it's better than leaving altogether like the Marais and the Stockwells. Uncle Cedric told me Oom Jaap Koen's trying to sell his place. It's hard to believe. Poor old bugger.' He had said it softly. 'What the hell will he do?'

Another homestead would stand deserted. Another farm. Gates would sag on hinges, unattended. Most weeks workers came to the door looking for a place. A hungry family waited in the road with a cart, a goat on a tether, chickens in a crate. They were turned away. There was no work here. There was no work anywhere.

And so Elsa did not discuss the matter any more. Jan had decided. She would stay and Petrus would look after the farm until the rains began and Jan came home.

An owl called somewhere in the pepper trees.

'Mama!' Nella cried.

'What's wrong Nellie?'

'The owl is frightening me.'

She climbed the stairs again. 'It's only an owl.'

'Why is it crying?'

'Lonely perhaps.'

'Mummy . . .'

'Sleep darling,' she said, bringing the lamp into the room. 'There's a little light for you.'

She went down into the hall and opened the living room door. The silence was gone. Jan had turned on the radio to listen to the weather report. He leaned over and tossed the newspaper to her. He had broad, big-knuckled hands—but gentle, able to deliver lambs, untangle goats from wire. Merciful hands. Once she'd seen him kill a *rhebok*, limp with disease, grey as the hillside on which it lay. She had watched, curious. Too tired to care, the *rhebok* had shown her all its secret pain. She had turned away, as Jan, unsheathing his knife, had cut its throat.

She had wondered if, in the moment of death, the whole of its life had opened out: the morning of its birth, the first feel of the sun, the smell of red grass at the edge of the track. Red grass fading to grey, bleached for want of rain. The taste of shoots—all these things.

The *rhebok* was a carcase—stiff, obscene, its throat gaping, its tongue thrust out. How quickly its eyes glazed over.

'Close them Jan.'

That night the jackals had come. She had heard them on the *bult*. And later, all of a season, up on the hill, searching for a strayed goat with Jan, Nella running ahead, she had stooped to examine the grass. She had found the skull. A furtive beetle crouched in the socket as though it had eaten all the visions from the tiny brain then defecated in the dust.

Jan turned off the radio and said, 'Did you speak to Nontinti?'

'No, why?'

'She was here just now when you were putting Nella to bed.'

'What did she want?'

'Something about going to Port Elizabeth.'

'Port Elizabeth?'

'She wants to try and find Abedingo.'

'Has she heard from him?' asked Elsa, startled.

'No—just that there are relations who might know. She had a dream he'd gone to find his mother.'

'She shouldn't go alone,' said Elsa. 'She's too old. She's never been further than Cookhouse in her life.'

Chrissie appeared, her apron white in the gloom of the hall. '*Ukutya*,' she said. Food.

'Chrissie,' said Elsa. 'Is Nontinti there?'

'She has gone home,' said Chrissie. 'She says she will come tomorrow.' She left them, moving quietly.

'When's Chrissie's baby due?' asked Jan.

'A week or two.'

'She's huge.'

'It is the fifth.'

'She and Petrus have a hell of a brood,' he remarked absently.

Elsa threw the newspaper on the floor. She did not reply. She could not resent Chrissie and Petrus's five children with their solemn little faces, their black eyes. Only regret that in all the years she herself had only one. Still, she had kept all Nella's baby clothes, in hope, neatly packed away in a drawer. She did not speak to Jan about it any more. He would be defensive, fold his arms across his chest and say, 'Don't get uptight, Els. You know, sheep are just the same as people. It's those neurotic ewes of mine that never lamb well. Forget about it and it'll come right. After all, we didn't exactly plan Nellie, did we?' He would ruffle her hair, grin—his old self. But it worried him, she knew. One little daughter, no sons and the Blackheath farmlands willed by Dick de Villiers to the male line. One day it might all belong to Adrian's boy.

'Come Els.' Jan put his arm around her. 'I'm hungry.'

He carved the lamb, forking fat-marbled slices onto the plate.

'That's too much,' she said.

'We've heard all that before. You've got to eat.'

Gravy, potatoes, pumpkin, parsnips.

His plate was full. He worked at it with concentration, mashing the pumpkin with his knife. 'Wine,' he said. 'Would you like some?' He reached for the glasses on the sideboard, the bottle in his fist. 'Uncle Cedric was at the meeting in the Co-op this morning. He asked if you'd go over sometime and help him replan the garden.'

'I was hoping he'd forgotten,' she said, frowning.

Uncle Cedric had always disturbed Elsa. It was his mouth. It was predatory like Adrian's with teeth spaced apart. His tongue seemed to crouch behind them. It could unfold, dab at her, curl itself around her and suck her in.

His head was big, skin stretched tightly over skull and cheekbones. His ears were big too. So were his hands. He smoked his cigarettes with a kind of angry vigour. His face was florid beneath the tan for he enjoyed his whisky and tobacco. He was tough, flinty even—but he had charm.

There was a quaint courtliness in his manner. He might be irascible now, growing older on his own, but his exploits as a young man were legend. He was wild, prodigal, inventive. Women had adored him.

Once he'd had a wife but no one could remember her. Then, in later years, he'd had a mistress. Elsa's mother, Dorothy Southey, had disapproved of Cedric and his mistress and they had never been invited to Kleinfontein while they had lived together. But Elsa knew all about them from Jan, who, when nine, had regaled her with stories.

'Do you know, there's this wife who's not a wife who eats tortoise livers?'

Elsa had recoiled. 'How can she eat tortoise livers?'

'She does!' He was triumphant. 'She has them fried with onions.'

When Elsa had seen Cedric's mistress buying cigarettes in the café in town she had watched, fascinated. The woman wore black helanca slacks stirruped at the instep and glittery kid-glove shoes. Her bosom was huge. Her hair was soft and flossy, a little pink. She held her head high: no double chins, and her skin was beautiful, carefully rouged. She had a wide mouth. Her teeth were big, like Uncle Cedric's and ivory-coloured from all the nicotine.

The men in the café had stared unabashed. She had greeted them charmingly if fleetingly and padded down the road to Uncle Cedric's car like a big Persian cat, the tips of her hair webbing light.

'Uncle Cedric also told me he's thinking of buying Jaap Koen's farm. He wants Adrian and us to go in with him,' said Jan.

'What'd you say?'

'How the hell does he think we could buy more land at this stage?'

'I wouldn't like to buy Brakkloof anyway,' she said. 'It would seem all wrong without Oom Jaap and Freek there.'

'Uncle Cedric says Oom Jaap would sell today but Freek's holding out for a better price.'

'Do you blame him?' she said. 'I wonder what Freek will do.'

'God knows.' He filled her glass. 'This bloody drought,' he said, pushing his plate away.

Elsa sat, her food still untouched, thinking of Oom Jaap Koen's son Freek with his sallow face and small moustache and his self-defensive bluntness. She thought of his wife Ria and the baby, always pale and croupy with a rattle in its breath and a runny nose as though it had been kept all its life in the back bedroom and had never felt the sun. 'Who'd run the farm anyway if Uncle Cedric bought it? I know him—he'd leave it all to you while Adrian sat in Grahamstown and stashed away the profits.'

'That's a bit unfair,' said Jan.

'It's not! It's true. And Brakkloof itself?' She looked at him. 'The homestead and things? They're kind of sad. You know, creepy. It's all those cypress trees.'

'And you hate cypress trees!' He grinned. 'I'll tell him Adrian can have the profits to himself because Elsa hates the cypress trees and doesn't want to go there. Freek's had bad luck,' he continued. 'He's a damned good farmer—but it's not the best bit of land. It's too small and there's not enough water, specially when the river's dry. We could only use it for extra grazing. I don't know,' he shrugged. 'The Koens have always been there. They're the kind of neighbours I like.'

'That doesn't seem to bother Adrian.'

'Funny how Adrian always used to despise that farm, only because Oom Jaap used to plough with oxen. I remember when he got a tractor and I went with Dad to see it. I suppose I was about six.' He laughed. 'Now Adrian can't snap up the place fast enough. He can do what he likes but he can count me out.'

Elsa cleared the plates and the vegetable dishes to the sideboard. 'Jannie,' she said. 'I thought we could go down to Bushman's for the weekend. Annatjie said we could have their cottage if we wanted to.' She turned to Jan but he did not look up from his poached peach and custard. 'Nella would love it. Don't you feel like fishing?'

'There's too much to do in the next few days. I have to be sure Petrus knows what he's about before I go to the dam.'

33

'But you'll be back every month. And I'll be here. It's not as if we won't be able to ask.'

Jan did not reply. A moth lumbered around the lamp. Elsa sat, leaned her chin on her cupped hand and said, 'I wonder what I'll do when you're gone?'

'Take a lover and keep him in the loft.' He took her hand. 'I'm not going forever Els. It has to rain in the end.'

'I think you're looking forward to it,' she said crossly.

'Come off it!' He glanced towards the window, sitting intent—a big man—listening to the wind.

Elsa got up and opened the door because the owl was calling and Nella might wake. Chrissie was still singing in the kitchen. Returning to the table Elsa poured the coffee from the enamel pot. 'Jannie,' she said softly. She stopped. He looked up but she did not say as she had meant to, 'I don't want to stay here on my own. I'm too afraid.' Instead she said, 'What do I do if the water runs out and the goats start dying?'

Jan did not wish to consider such a possibility. 'It will rain,' he said. 'It has to.'

Above the sound of the wind Elsa heard the latch on the kitchen door click closed. Chrissie had gone. The clock struck in the hall. Jan was talking between mouthfuls of coffee but the silence was deep.

The next day when Elsa went to the kitchen in search of Chrissie she found Nontinti waiting.

'*Molo Mama*,' she said tentatively.

'*Molo wethu*,' said Nontinti. She held her blanket close. Her old brass wedding ring hung loose between the joints of her finger. She said '*Mama*'—she glanced first at Chrissie, then at Elsa—'I am going on the train to Port Elizabeth.'

'*Nkosana* has told me.'

'*Mama*,' Nontinti, addressing neither Elsa nor Chrissie, speaking from the doorway, seat of ancestors, to be heard by those living and those that had gone before, 'In Port Elizabeth I will find that boy Abedingo.'

Elsa knew Nontinti, she knew that she had waited for her time and that now she made the journey for all the people who had walked out in the road: for her daughter Funeka

34

who had gone long ago, returning only twice to bring her sons to Nontinti to care for and for Abedingo Ngubane who had left, a fugitive, so many months before.

'I will take you to the station if you are sure,' said Elsa. Then she said, 'How do you know he is in Port Elizabeth?'

'It is said.'

'Where will you stay?'

'There are people.'

Elsa asked no more. Angry at her own inability, in all the time, to help, to find another way, she drove Nontinti into town. Chrissie accompanied them. She sat in the back of the car in her black shawl, Nontinti silent beside her.

Nella and Chrissie's daughter Tombizodwa shared the front seat. They ate boiled sweets. Tombizodwa sucked hers, inspecting it at intervals, to see how the stripes and colours changed. Nella crunched carelessly. She knew where the others were hidden in the house.

The dust from the wheels spiralled out, coating the brush and *besembos*. Nella traced pictures on the side window with a sticky finger. Tombi stared ahead.

The road led past Elsa's family farm, Kleinfontein, hidden in the trees. The gates were old, whitewashed and elegant, the poplars thick and tall. The ironstone walls curved out of sight to where the homestead lay on a ridge above the dam.

Elsa went on down the long, long road, past the Cloetes, the Frasers, the Pringles and de Jagers, each farm announced by a different signpost, a painted ploughshare, a board with a tractor-dealer's logo, Annatjie and Kobie's rather ostentatious entrance topped with a palisade of thatch, an ornamental edifice, bare and alone in the *veld*.

Down by the river a causeway bridged a watercourse. A deserted school stood so close to the track Elsa could see right through the arched windows of its shell to the hills beyond where *garingbome* stood against the sky. She drove on towards the outskirts of the town and turned in at the station.

Nontinti got out of the car and lifted her bag to her head. Chrissie followed with a string parcel. Elsa called Nontinti

35

aside and gave her all the money that she had. Nontinti folded the bunch of notes into her bodice and went with Chrissie to buy a ticket.

The man at the counter chewed a match stick. He took Nontini's money as though it had offended him and dropped it into a drawer.

Elsa waited on the platform and watched Nella hopping on the shadows cast by wooden eaves.

'Come and play Mama!' cried Nella. 'Come Mama! Come!' she urged, jumping big-shoed, thin-legged, startling brown sparrows. She climbed on some *mealie* sacks and slid down laughing. 'Let's slide, Mum!'

Elsa had played the same game with Jannie long ago, leaping the shadowed struts together. Older than Nella—eight or nine—they had waited for the train from Grahamstown, for Jan's big brother Adrian, coming home from school.

'Elsie, come and slide!' Jannie had commanded, bounding to the top of the pile. She had followed carefully for the sacks were heavy and they might fall.

The stationmaster had appeared and shouted at them. 'Get down from there at once or I'll send you on the next train to Doringbult and you'll never be seen again! And you know,' he had added, 'Doringbult is a terrible place!'

Doringbult hadn't bothered Jannie. He'd waited till the stationmaster went back to his office (timetables sagging on the notice board, an old fan like a propeller droning round and round) and then run up the stack and leapt down the other side, bare feet thudding on the concrete.

'Where's Doringbult, Jannie?' Elsa had asked.

'Don'no!'

She had thought of it often, wondering. Doringbult— a siding somewhere between *koppies*. Thorny. Grey. A side track with no turning. An iron building and a gum tree, its bark strips rattling in the wind. No water in the pump. Abandoned carriages. No stationmaster. Nothing. Perhaps there were rats in the grain shed. Maybe a grave.

There had been the day when she and Chrissie, Jannie and Petrus, the senior stockman's son, had played in and out of the cattle trucks at Melkbos Siding and the train had suddenly lurched forward, wheels screeching on the rails.

'Chrissie's still inside!' Elsa had screamed. She'd seen Chrissie's small face peering back in panic. 'Perhaps it's going to Doringbult and we'll never see her again!'

A moment's apprehension, then Jannie had laughed. 'Silly! There's no such place!'

Petrus had run beside the train. It had moved slowly, the trucks rocking. '*Tsiba!*' he had cried, holding out his hand to her.

Chrissie had jumped blindly, not choosing her time. Flung to one side by the jolting cattle car she had fallen on the gravel at the edge of the track and rolled over and over, small grey stones digging into her hands and face.

Jan and Petrus had looked frightened then. Chrissie had shaken herself, mute, a cut bulging above her eye. Jan's father, Dick de Villiers, had been very angry. He had beaten Jan and Petrus and sent Chrissie back to Kleinfontein in the Scotch cart. Elsa had sat close beside Chrissie, knees touching, glancing every now and then at Chrissie's fingers, closed around her swollen palms, and wondered which was worse — to have fallen from the train or to have gone to Doringbult with its gum tree and deserted iron shed.

Old Nontinti walked down the platform. Chrissie followed, balancing her weight. Nella jumped from the *mealie* sacks and ran towards them.

'Nella!' Elsa cried. 'Not so close to the edge!' She reached for her arm and jerked her back, seeing gravel lying grey in the shadow of the train. Elsa said to Nontinti, 'You will be all right Mama?'

Nontinti nodded. She stood by Chrissie and the child Tombizodwa. Elsa drew away.

'*Eehe,*' said Nontinti. The word was brief, a small, gruff sigh. She touched Tombizodwa's head. She mounted the step and stood alone among the packages at the door of the carriage. As she turned away she ran her fingers across her eyes — a small, discreet gesture.

The joints of the train creaked. Luggage was passed up. Men boarded. Women. Boxes tied with string, blankets tightly rolled, were tossed to the passengers leaning from the windows.

The whistle blew. The train drew out of the station. Nontinti sat on a bench, the money Elsa had given her safe against her skin.

The station lingered a moment, then it was gone: the cattle pens, the tin rooves, the ornamental flower beds. Wasteland streamed by, a siding, a water tank. Someone stood near the rails watching. The train sped out. Way behind the town the ridge of hills sank into the abundance of the farmlands, mist against the sky.

Elsa, sitting in the car in the station yard, leaned her head against the door and closed her eyes. In the back were Chrissie and the children, saying nothing. The train had gone, heading out towards Cookhouse with Nontinti Ngubane, matriarch of vagabonds. Cookhouse, Middleton, Alicedale—it might as well be Doringbult.

# ❧ 3 ❧

When it was time for Jan to go the land was still dry. The leaves of the poplars were turning. The air was mellow at mid-morning. The *garingbome* stood tilted against the *dongas* behind the shed where the ground was leached and empty.

Jan and Petrus worked together. They cared for the goats, they repaired the machinery, they watched the level of the reservoir. They spoke with the stockmen, with each other. As boys Jan had given over his pet crow or his orphan lamb, his wire cars and catapults to Petrus to care for when he went back to boarding school. Petrus had made them his own for the time, had returned them uncomplainingly when the holidays came. They went from Jan to Petrus to Jan and finally, when discarded, to Petrus again, where, somehow, they belonged.

Jan was not possessive of his things, he never had been. He was generous. He gave Petrus anything he thought he specially liked. But by his generosity he excluded Petrus from bargaining or from making gestures in return. It held Petrus in bondage.

As children, when they trundled their wire cars down to Langa Store by the drift and bought sweets — banana, buttermilk or molasses toffees from the glass jars on the counter; rainbow suckers, orange gobstoppers — it was Jan who paid for them and divided them up.

When they stole wire from the roll in the shed to make *ingqola* cars, it was Jan who found the pliers, clipped the strands and decided who should have which strip. They had known it no other way. But when they spoke, it was Petrus's language that they used. *Xhosa* fitted, and why it did no one ever bothered to question. It was so — that was all.

Workers were part of a farm, like the earth and the shed

and the best pepper tree by the *kraal*. They belonged, and the idea that they might choose differently was seen, always, as a typical inconsistency, a lack of gratitude, an aberration —like a thunder storm in the middle of the dry season or a mist at midday. A defection indicated a fault in the worker —that he might have a good reason for going was not considered. Such a possibility made everyone uncomfortable.

Jan was leaving Petrus—not with a lamb or a crow but with a farm, hundreds of head of stock and his family to care for. The exchange was the same as it had always been, the stakes were different. Jan handed over Blackheath reluctantly, feeling the process of abdication. Petrus accepted the responsibility without emotion. He would do his work as he always had; for the rest, there were more important things on his mind. He had acquired his own land on Mpumalanga. He had sent his mother and his younger brother up there to live. A homestead was being built. Jan knew about it. He had helped by collecting the materials from town, but he had never been to see Petrus's plot and Petrus had never thought to invite him.

For Petrus Blackheath had become a place to work: a good place, but no longer home, even though he had been born there, in the same year as Jan, when the rains were good and the mohair fetched a record price.

Jan knew he could rely on Petrus. He had counted on him all his life to be there when he wanted him, to go away when he did not. It hadn't occurred to him that he had always made the terms. Such a notion would have angered him, he would consider it ungenerous. And yet, in all the time, in his deference, his acquiescence, it was Petrus who had known how to keep their friendship just beyond the test. It was Petrus who had always held the links—only he seemed to realize how fragile they might be. He preserved them with a kind of wry prudence, aware of what was best, aware that Jan, unconsciously, could play the 'white man' when he wanted.

Their daily tasks might be the same and somewhere was an old affection that had never changed, but Jan made his life, Petrus his, beyond the possibility of sharing. And Petrus had preserved, in silence, and often in retreat, an autonomy for which he'd always fought: he went often to Mpumalanga where the small homestead was growing from the earth, and ironstone lay on ironstone around the goat *kraal*, and a patch of ground was hoed for *mealies*. From his doorway Petrus Ngubane could look out, not across the farmlands to Black-heath and Brakkloof and Melvynside, but east towards the hills where cattle, goats and sheep grazed among the thorn brush and the *gwarri*.

'I wish you weren't going tomorrow Jannie,' said Elsa. She poured him a cup of coffee from a flask and stirred it as he sat at the desk in the shearing shed checking the records for the last time. 'Adrian isn't short of money. He'd still sink some into the farm to see us through.'

'We've been over all that before,' said Jan shortly.

'Adrian said . . .'

'To hell with Adrian.'

'That's it, isn't it Jan?' she went on relentlessly. 'You'd rather leave home and be a foreman on a damsite than ask him for a cent. Kobie and Andrew have no choice—but you have. Blackheath belongs to Adrian as well. Why should you take all the responsibility? The drought isn't your fault.'

'What does Adrian care about Blackheath?' he demanded. 'Blackheath's a profit margin for him, a tax dodge. He seems to think I'm some kind of a labourer on his estate. Well, I'm sick of taking hand-outs from Adrian and I'll work on the dam for a year if I have to rather than be in debt to him.'

Jan dipped his rusk in his mug. His socks hung over his boots. His legs were scarred from walking through thorn scrub. His thick straight hair stuck up on the crown of his head. He wiped his face on his sleeve—an impatient, boyish gesture.

'Let's go for a walk Elsa,' he said, flinging down his ledger.

'Aren't you tired?'

He shook his head.

'I'll find Nellie.'

41

Nella was playing hospitals, her tongue stuck out in concentration. She breathed noisily through her nose as she bandaged a doll's head with sticking plaster.

'Are you coming for a walk Nell?'

Nella nodded. She laid the doll in its cot and tucked the square of crocheted blanket round it.

Jan was waiting in the yard, hands in his pockets, staring up at the roof of the shed, his sheepdog at his feet, its nose close to his leg. It sensed his restlessness.

They walked towards the *bult*. It was a favourite place where they had always come to talk and plan. Climbing up through the grass the sounds of the homestead reached them from far below. They were different from when they'd last walked that way. Before, there had always been the exchange of voices from the workers' houses, cattle lowing in the *kraal*, the bleat of goats down by the shed. Now the noises were sporadic, discontented. The sun slunk out of a pewter-coloured sky. Still the air was fierce with dust and a cold wind blew. Looking down, Elsa felt an anxiety too vague, too amorphous to explain. A small unease seemed to flutter at her skin.

Jan took Elsa's hand. She wound her fingers through his and said, 'I'll miss you Jannie.'

'I'll be back with the rain.'

She leaned her head against his arm. Nella ran ahead, kicking at stones, the sheepdog trotting at her side. They walked through a deserted dusk, against an ash-grey sky, across an ash-grey hill. As children they had run as Nella did, with the red grass bending to the wind, bush willows green by the *spruit*, the *kannabos* on the rock cleft clenching the fissures with its roots.

Then, the skin of mud from a light rain could be rasped off the ground and collected in a ball. Jan had always made clay oxen but Elsa had fashioned hares, ears laid flat against the back, the mud gritty with sand grains. No bigger than Nella, Elsa had sat on the edges of the track watching Jannie make his big clay ox, sticking in a tuft of grass for a tail. She would hold her hare, warm in her palm. Jan, red-faced, would look up and say, 'Why always a hare? Make a cow or a horse, silly.'

'I like hares,' she would reply crossly.

Rooikloof lay to the east, blue with dusk. The rocks fell bare and dry into the shadow. To the west the workers' houses straggled in an uncertain line, smoke drifting. No sound. No sound at all except the wind. Another day gone and still no rain.

Elsa stayed close to Jan that night, in between packing clothes and writing lists of things to remember. She talked brightly, going over his instructions once again: who to contact, what to do, if things went wrong. She made him coffee after Chrissie had gone and they sat on the steps and looked at the stars, side by side, her hand in his. The Bushman star gleamed above the ridge of hills: the young girl taken up into the sky to bloom. Elsa watched it, saying nothing. Jan might have laughed.

Jan was gone and autumn faded. The first frost came and the trees in the orchard were black in the wind. A team of men were still planting *garingbome* in the land behind the shed. The stockmen were out in the camps checking the goats and the sheep. Elsa returned to the house to hear the weather report, more from duty than any hope of a change. The sky was clear and wide and white. It seemed as if it would never rain again.

Elsa turned on the radio and left it to play softly as she waited for the bulletin. She went into the living room. Since she'd been alone she'd often caught herself hesitating in a doorway, aware of her own breathing, listening.

When she had married, Elsa had made new curtains. They were shabby now, the modern design at odds with the room. Even the curtains—the small attempt of a newly-married girl to imprint herself on her home—could not change it, faithful as it had always been to Jan's mother's taste and generation.

It was only when Jan sat at breakfast with the morning sun coming in, with the homemade loaf and the marmalade, the tea pot and his plate of eggs and Nellie, first in a high chair and then in her own seat, chin level with the table, that the house was full of living.

It was time to change the rooms around, to remove the

coldness that had crept in imperceptibly since Jan had left
—Jan with his untidiness, his catalogues and dip kits, his
discarded jackets, boots and ledgers.

Soon after she'd come to Blackheath Elsa had redecorated
the bedrooms, but the living rooms downstairs had been too
big, the furniture too cumbersome, the task too daunting
to start again. They had not had enough money to upholster
the sofa or buy new carpets for the wide, polished floors.

Elsa fetched a packing case from the shed, placed it in the
middle of the hearth rug and looked around. She began with
the plant stand in the corner on which had always stood a
maidenhair fern. She put the plant outside where, she secretly
hoped, it would die in the wind and heat.

From the tallboy she unearthed an ugly carved dancing
bear holding a brass ashtray. Nella was delighted with it when
she saw it but Elsa remembered it next to Dick de Villiers'
big easy chair, always piled with old cigarette stubs and ash,
smelling stale.

She gathered up many of the things that had been in one
place so long they went unnoticed: a cuckoo clock with dusty
chains, a black-framed picture of a Victorian wicket gate,
a collection of china dogs, a shepherdess and a clown with
a china ruff, a host of small ruched taffeta shades from the
wall brackets. They had never bothered her before—she had
even liked them for their familiarity.

The more she tossed in the box the more she found to
discard. Like an exorcist she dismantled the room as far as
she could, wondering how she would fill the empty spaces
on the tables, pelmets and walls. Nella enjoyed it all and
got in the way, taking a new and irritating interest in objects
she had never noticed in the past. As fast as Elsa filled the
cardboard box Nella unpacked it and ran off to secrete the
best treasures under her bed, where after a little time they
lay forgotten, gathering cobwebs and dust, until Chrissie res-
tored them triumphantly to the living room. With irrational
anger Elsa swept them into a packet, breaking the clown's
head from its ruff, and carted the remnants up to the loft.

The loft ran the length of the old house. A wooden balustrade, its railing hidden by the ancient wisteria that grew

around the pillars of the *stoep*, led up the side gable to a green door. Chairs, milk churns, books, trunks, *biltong* racks and tools lay in the deep, warm gloom.

There was a stillness, a waiting in the loft. The order and the coldness of the rooms below did not exist up here. Elsa had once thought of tidying it but she decided there would be something wrong in washing out the corners with Jeyes Fluid and disturbing the patina of four or five generations crammed together under the rafters.

She went to find replacements for the things she had removed—for something warmer, simpler, gayer than Dick and Gladys de Villiers' bric-a-brac. Quietly she walked between the old chests of drawers, the boxes of kitchen utensils—an ancient mincer, butter paddles, a chipped blue enamel dish with embossed white daisies. She unearthed a brass preserving pan, a quaint painted samovar and a china dish from a washstand. It was cracked but she would float dahlias or roses in it when they grew in spring.

A pile of picture frames leant against a chair. The rusty hanging wires were tangled together. She bent down and glanced at them. There was an etching of a windmill, a Virgin and Child, a series of sports photos. She wiped away the dust from one. There was Dick de Villiers at school, the famous rugby team of '26. He stood on the left in his small, navy, silver-tasselled colours cap, his expression grave. A second picture, taken forty years on, an echo of the other: Jan in the first fifteen. As backdrop was the stone school building, an arched door, the overlapping shingles of Virginia creeper. Jan sat in the same way as his father had, hands crossed, collar of his blazer turned up as dictated by tradition, the velvet rugby cap on his head, silver tassel nudging at his eyebrow: a boy's face, still round, the familiar grin which crinkled his eyes. Elsa had always found it difficult to reconcile the mannish legs with the boy's face when Jan was eighteen. She smiled and laid the photo aside.

She discovered a picture she had painted herself. She propped it against the side of the chair, squatted down and looked at it. It was small, foxed and spotted where fishmoths had eaten through the mounting. She had forgotten all about it. She had painted it on Blackheath seven years before: the shed, the sheep-dip, the patch of yellow *veld* beyond the fence.

Jan had said to her, 'Paint me a picture Els.' He had said it in his new stranger's voice as he repaired the dip. He had spoken to keep away the silence.

She had sat in the sun, her legs browning, her long pale hair falling across her face as she worked at her sketch pad. He had watched her. She had pretended to be unaware of his self-conscious gestures. When she'd finished they had sat together in the cool, quiet shed and drunk tea, cold from the bottle. Jan had lounged on a wool bale, his back against the wall. They did not speak much. Elsa kept her distance for the time with a kind of empty banter, not ready yet to think of what she'd done.

The night before they'd driven in from town. Jan had not taken her home to Kleinfontein, nor explained at all. Blackheath house stood big and dark among the pepper trees. She had followed him inside, laid down her evening bag and wrap and absurd pink paper hat from the Christmas party.

'Shall we have some coffee Els?' he'd said.

He'd gone into the kitchen and turned on the light. His dog had greeted him and wagged its tail lazily.

'Go on Els. Make the coffee.'

He'd disappeared into the hall again. Elsa had pushed the kettle onto the plate of the stove and searched for mugs. Outside the wind was rising.

Jan had returned with an old paraffin lamp. He'd switched off the overhead lights and put it on the table.

'Are you trying to be romantic Jan?'

'Where's the coffee?' he'd demanded.

She had made it slowly, stirring it round. 'Listen to the *dikkops*.' She'd inclined her head. 'Listen to them crying. You always had more than us.'

'Bugger the *dikkops*,' he'd said. 'Come here.'

She'd put down the coffee in front of him and sat opposite, silent. He'd leaned back in his chair and looked at her. She'd turned her eyes from his and when he'd tried to start a conversation she had not replied. She'd drunk her coffee, saying nothing, and taken his cup and gone to the sink to wash it. He'd come up behind her and put his arms around her. 'No more playing Els,' he'd said.

'Don't push your luck Jan.'

He'd stepped back angrily. She had repented then. 'I'm sorry. I didn't mean it.'

He'd led her upstairs. Automatically she'd missed the fourth as they always had when they'd gone to steal sweets from the cupboard in the spare room. They had not gone there then. Jan had closed his bedroom door. His bed was just the same, sagging in the middle, with a faded blue weave spread.

He'd undressed her in the dark. She'd only looked into his face that night, looking for Jannie. She had looked no further—not yet. She had not seen him naked since he was twelve, Jannie ducking her in the dam, leaping and splashing. She had reached for the familiar hands that had made clay oxen for her or struck her in anger when they'd fought for the possession of a bicycle. His fingers had held hers closely.

It had started as a game weeks before Christmas on her return to Kleinfontein from nursing college: teasing, laughing, touching. It was over now. After this there would be no more Jannie. Only Jan who watched her. A stranger now.

They had spent every day together after that. Elsa had escaped the emptiness of Kleinfontein, without her father there. She did not know how to cope with her mother's stoicism at his death, her inability to share her grief or memories, to speak about him or to cry. Excluded from the right to mourn, Elsa retreated to Blackheath and to Jan. And having lost his own father some years before and carried through his loss alone, Jan knew when to talk, when to reminisce and when to leave some things unsaid.

They rode, they swam, they went around the farm and Elsa watched him at his work, cooked for him when Nontinti would allow and returned to Kleinfontein at night because she had to.

'I don't want to go back to the hospital,' she had said.

'You've only done your first year.'

'I don't want to be a nurse.'

'What do you want to be?'

47

'An archaeologist or something, like Dad had hoped.'

'I thought you'd given up that idea,' he'd said with a puzzled grin, not really understanding. 'Your Ma says you've got to finish your course.' He'd bent and rubbed his knuckles against his sheepdog's head. 'Anyway, why's she complaining?' The dog had wagged its tail. 'She's got all those smooth doctors to entertain her and she'll forget about us, hey?'

'Won't!'

'We'll see.'

She had looked at him, puzzled in her turn.

'Come on Els, I've got to check on things,' he'd said briskly.

He would never have admitted his anxiety—something he had always had—that he might lose her, that she would find a world beyond the farm, somewhere where he could not follow.

Just before her leave was up Annatjie and Kobie had got married and Elsa, a little wistful at Annatjie's exuberance, had helped with the final preparations, the dresses, the flowers.

'I'm having the whole catastrophe for my wedding,' Annatjie had said. 'The whole bloody catastrophe! I'm having four bridesmaids and two flower girls, a best man and three groomsmen and a page. We can't leave out any of the brothers and sisters, after all. I'm ordering the cake from Mrs Koen and she's going to make it in four tiers and decorate it with bells, butterflies, the works!'

The wedding was held in town when the temperature stood at thirty-three degrees and a dust storm howled. People had arrived from all over the district and from Cradock, Graaff-Reinet, Steynsburg and Port Elizabeth. A fierce wind sent dust devils spiralling out across the cricket ground, the stock pens and the dusty roads of the township.

The Southeys had set out from Kleinfontein, Dorothy driving, Aunt Vi ensconced in the front, Elsa at the back with Bruce, irritated that his mother had made him wear his school uniform. He had sulked, his well-scrubbed ears sticking out from his cropped hair.

Elsa had inspected her shoes, unsuccessfully dyed in orange

48

splodges to match her straw Breton sailor hat. Her suit had been tight and hot but she'd dared not open the window to let the dust fly in.

Jan, whom Kobie had appointed as an usher, had waited for her at the door of the church, his hair plastered flat, the carnation wilting in the buttonhole of his father's last grey suit. He winked at Elsa. 'Keep a place for me, Els,' he'd said as he conducted the family down the aisle to a seat near the front.

The pews had been decorated with silver-painted wishbones and posies of dried pink flowers tied with curly ribbons. Dorothy Southey had cast her eye upon these fripperies disdainfully. Huge arrangements of chrysanthemums and greenery stood at the altar. Strelitzias stuck up above the pulpit, a regiment of long-necked birds.

Bruce had fiddled with the prayer book and picked his nose. Elsa had nudged him. 'Cut it out, Bruce!'

Kobie and his brothers had taken their places in the first pew. Kobie's face was red, so closely shaved it shone. His moustache had been trimmed, the hair clipped close.

Elsa had heard the crunch of wheels on gravel as the bridal car drew up at the door. There was a flutter in the porch, women's voices, everyone turned, craning to see the bride.

Annatjie, in a torrent of tulle and stiff satin, embossed with pearl-embroidered roses, had appeared in the arch on the arm of her father. They had paced slowly up the aisle, Annatjie's big-bosomed sisters following in peach georgette. The two flower girls had gone before, balancing little baskets of confetti and glancing about apprehensively like small lambs exploring a new pasture.

After the ceremony the guests had been herded across to the town hall by the ushers while the bridal couple were driven away in Annatjie's father's blue Pontiac to cruise the streets until the guests were seated.

The old overhead fan had whined round, dust thudded against the windows. Swans made from pipe cleaners and throttled with ribbon had announced each place at the feast. Net parasols bulged with sugared almonds and festoons of streamers and balloons hung from the ceiling.

'Where's the bar, for God's sake?' Cedric de Villiers had said, pulling off his jacket and dragging at his tie.

'You've got to wait for the bride!' Adrian had been patronizing. 'Not a drop till she arrives!'

'To hell with the bride!' Cedric had grumbled, collaring a perspiring waiter and demanding a beer.

At last Annatjie and Kobie had swept in while the band played and the guests applauded, not the least Uncle Cedric who downed his beer at a gulp and was then prepared to be affable.

Oom Seppi, a relation of Kobie's mother from the old people's home, had pottered about the tables helping himself to the cigarettes set out in their stiff display packs. He never removed his hat in public and he had not bought a new one for years. Toothless and simple he had sat in the corner and puffed, his breast pocket crammed with booty, a paper plate of sausage rolls on one side, a cup of tea on the other and a glass of brandy and coke placed discreetly among the pipe cleaner swans and parasols of almonds.

Dorothy Southey would never have invited someone like Oom Seppi to a family wedding. She did not have relations like him and somehow Elsa regretted it. Hers were so well-connected, so predictable.

Long after Kobie and Annatjie had gone, clattering cans behind their car, lavatory paper trailing from the hubcaps, Andrew, Joy, Jan, Elsa and the others had continued with the party.

Elsa had been making coffee with the bridesmaids in the kitchen when Jan, drink in hand, had pulled her outside.

'Let's get married,' he'd said, offhand, as he sipped his beer.

'You really are romantic, aren't you Jan?' she'd retorted. 'Let's ride bikes, let's play marbles, let's get married! All the same!'

She'd shaken him off and stalked away. She had poured a glass of wine and gone to talk to Joy and Andrew. Sometime later Jan had come in, leaned against the wall and looked down at her. He'd grinned, not at all contrite. Infuriating Jan. She had paid him no attention.

'It's time to go home,' he'd said.

'No. I'm staying.'

'You're not!' He'd dragged her from her seat and marched her out.

At the truck he had turned to her. 'Elsie,' he'd said. 'Will you . . .'

'Where's the ring?'

He had bent and pulled a long stem of grass, broken it to size and twisted it into a band. 'There, Madam, is your ring. Now,' he had looked at her gravely, 'will you marry me?'

Elsa had burst out laughing. 'Of course I'll marry you, you silly arse! Who else could I possibly marry?'

Elsa put the painting aside with the other things she had chosen. She turned to the dresser and was looking through the drawers when she heard Petrus's voice. He tapped at the back door, a small sound echoing through the house.

Elsa climbed down the stairs and went into the kitchen. In his haste to find her Petrus had gone into the hall and was calling her name. He had rarely been in the house since he was twelve—Jan's *kwedini*—seventeen years before. He held his hat as Chrissie might have held her apron— with slight, respectful fingers.

'The baby is coming?' asked Elsa breathlessly.

Petrus nodded.

'There is something wrong?'

'It is taking a long time.'

Elsa went to the bathroom: cottonwool, scissors, cord-powder, a blanket from Nella's cupboard where her baby things still lay, laundered and folded, good for use again.

She was apprehensive. She had not been called to a birth for years. Nontinti had always been the midwife. The day after a delivery Chrissie would appear in the kitchen and lay the baby in a box near the stove until it was old enough to be carried on her back.

Elsa followed Petrus into the yard. Nella and Tombizodwa balanced on the stone wall of the orchard. They were shooting loquat pips into the grass, seeing who could make them fly the furthest.

The path to the huts was rutted. A goat, startled by their passing, jerked its tethered head. It watched them go, dragging its short rope, the wind fluttering its beard.

The houses circled the stretch of beaten earth: abandoned tins, washing spread on bushes, fowls, a clump of cannas. The children stopped their playing, stood close, foot to foot. A small boy sat on a box, snot-rimed, his hands hanging slack between his knees. He watched Elsa intently then turned his gaze away as her eyes found his.

Petrus's house was dark. The window had been boarded up. A fire made in a perforated tin smoked in the centre of the room, fiercely hot where ash and embers trickled through. Chrissie's bed was propped on bricks. The women standing round stepped back for Elsa.

Chrissie lay, hands clenched against her chest, knees drawn up. Her eyes were closed, a small scar running down from brow to cheek. Chrissie was mute, unmoving, as muscles tightened once again. The watching women murmured, a sibilance of voices. A drop of sweat edged down Chrissie's lip into the corner of her mouth. She licked it away with a small, quick movement of her tongue.

Once they had watched a ewe give birth in a bleak camp on a hillside. Chrissie had pulled grass husks from their stems and played two-stones with Elsa in the dust. At a distance a young sheep had gazed on curiously, the older ewes grazed unconcerned. The lamb had slid to the ground. The mother had turned to watch it, afterbirth trailing.

Chrissie's hands curled tighter to her chest and tighter. Another drop of sweat ran down her lip. The women looked at Elsa. Petrus waited outside the door.

'Petrus, fetch the truck.' Elsa spoke quietly, in his own language, to reassure him. 'We must take her to the hospital.'

Petrus went. She heard him go—the sound of boots, the brush of overalls. The children followed. He sent them back and hurried on past the tethered goat.

Elsa waited, squatting by the bed, her fingers touching the rough edge of blanket, breathing in the stifling smoke, the smell of sweat. She was afraid. The women were silent. Then Alzina, the stockman's wife, beckoned her outside.

'They must not take the *makoti* to hospital,' she said.

'Why?'

'When Ngubane was taken, that time in the truck, when he was old—did he return? He did not. When Funeka went, long before you came here, she bore a child in the hospital. It died. We remember these things.'

She looked into Elsa's face. Elsa, standing in the sun, felt the sweat crawl down her back. 'If there is something wrong,' she said, 'we cannot help, Alzina. At the hospital . . .'

'She does not want to go,' said Alzina simply.

Elsa heard the truck. The children ran along the path to meet it. Sounds came from the house. Voices urging. Elsa turned back and stooped through the doorway.

'*Luzalile.*' It is born.

A cockroach scuttered down the walls, its shadow flitting across the floor. The baby cried. The women stood back so that Elsa could see. The child—a girl—lay in blood and vernix. Elsa cut the cord. The women took the child, wrapped it in a blanket. Alzina was brisk. She knew her work.

Elsa stood beside the bed, wanting to speak, to acknowledge somehow, the weariness and triumph. But Chrissie's head was turned away. Her eyes were closed. One hand locked around the other as though there was no one else to hold it.

Elsa took the baby and brought it to Chrissie. '*Yintombazana*, Chrissie. It's a girl,' she said, feeling her own emotion tight in her chest.

Chrissie looked at her and smiled and Elsa bent and took her hand. 'She is beautiful,' she said.

Elsa went to Petrus waiting in the yard, barred by the women. Alzina's old husband stood expectantly beside him, fingering his beard. He raised his hands in greeting, sang out a praise in celebration of the birth. The children, hearing him, scattered about the yard, chasing and shouting, the waiting over.

'So many daughters Petrus,' said Elsa.

'Indeed, there are many.'

'It is a good day to be born,' said Elsa looking up at the sky.

53

'Indeed, it is a good day,' echoed Petrus.

When all was done, Elsa took the path across the hill. She could hear the excited cries of the children, the old man's voice sending the news across the camps.

She went down to the homestead. The sounds far behind her faded. She opened the yard gate and stood a moment as she fastened the ring to the iron hook. She let her breath out very slowly. It faltered in her throat as she remembered Chrissie's face and the small, warm weight of the baby in her arms.

Elsa became the farmer. Each day she carried out the tasks that Jan had left for her to do. She paid the workers, handed out rations, listened to the weather report, collected feed from town. She recorded everything for Jan as he would want it.

She tidied his desk in the shed, and, daring his displeasure, recruited a team of women to clean, dust and return the implements to their places. He might not like the new initiative but she would take the chance.

In the day she left the chores to Chrissie and escaped into the lands. Chrissie cared for Nella and Tombizodwa and went about the house singing, her baby snug against her back. She cooked and cleaned and sat in the shade of the cypress to feed her child while Nella and Tombizodwa shared a plate of beans or a mug of *maas*.

Elsa felt detached from the homestead. It seemed empty without Jan despite the changes she had made. The rearrangement of the furniture had pleased her to begin with. She had tried, with what she had, to recreate the rooms, to reflect herself in the choice of plates and pictures, the ginger jars of dried *veld* flowers, the teapot full of daisies. But even these seemed insignificant against the brooding of the old house.

This had always been Jan's place and he had brought her here because he loved her, because she belonged to him, because she should be happy where he was.

Her sense of self apart from Jan was something she had rarely questioned or felt any reason to explore. Her aloneness now he was away frightened her, the quiet of the evenings when Nella was asleep and Chrissie had gone home. She lis-

54

tened to the radio, she played her records, wrote Jan letters, did the accounts, fell asleep in bed over a book. And waited —holding Jan close against the feeling that Blackheath, as she'd always known it, was slipping away.

One day she drove up to the top camp to repair a fence. Along one side ran the boundary where three properties met: Blackheath, Uncle Cedric's Melvynside and Brakkloof, the farm of Oom Jaap Koen. A beacon stood at the place where the fences converged. Way below, the river lay empty, boulders bleak in its bed.

Elsa went with Petrus and a group of workers to a place where posts had fallen, victims of ants and dry rot. They had gone in the early morning, workers in the back of the truck: spades, posts, a roll of wire. Elsa left instructions with Chrissie to make a sponge cake for the stork party her mother and Annatjie had arranged for Joy Fraser at Kleinfontein that afternoon. She piled the ingredients on the kitchen table and walked out. Chrissie could preside. She had more important things to do.

She turned the truck along the western side of the farmland towards the boundary fence. The road rose steeply. The *kannabos* grew through rock. *Kiepersol. Gwarri.* At the edge of the culvert *kapokbos* flowered, the frosting of white down lying in drifts.

A herdboy huddled in a scrap of blanket watched them pass. The hillsides opened out, the farmland began again. Only fences were evidence of ownership.

Elsa went down towards the ford in the river where it ran out of the *poort*. When she and Jan were at school she had spent long summer days there with Joy and Andrew and Annatjie and friends they'd brought home for the weekend to stay. They'd laid cold drink bottles in the stream to cool and eaten homemade fudge—Annatjie's speciality—while Andrew handed round cigarettes bought from Langa Store.

Years later Elsa had walked down there with Jan to be alone, away from Blackheath and Chrissie always cleaning somewhere in the house, Elsa's family at Kleinfontein. They had swum in the cold water and sat in the sun to dry. Jan had drunk beer and eaten cheese and biscuits and made love enthusiastically. He was happy then. He had done well at Agricultural College, he had a farm of his own, Elsa Southey was his and he had acquired an almost permanent erection. Elsa went on up the steep incline. The workers in the back shouted greetings at a woman walking down the road. A sneeze wood stood sentinel at the bend. The track turned into the wilder hills. Only the wind was left.

Elsa stopped at a gate, a square of silver-painted iron fastened to it—a reflector for vehicles travelling at night. Petrus jumped from the cab and opened it. The truck bumped on.

The wind was keen on the hillside, a sound beyond the noise of men. Wind in grass, wind breaking on stone, birds and their thin upland piping. Way below, where Uncle Cedric's lands lay in shadow, shaven to the earth, two blue cranes stalked the stubble.

Elsa inspected the fence with Petrus, watched as a man began to dig a new hole for a post. She walked along the wire, testing it, the gazed down the slope beyond.

There, on the incline of the hill was a shearing shed, stark and white in the fall of land. It was the oldest building on Jaap Koen's farm. A thorn tree, divided at the crown, grew in the shadow of the walls. The great doors were closed. A wagon stood nearby. Behind, a strange, sculpted pair of *kokerbome* grew at the rim of the valley's fault. A wall had been built at the edge: ironstone piled on ironstone, a refuge for cobras in the warm incubating hollows between the rocks. No one ever went there to disturb them.

Elsa climbed through the fence and walked down towards the shed. She looked up at the craggy sweet-thorn. If it had been summer it would have been bright with pollen balls. Now it stood bare in the wind. She opened the double doors with difficulty, grating them back just far enough to slip through. She waited, very still.

The shearing pens were empty. A fleece, smelling rancid, lay on the floor. Near it, small and fragile, the corpse of a bird. In the middle of the shed were the slatted classing tables and the old press, worn and silky with the polish of decades of wool-clip.

Once, Oom Jaap Koen with his thick grey hair and his blacksmith's arms had watched at those tables as workers sorted mohair. The shearers stood to one side, the goats between their knees. At last, shorn but for a sheen of white, the pink flesh showing through, nicked here and there— a wound weeping with hastily-applied healing oil—they were chased into the pen outside. For each goat shorn the shearer would toss a round tan *boerboon* into a tin—a tally of his day's work.

Deft fingers flew among the mohair, the *boerboon* seeds rattled in the tins, the goats cried. Oom Jaap, his hat on his head, his face burnt brown with sun and wind—strangely pale on the forehead—moved along his men, guiding them.

Elsa stood in the big empty shed hearing the tapping of the thorn tree—threads of sound, the branches grating against the walls, the creak of the roof. She listened to the wind.

The wind had always gathered on those hills. Faintly it began, rising, a murmur far out in the desolation of the *poort*. Then it swelled, grew, tunnelled down with a roar, like a train hurtling out across the wilderness. After that the silence ebbed back, deeper than before. The old grey cypress trees stood breathless in the hush.

Elsa went out again, closing the door behind her, thinking of the people who had come there once. The shearers: the spare, the gaunt, the young, the dark, and those descended from the hunters of the valleys—the men who'd crafted bows and quivers, who'd stalked the *springbok* and the *vaal rhebok*. She thought of her father with the face of an ascetic, dressed like a farmer who had gone too. And of Oom Jaap Koen, defeated by the drought.

As Elsa went outside she noticed a lean yellow dog intent upon something in the grass. She walked towards the place where it sniffed and whined, absorbed as only starving creatures can be on so small a prize. It did not see her, so intent was it, until her shadow touched it. It winced and cowered, a dog accustomed to the boot. It snarled, its lip drawn back and then, as though she'd kicked it, slunk away, hunched over, sheltering the softness of its belly from her blows.

She called for Petrus. Stray dogs were not tolerated on

the farms. They were scavengers. She knew that it would have to be destroyed.

'Petrus,' she called. Her voice was thin in the wind. 'Come!' He came towards her.

'There is a stray dog,' she said.

He went ahead, looking for the fugitive. The dog turned, jackal-like and timid, watching his approach. Suddenly Petrus stopped. He was peering down the slope. Then he turned to Elsa. She stood with him on the edge of the hillside where it fell sharply to the district road that marked the boundary of Cedric de Villiers' farm. In a hollow, well secluded from the track and hidden in a clump of *boerboon* bushes, pressed, it seemed, against the hillside, was a hut, built long ago for a herder or a stockman. Before it, on a stone, a blanket was spread in the sun.

A filthy sheepskin dangled in the doorway. The inside was still raw. Elsa could hear, listening minutely, the whine of flies hovering and settling round its edges. The dog that they had followed detached itself from a bush and growled.

'Who are they?' asked Elsa.

'*Andazi.* I do not know. Maybe people who were working here before Baas Koen left.'

'He has been gone too long,' said Elsa doubtfully.

'Who can know this thing?' replied Petrus.

'I wonder where that sheepskin came from,' said Elsa.

'Maybe they are *treks*,' said Petrus. 'Those that go up and down, up and down.'

'Squatters, perhaps,' said Elsa. A man dismissed from another farm, finding shelter. Perhaps it was one of those families that wandered round the district in a cart looking for work, unable to find it without references or connections, considered a liability to employ. Perhaps these people were they who had sometimes brought the pelts of trapped animals to the homestead door: twelve rands for a *rooikat*, five cents a *dassie*, two rands a jackal skin. No more the sleek, fierce amber of a lynx pelt enclosing sinew, muscle, heart. Drab and stinking they became a curiosity to fling on the gun cupboard floor and forget.

Petrus waited a moment, anticipating that Elsa might say

58

something but she only nodded. So he went back to restring the wire and secure it to the upright standing in its place.

Below, the half-cured hide rotated in the wind. There was a movement in the doorway. A black woman came out. On her hip she carried a baby. She let it down in the open space while she shook and turned the blanket on the stone. The baby wailed plaintively. Its hair was tinged orange, its belly distended, its legs and arms were thin and frail.

Its mother walked around the clearing. She gazed off down the road intently as though she was waiting and then she went to the child. She picked it up, dug in her blouse and drew out a flaccid breast. Greedily the child drank, then pulled away and wailed anew, dashing a fist at its mouth and sucking, sucking. The mother hunched over the baby, held it against her. Quietly, unobserved, Elsa climbed the hill out of sight, returning to the waiting men at the boundary fence.

When they had finished she drove on with Petrus and the workers back into the lands of Blackheath. She talked of goats, the drought, the feed that would be arriving at Melkbos Siding in the morning, postponing for the moment any thoughts about the woman in her shelter in the bush. They went on down the track through the old stone gates towards the green enclave in the hills where the house and windmill stood, shaded by the pepper trees.

Elsa was in the kitchen with Chrissie admiring the cake she had iced—with shy pride, for she had not done it before—when the telephone rang. Elsa answered it. It was Cedric de Villiers.

'Elsa my girlie,' he began.

'Yes Uncle Cedric?'

'How are you?'

'Fine.'

'What's the matter? You sound nettled. Have you got a problem?'

Elsa knew that she should tell him about the dog scavenging near his lands. She knew that the sheepskin hanging at the door of the crumbling house had probably been stolen from his flock, or even hers. She could prove that she was the farmer now—and tell him. She did not. Instinctively she said no word to Cedric.

'No Uncle Cedric,' she said. 'I haven't got a problem, but . . .'

'Don't ask me about goats Elsa. I hate the bloody things. Sheep—yes! Goats? No! Don't ask me about goats.'

'It's not goats, Uncle Cedric,' said Elsa patiently, regaining her composure.

'I phoned,' said Uncle Cedric briskly, 'to find out when Jan will be back for a visit.'

'Not for a couple of weeks still. Why?'

'You know that Jaap Koen left?'

'Yes.' The shearing shed, the wind, the thorn tree tapping at the walls. Below, the hut, the woman, a hunted thing, watching for someone in the road.

Cedric was speaking. He was saying, 'Jaap Koen couldn't get rid of his farm at his price. Now it's going dirt cheap. I just spoke to Adrian about it and we've made an offer. The land's in shocking condition but if we buy it and Jan comes in with us we can get stuck into it and improve things. It could be very worthwhile.'

'What about Oom Jaap?'

'I believe he's gone to relations in Uitenhage.'

'I didn't mean that.'

'He and Freek really let that place go to rack and ruin.'

'Oom Jaap was sick,' said Elsa.

'Sick?' Cedric snorted. 'He was too fond of the bottle.'

'It doesn't seem fair with the drought and everything.'

'Now, my girlie,' said Uncle Cedric. 'You mustn't be sentimental. Forget all that. Why should it affect you? Jan would do well to join us, mark my words. The grazing would be a great asset to Blackheath, adjoining as it does.'

'We haven't got extra money for land.'

'Now my girlie, that's not for you to decide. I'll speak to Jan. We can't miss an opportunity like this. By the way, when are you coming over to Melvynside to talk about the garden? I need advice from green fingers.'

'Green fingers are useless in a drought,' returned Elsa

coolly.

'We can always plan,' he said. 'Phone me as soon as you know when Jan will be home.'

'When he comes back it's for such a very short time,' she replied plaintively.

'Well that's all right. Adrian said he'd fit in with Jan.'

There was a pause. Then Elsa said, 'Yes Uncle Cedric. Goodbye.' She replaced the receiver. 'Adrian will fit in with Jan,' she said loudly in imitation. 'Bloody Adrian!'

She sat a long time in the hall. The empty white wall was reflected in the mirror of the dresser. Only the oranges in the fruit bowl were bright in the shadows. She trailed upstairs. A *berg-wind* was blowing. It shook the windows. Way beyond the shed, above the sporadic sounds of goats, she could hear the workers' voices. A woman in the vegetable patch broke clods of earth with a hoe. Up on the *bult* the aloes budded among the thickets of euphorbia. A *witgat* tree grew hunched against the cold. The dust was streaming out across the sky.

'Forget all that Elsa. Why should it affect you,' Uncle Cedric had said. How could she forget: Oom Jaap's shed, the small, broken body of a bird, the door shoring up leaves and withered grass, the hut, the sheepskin turning in the wind. Nontinti. Sipho. Jan. And somewhere Abedingo.

Long ago Nontinti had used the word *ithinzi*, in some old love story, a parable of honour. *Ithinzi* was a small, black panic that rose, that could follow, shadow the spirit of a man and bring him grief. What did Adrian or Cedric know about *ithinzi*? Did no shadow follow them and wait to stir unwanted tears?

Out on the lawn Elsa could see Nella and Tombizodwa turning circles round each other, arms held out towards the sky. Only they—laughing, small child delight—held everything for that moment that was certain, that was possible. She turned from them into the darkness of the house and wept.

# ☙ 4 ☙

---

Nella curled up on the bed, thumb in her mouth as Elsa changed for Joy Fraser's stork party.

'Hello my Nellatjie.' Elsa sat down next to her.

'Guess what?' Nella took Elsa's face between her hands. 'Matthew and Kippy will be at Grandma's. I think I'll let them kiss me.'

'You do that,' said Elsa, smiling.

She turned to her cupboard, to the ranks of dresses, red, yellow, green, made from material from the local shop. She seemed to have had them all for years. Where amongst them was something that looked right for Elsa now? The drab slacks, the unmatching blouses. They hung there, a testimony to Elsa as she was—a sparrow living in her patch of grass, never venturing beyond.

There was no allure in the wardrobe, nothing that couldn't be found in every other cupboard in the district, except for the necklace. She had bought it in Grahamstown. It was made from Moroccan trade beads with ostrich eggshell discs in between. Jan did not like them. He thought them clumsy.

Jan liked girls with bosoms and bottoms and slim athletic legs. He liked solitaire diamonds and gold chains. He liked elegant ankles and short skirts. He liked girls in sports clothes. And here was Elsa—short, a little dumpy, with thick pale hair cut to the chin, always tucked behind an ear. She had a square face with a long mouth and wide cheek bones. No one noticed her eyes, for they were dark and her brows were heavy and defined. She was not as pretty as her sister nor as glamorous as Elizabeth. Like her mother, Elsa was handsome—too healthy, she thought, to be interesting.

She dragged dress after dress from the rail and looked at each. Nella, lying on the bed, had made her own choices.

62

She wore grey shorts, long brown socks, lace-up shoes and a pink ballet jersey handed down from one of Elizabeth's children—a shrieking combination. Elsa knew that Annatjie would say: My God Elsa, you sew so well but look at Nella! She looks like she comes from the orphanage! The colours! Nella, with her small, pale face, one ear pushing through the cropped hair, could wear what she liked. She was a combination of all the things most dear to her: school children in lace-ups and socks, ballet girls in cross-over jerseys, boy cousins in rugby shorts. Underneath, Elsa knew, would be her favourite panties—Mary-Mary-Quite-Contrary with a watering can and a nylon row of hollyhocks.

Elsa chose a skirt, a jacket and a pair of boots. She dressed and stamped downstairs. Nella slid on the bannister behind her, her legs sticking out of the absurd grey shorts.

''Bye Tombi,' she called to Tombizodwa who was eating lunch on the back steps with Chrissie.

Tombizodwa watched Nella walk towards the car with the cake tin in her arms. Then she lowered her eyes to the plate of beans in her lap. With the same light delicacy as her mother she spooned them into her mouth.

Elsa drove along the edge of the *spruit*, the afternoon light was harsh. Even the soap bushes were withered, casting short, dry shadows. She took the road to Kleinfontein, turning into the thick shade of the drive. Nella looked out excitedly and clung to Elsa's skirt.

'What is it Nellie?'

'I'm shy.'

'Don't be silly!' She said it automatically. Then she held Nella's hand more closely to make up for it, knowing the desire to escape. 'There's no one here yet. You can help Grandma set out the tea things.'

Nella ran off down the path to the vegetable patch where she could see Dorothy Southey picking parsley from a sandy furrow. Elsa went inside.

She stood a moment on the red-polished floor of the back *stoep* and listened. The unused meat cupboard was in place, filled now with dusters, brushes, floor cloths. She stopped instinctively to hear the voices, the sounds of the old house as it had been when she was small: the slap of dough as Sophie made the bread, the wandering click of the dog's nails as it came down the passage, the cries of children—sisters, brothers, cousins, her father's laugh from the office at the end of the house. His boots stood there still, polished every week.

Elsa opened the door of his room and went inside. She had rarely been there since he had died. She crossed to his desk and sat in his chair. The cushions were hollowed and comfortable from years of use. She opened a drawer. Among the pencils and papers, seed catalogues and envelopes she found a small San arrow. She took it out and examined it. She turned it over in her hands. It was delicate and beautifully crafted of reed and bone and sinew.

She remembered when her father had found it. They had gone out one Sunday, far from Kleinfontein and explored the slopes at the head of a valley so desolate and abandoned that no one ever ventured there except a herdsman with a flock of goats to camp out through the summer. In winter it was left to winds, bleak and cold, blowing off the Winterberge.

She sat there, the arrow balanced in her hands, and looked over at the bookcase. On the upper shelf was Norman Southey's collection on Rock Art, Anthropology, Archaeology, the San. Next to them, carefully numbered, were boxes of correspondence. Elsa lifted down a file and examined it. It was full of annotated notes marking sites of rock paintings on Kleinfontein, Blackheath and the surrounding hills, letters from Dr Balfour, an archaeologist, who had been Norman Southey's oldest and most valued friend.

Elsa had often accompanied her father to see Dr Balfour at the Museum during the holidays or on an afternoon outing in her last year at school. She remembered the tall Victorian building, the permeating coldness of the galleries, being ushered through a side door by an attendant in a white coat to a collection of buildings at the back. She had sat and drunk coffee and powdered milk from a Pyrex cup while her father and Dr Balfour had discussed a dig.

Her father had been at home in the archaeologist's office

among the litter of papers and files—more at home than on the farm among his sheep. He had developed an apologetic air towards his workers and had spent more and more time in his room at the end of the passage, writing notes and reading journals. She shared it with him then, going with him on inspection tours that led them higher and higher up the *koppies* and the valleys as they visited the old rock shelters of the extinct Southern San, searching always for evidence that they had lived there once.

The end of the search was the building at the Museum and she and her father the link between the two. It was strange to see the little arrows they had found among the ironstone of the hillsides, numbered in ink and lying preserved in the storeroom, no longer theirs to touch. The only evidence of their part in the preservation was the entry in the bottom corner of the catalogue card: donated by Norman Southey, Kleinfontein and the date.

Elsa had been intrigued by the people at the Museum. There was one young man she had noticed often, who walked with hands thrust deep in the pockets of his lab. coat, his hair very black, a little wild. He wore ankle *velskoens* with his jeans. He drove the Museum Land Rover and he was always alone.

He did not notice her, she knew, for she looked like what she was—a schoolgirl in a lumpy green uniform with no accomplishments.

When she had begun to read her father's journals and search for artefacts for him and talk about the Museum, Jan had been annoyed. 'Come on Els. What do you want to keep all this crap for?' he would say, knowing it would annoy her as he (dismissively) inspected her little collection of stone flints.

After her father had died Elsa did not go to the Museum any more. Her small collection of arrowheads had disappeared. She did not know what had happened to the young man, but for years, out of habit, she scrutinized the drivers of Land Rovers in case he was behind the wheel with his wild black hair. She never saw him though. It was always with a sense of disappointment that she encountered fat farmers and their wives taking goats to town or a group of men, like small boys out of school, embarking on a fishing trip, and who might return her interested stare with waves and hoots.

Elsa became a nurse instead of an archaeologist. Her father was dead. He was not there to support her choice and her mother had simply said (perhaps out of her own resentment at his preoccupation), 'Archaeology's impractical Elsa. You'd make a good nurse. You always wanted to be one.'

'Only because you were.'

'No better profession darling. It's always something you can fall back on.'

And so it was.

Elsa closed the door to her father's room. She could hear Nella and Sophie singing in the yard. Nella ran round the side of the house. 'Can I come in?'

'Of course,' said Elsa. 'Pick some flowers for the tea table. I'll find a vase for you.'

Elsa went down the hall, past the big bedroom where her parents used to sleep. Her mother had a smaller room now. It was dark, shaded by a deep verandah. All the jars that Elsa had kept as a child—packed with seeds, stones, dried helichrysums—were gone.

The wardrobe stood squarely in the corner. The chair with its tapestry cushion faced the table. The gardening books were regimented on the shelves.

'Here are the flowers,' said Nella, coming in with a handful of marigolds, a tuft of sweet-thorn leaves. 'There weren't any others.'

'Those are fine.' Elsa smiled. She took a small china jug from the dressing table and filled it at the basin. The tap sputtered and the pipes knocked somewhere in the walls.

'I'll put them on the table. Grandma says do you want some tea?'

'That would be nice.'

Nella skipped back to the kitchen. Elsa listened to the sound of her feet, unhesitating, unconscious of the manikins in the

66

laundry chute or the one-legged *mazimuzimu* lurking near the bathroom door. For her it was a place inhabited by no one but Grandma, Sophie and Johannes. No creatures called *'gunqu, gunqu, gunqu'* as they thudded down the *bult* at night, making the jackals howl. No horned eagle owl waited on the windowsill to swoop in, black-winged to seize her. Sophie did not tell tales to Nella by the coal stove as she had to her daughter Chrissie and to Elsa long ago.

Sophie had taken the tea to the verandah. Nella sat on the wall swinging her legs. Dorothy Southey poured milk into the cups, leaned back in her chair and looked out across the lawn. A small vein fluttered in her temple. Elsa saw her put her hand up furtively to still the pulse. She handed her mother a cup of tea, saying nothing, for Dorothy could not talk about her feelings or share her thoughts with Elsa. She was always brisk and cheerful.

She had, Elsa knew, subconscious though it might have been, a need to hold exclusive rights to memories of Norman Southey. Elsa had always wondered at the contrast between her parents: her father's easy warmth, her mother's cool, dry wit. Perhaps Dorothy had thought him profligate with his time and generosity and whatever residual love was left behind she took as hers, by right.

Elsa's father had often spoken of the continuity of living, of love and life being gifts passed on from one person to another, and of the interdependence of man and animal and earth, of renewal in each day. It seemed to Elsa that her mother had arrested any real sense of living when her husband died, afraid to go on. Her exclusion of her children from her grief made it impossible to reach her or to help dispel the loneliness.

Dorothy Southey lived out the ritual of her hours the way she had when Norman was alive. She did flowers in his study, ate at the big dining room table, Sophie serving, the candles lit.

And so the days went on unyieldingly and a deserted Sunday feeling clung to Kleinfontein now that there was no more busyness to keep out the sounds of the leaves tapping at the windows or the creak of the roof contracting as the sun went down.

Dorothy Southey poured herself another cup of tea and said, 'I do wish Bruce was finished at Grootfontein and could come home and run the place for me.' She thought a moment and then she said, 'Bruce is not like Dad though. He'll need guidance and I'm too tired to think about farming any more.'

'He's doing well at College Mum,' said Elsa. 'He'll make a good farmer. He might be a bit wild now but he's only twenty.'

'It's not that. He doesn't seem to be committed to anything. He's so irresponsible.'

Bruce, always in boots, even in the height of summer, his jeans faded to perfection on his thighs. Bruce with his knives and guns, a motorbike between his knees, flying down the roads of Blackheath and of Kleinfontein.

'Let Bruce get on with it,' said Elsa. 'The farm's his now. Dad would have wanted him to make his own decisions. Give him a chance.'

Her mother was about to argue, changed her mind and said, 'I bumped into Cedric in town this morning when I went to have my hair done. He tells me you're doing all the work on Blackheath yourself.'

'With Petrus and all the others,' she said. 'I'm enjoying it.'

'I still can't understand why Jan chose to go to the dam. Surely Cedric or Adrian could have helped.' She looked disapproving.

'Leave it Mum. He's there and it won't be for long.' She suspected that her mother disapproved of Jan working as a foreman more than of his absence. Foremen were not part of Dorothy Southey's experience.

Elsa was relieved to see Annatjie's car bumping along the road near the dam. It turned into the yard and stopped.

'Annatjie's early,' said Dorothy. 'I didn't expect her till two.'

Annatjie walked across the yard, followed by her daughters. A young black woman in her pink print uniform struggled behind them, laden with two big hampers.

'Cooeee! Anyone at home? Auntie Dot?' Annatjie called.

She came down the passage. Her small daughters, dressed identically, trouped behind her.

'Hello Annatjie,' said Dorothy Southey, rising graciously, offering a kiss. 'You're early.'

'Thought I'd get here in good time and help lay out the eats. After all, the party was my idea and I didn't want to put you to trouble.'

'Hello Annatjie,' said Elsa.

'Hi Els! Did you remember the cake, hey? I can't think what I asked you to bring. Was it Swiss roll or chocolate chiffon pie?'

'Vanilla sponge.'

'Right! That means Petra will have made the Swiss roll. I tried to phone you this morning, by the way. The girl said you were out on the farm. It's impossible to get hold of you these days. What were you doing?'

'Fixing a fence.'

'What's the matter with that famous bossboy of yours that you keep praising to the skies?'

'Would you like a cup of coffee Annatjie?' said Elsa, ignoring the remark. 'There's time before the others arrive. Hi girls!' She turned to Annatjie's daughters. 'Nella's gone round the side to look for Sophie. See if you can find her. She brought along a lot of toys so you could all play.'

The guests arrived in cars and trucks. The dust hung red and heavy in the driveway. Everyone was dressed up for the occasion—there were few opportunities to show off a new outfit, to exchange patterns or admire handiwork.

Joy came last, exclaiming in surprise at the gathering, playing the game generously to the end. She hugged Annatjie in thanks and kissed Dorothy Southey. She sat on the floor surrounded by presents, her big tummy held before her under the folds of the maternity dress, and read the messages on the gifts she had been given, trying to guess the senders.

Elsa perched on the arm of her mother's chair. Mrs Harcourt, Dorothy's oldest friend, leaned over and whispered loudly, 'I'm sorry your husband left you dear.'

Annatjie caught Elsa's eye and repressed a smile. Her bright red bauble earrings bobbed at her plump lobes. She lit a cigarette and looked away.

When Joy had opened all the gifts and everyone had gathered near the tea table Annatjie turned to Elsa. 'Kobie says the dam is too terrible!' She helped herself to asparagus tart and continued, 'I worry about them—the town's full of contract workers. They're rough types Elsie! All the boozing! It seems there's girls too. What will they get up to—I mean, you know Kobie.'

Elsa nodded automatically. She could imagine what Kobie might do. He had always been loud and over-enthusiastic. He reminded her of a bullock butting away at something. He had often picked fights at the Club.

She remembered a New Year's party in the town hall when she and Annatjie had been eighteen and Kobie had been sulky because Annatjie had brought along a fellow student from the Teacher Training College in Graaff-Reinet. Kobie had leant across the supper table and hit him on the mouth, splitting his lip.

Andrew Fraser and Jan had parted them and dragged Kobie outside. He'd glared over his shoulder at Annatjie who was fussing around the injured boyfriend and said, 'Ag man, that guy's such a toss! She only fancies him because of that big puss-catcher of a car of his!' Annatjie had looked at him scornfully but it had only taken a weekend before the boyfriend was packed off, back to Graaff-Reinet and Kobie was reinstated, suitably contrite.

'You're lucky you don't have to worry about Jan,' said Annatjie pouring herself another cup of coffee. 'He's just not likely to run after girls. Anyway Els, how are you man?' She smoothed her short hair and plumped up the crown.

'I'm fine Annatjie. Sorry I haven't phoned for ages but I knew I'd see you today.'

'What have you been doing? Why are you so antisocial? Every time any of us come round you've gone off somewhere.'

'Not at all,' said Elsa. 'What's your news?'

'Cheryl's been sick,' said Annatjie. 'Tonsils. She's always got a cold. That doctor in town's useless, s'trues God. I'm taking her to a specialist in East London next time I go. She's been on antibiotics every two weeks.' She squashed out her butt. 'I've been looking at Nella. You must get a tonic for her. I've never seen such a pale child. There's some stuff—it's fantastic! I can't remember the name but I'll phone you.'

She scrutinized Elsa. 'So, Elsie, how are you hey? What else have you been up to?' she repeated, anticipating intimate revelation.

'Have some cake,' said Elsa evasively. 'It's Ma's speciality. You must ask her for the recipe.'

A little exasperated Annatjie turned to Joy. 'Listen Joy, all those blue things hey? And I know it's another girl! Give me a hair and I'll do the test with your wedding ring. It always works.'

She threaded one of Joy's hairs through the wedding ring and let it swing above her wrist. Everyone crowded round to see its movements.

'It's going to be a girl!' said Annatjie triumphantly. 'I told you so!'

Elsa glanced out of the window. Nella was running up and down the lawn in her big shoes, Matthew after her— all knees and knuckles and ribs.

'Do you know what?' said Petra Steyn to Annatjie. 'Hannah *is* having an affair with that lawyer from Grahamstown.'

Elsa, embarrassed, took up a small cheese puff and fingered it. 'Sssshhh,' she said softly, for Hannah was sitting on the window seat nearby talking to Dorothy Southey.

'Don't be ridiculous!' said Annatjie. 'Who'd want such a pale, thin thing? I mean, she's just not the sort!'

'It's true!' said Petra loudly. 'Have you seen him? He's helluva good-looking.'

'Well, do you blame her? How'd you like to be stuck with that pompous twit of a husband? Is the lawyer married?'

'Yes,' said Petra primly.

'I believe he's separated,' said Joy.

'So? Hannah's the cause of it, let me tell you.'

Elsa did not know Hannah very well. She'd been a contemporary of Joy's elder sister—eight, ten years their senior,

71

her children already adolescent. Their circle of friends had been different.

Elsa glanced across at Hannah wondering if she'd heard Petra's strident whisper. Evidently she hadn't for she sat there, still in her repose. Hannah, who had always been too quiet and unassuming to arouse any interest, had suddenly become the subject of covert speculation.

There she sat, neither distant nor aloof but somehow free. It wasn't possible to harness Hannah. Elsa envied her her independence. The disapproval of the others had arisen, Elsa realized, not because of what Hannah might have done— by that they were secretly intrigued—but from a fear that the order of their own lives was also tenuous and that it could be overturned as easily as Hannah's had.

Afraid herself of isolation Elsa had always allowed her friends to cajole or bully her to be like them. They had dressed her in their clothes, told her her hair was awful, taken her shopping to improve her and she, like a puppet, had mimicked and was theirs.

They had even argued over her wedding dress. It had been straight, severe, classic. She had dreamed of a dress that was soft and light, of freshly-picked *veld* flowers, her hair wild and loose.

Instead she had worn a chignon, well lacquered and pinned into a plain headdress. She had carried roses, cold from the florist's refrigerator.

'You look magnificent Elsa,' said her mother.

'Stunning!' declared her sister.

'Don't drop anything on it!' Annatjie had warned. 'It would be so typical.'

'Stop staring!' said Annatjie in Elsa's ear.

'I wasn't.'

'Yes you were.' She looked at Elsa a little patronizingly. 'Some people do have affairs you know.'

'I wasn't thinking of that. I was thinking of something else.'

Hannah got up. She went to Dorothy Southey. She kissed Joy and she wished her luck. She went from the room saying goodbye to those near enough to notice. She walked away across the lawn.

'She's gone now,' Petra said. 'But I can tell you, they were seen at Port Alfred together. My sister said that when she took the kids out from school she saw them there. Can you credit it?'

'What's his name?' asked Annatjie, displeased to know less than Petra.

'I don't know,' said Petra, 'but he works with Hannah's brother.'

'Who's Hannah's brother?' asked Annatjie.

'Don't you remember that chap from College—Nick Chase? He might have been at school with Andrew and Jan —no I'm wrong, he must be quite a bit older. He's an Advocate in Grahamstown. He's weird though. He and this chap Hannah's involved with do cases for the natives free, you know the sort of thing?' said Petra, enjoying her audience. 'I tell you, Hannah's gone funny herself. She's got some very liberal ideas all of a sudden. Have you noticed?'

'Chase?' said Dorothy Southey. 'It was a Miss Chase who had something to do with the Royal Tour in forty-seven. Something about a Captain in the Navy.'

Elsa turned away. Her mother was using her usual ploy for raising the tone of someone else's gossip.

Petra pretended not to hear. 'Allan says this Nick was a good guy at school—played first team cricket—but you know those students from Rhodes get a bit out of hand, hey? That's why my Dad sent my *boet* to Potch.'

Elsa talked about Kobie with Annatjie, childbirth with Joy, she admired Petra's macrame, she sat close to Mrs Harcourt. She went to each person, looking into their faces, speaking to them, hearing them: Annatjie's errant maid, Joy's drunken gardener, Mrs Harcourt's cataracts, her mother's marmalade that wouldn't set, Petra's visit to the smart interior decorator in Port Elizabeth. She listened carefully as if hearing for the last time, not with impatience, not with contempt, but with a sense of detachment. The most familiar things suddenly seemed strange and distant.

73

When Elsa got back to Blackheath she carried Nella upstairs and laid her gently in her bed without waking her. She did not want a grumpy child whining round her in the kitchen.

Petrus came to tell her the doings of the afternoon and then he went, Chrissie following, a long bundle of wood balanced on her head as they walked towards the workers' houses.

Elsa switched on the lights and waited for Jan to phone. She made coffee and fed the animals. The night wind got up. It was moaning in the pepper trees. She stood and listened as she opened the back door to let out the dogs. She watched them sniff along the hedge, squeeze under the fence and disappear.

She could hear the wind in the reeds of the *vlei*—a sound like fire eating through dry grass. The clock in the living room struck the half-hour. The chime was deep and old.

Jan phoned after eight.

'How is it love?' she asked, relieved to hear his voice.

'Bloody awful. It's just like being in the army again.'

'Your weekend's nearly here. How are Kobie and Andrew?'

'Fine. I hope you've been seeing Annatjie and Joy? You wives must stick together. It'd be the right thing to do.'

The right thing to do. Elsa kept down her irritation. She did not say—I do not want to sit and discuss macrame. I do not want to go to meetings of the Women's Institute any more. I do not want to make salads for the Club. I do not want to play tennis on Mondays. He would not have understood. He would have been stung.

'Yes Jan, I've seen Annatjie and Joy.'

'How's my Nellie?'

'Fine. She had a very happy day with all the kids at Grandma's.'

There was a pause. 'I wish I wasn't in this bloody hole,' he said.

She told him everything about the farm, passed on messages from Petrus. She mentioned the fence but not the small house sheltering in the scrub, the sheep-pelt turning in the wind or the woman with the child cradled on her breast.

When she put down the receiver she felt angry—not with

Jan, for she touched his old raincoat which hung on the hall stand—but with Annatjie and Joy for existing at all.

She had known them all her life, but now the names, the associations, brought back a sense of displacement she had felt increasingly since Jan had gone.

Beyond the world of Annatjie and Joy, her mother, even Jan, was another place. She had shared it with her father. He too had been displaced in the midst of a secure and loving world. His too was the mythology of the stars. He only could have understood why she could hear, just beyond the conscious sounds, the pulse of something bigger, something not quite understood.

Even when Norman Southey was buried Elsa had not wept as she sat in the district church among the short-haired farmers. Jan was solemn in his dark jacket, his big wrists sticking out of the cuffs, disturbed, she knew, by her composure.

Elsa had paid her tribute later, out on the hills of Kleinfontein. She had gone to their favourite San shelter, down a small, blind valley, obscured by boulders and scrub. She had walked through the *veld*, the tufts of grass so dry that the stems pierced the canvas of her shoes. She had climbed to where the *kannabos* grew and the *gwarri*, up to the crests where the helichrysums bloomed in the wind. They budded, opened and remained, petals whorled in layers, evidence of the men and women who had gone before, reaffirming life. Immutable.

Elsa poured herself another cup of coffee. The cat, which had been asleep in a crate in the pantry came out, stretched and yawned. Elsa stroked it and gave it a little milk in her saucer. When the phone rang she started so much she spilt the coffee and the cat looked at her in surprise. Elsa went to the hall and answered.

It was Annatjie with the name of the tonic she had recommended for Nella's pale face. It was all Elsa could do to stop herself from flinging her cup at the wall.

She closed the doors and went upstairs. She looked in at Nella's room. Nella lay, still in her shorts, her small dirty feet tucked up. Elsa covered her and touched her head,

75

smoothing her hair. Nella seemed so small and solitary in the big oak bed.

'We'll have six children Elsie,' Jan had once said after they had become engaged.

'Six!'

'Why not? Three of each. A whole de Villiers span.'

'Who's going to run around after six children?'

'They'll take care of each other. Look at Andrew's family.'

'I'll be pregnant for years!'

'So? I think pregnant women are beautiful.'

'Just like you think cows in calf are beautiful,' she'd snorted, knowing how he loved to stand and admire his expectant Frieslands.

But there was only one. Nella—with her small, pale face, the hint of a cleft in her chin, hair thick as Jan's, blonde as Elsa's. She followed Elsa like an orphan lamb, hopeful of games. She needed a brother or a sister to fill her days. In September she'd be six. Boarding school on her own would devastate her.

Nella had been conceived with a joyous defiance just before they were married. Elsa had rejected any notion of guilt. Now the irony disturbed her.

She had returned from the hospital—a stolen weekend— leaving the smokey flats of the city behind her and driving out on her own, taking a back route, heading secretly for Blackheath and for Jan. They had locked her car in the shed, left the telephone unanswered and retreated to the house.

On Sunday afternoon they had gone to the loft to choose some *biltong* for Elsa to take back with her to town. There was a *berg-wind* blowing down from Mpumalanga and ants plied along the brickwork of the back *stoep* looking for the small, shrivelled raisins that had fallen from the vines. The sheepdog followed them and lay outside on the landing in the shade of the wisteria creeper.

Elsa had stooped through the low doorway and sat on the old tin which Grandma had used for making soap from ostrich eggs and mutton fat. Jan had examined the *biltong* hanging in strips from the wire racks. 'It's *springbok*,' he had said. 'Adrian shot it last time he was up.'

76

She had watched him. In profile his nose was straight but unpronounced—not like Adrian's: a beak over a lazy lip. Jan's mouth was firm. It could never slacken into discontent like his brother's. And always it was Jannie's hair—astonishingly thick and dark and straight, curving in at his neck. He had farmer's arms, very tanned, the veins pronounced, the compliment of blood to muscle.

'What are you looking at?' he had asked.

'You've got interesting forearms.'

'How can anyone have interesting forearms, for God's sake?'

'I don't know!' she'd laughed. 'Like girls can have interesting ankles. You're always going on about thin ankles.'

'Pity yours are chubby, hey?'

'They are not! You've got rugby player's thighs anyway.'

'So? I thought rugby players turned you on.'

'Well, they don't!'

'Is that so?' He'd wiped his forehead on his sleeve and thrown the sticks of *biltong* onto a dresser. He'd pushed the door closed. 'You'd better go back to the Museum then,' he'd said mockingly, 'and start digging around among those archaeologists. You never know—you might find a prehistoric prick. Wouldn't that be exciting?'

The wind stirred outside. They could hear a ram calling imperiously in a pen by the shed. Jan went down the attic, glancing into boxes and drawers. It was dusty and he rubbed his nose and sneezed. An old sofa, brocade-covered with embossed fleur-de-lis and gold tassels, stood in a corner.

'God, Grandma had some furniture! Can you imagine hauling all this stuff around in an ox wagon?'

He lay down on the couch and stretched out his legs, pushing off his boots, foot from foot, and putting his hands behind his head.

'Come Elsie,' he'd said.

Elsa had sat next to him, leaning against his knees. Between the slats of the air vents, soft with dust, the light crept in. Through holes in the roof where bolts had worked loose it lanced down, trembling in patches—not liquid and pale, but thick and tactile, like star-flowers opening on the floor.

It was strange to recall, to remember, after all the years of living with him in the house, the wonder, the newness of Jan. He'd dragged her sundress over her head and smacked her bare bottom playfully, pulling her down. She had curled within the crook of his warm arm and kissed his temple— that small, vulnerable place beside his eye, and at the hollow below the muscle of his hip where the skin is soft, most naked of all.

He could go away and be as full of pretences as he liked: she had seen him playing rugby often enough, filthy with grass burns; drinking beer at the Club or driving too fast in the *bakkie* for the hell of it. She had seen him with his friends at the Cricket-*Braai* where he was sometimes loud, occasionally awkward. But here alone, he was Jannie. She had known it always—within Jan, somewhere—very seldom seen by others, was a stillness, a kind of gentleness he kept for her.

She held him, the light trembling on the floor beside them. Much later they had dozed, his hand heavy on her collarbone. Squeezed between his side and the musty couch, uncomfortable and damp but not wishing to move, to spoil the moment, Elsa had listened sleepily to the wind in the pepper trees outside and a barbet tinking, tinking somewhere on the *bult*.

They must have slept a long time for when they woke there had been a deep blueness in the loft and the sheepdog was barking, and in the yard she could hear Andrew shouting for Jan.

He had woken with a start and muttered 'shit' as he'd pulled on his pants and shirt. He'd done up the buttons hurriedly in the wrong buttonholes.

'Bugger off, Andrew!' he had yelled good-naturedly down the stairs. 'Don't you know three's a crowd?'

Elsa had scrambled to retrieve her clothes and had followed him to the landing. She'd smiled sheepishly. 'Hello Andrew.'

Andrew had looked up at them. As he'd turned his head Elsa could see his ears burned fiercely as they always did when he was embarrassed. 'I'm sorry, hey? I didn't know you were here Elsie.'

78

'Do you want some *biltong*?' Elsa had said as she twisted her engagement ring round and round her finger self-consciously. 'We were just getting it when you came.'

'Thanks hey,' Andrew had mumbled. He'd rubbed his hand across his woolly hair. Elsa had turned back into the room as Andrew plunged up the stairs.

Jan had leant on the door frame adjusting his buttons slowly while Andrew studied the racks, inspecting each strip of meat.

Elsa had frowned at Jan and mouthed, 'Stop it—don't show off.'

But Jan had ignored her, too pleased with himself to care.

Elsa knew—there was no doubt in her—that Nella had been conceived that afternoon in the hot, dusty loft, with the tinker barbet calling on the *bult*. Her mother's disapproval had hardly seemed to matter. Admonitions did not count any more. She had returned to Kleinfontein with relief and a sense of triumph and Jan had only laughed out loud when she'd told him and kissed her and wondered whether they should call the baby Richard after his father, or Louis after Oupa, and Elsa had said, 'We'll call it nothing of the sort! It's a girl and her name is Nella!'

In her own room Elsa took one of Jan's T shirts from the cupboard and put it on. She got into bed at his side, holding his pillow. She did not stretch out her legs for the sheets were stiff and cold. She curled up tighter, her knees drawn in. She turned out the light and held the pillow closer.

She lay alone, Jan gone, high up in the house. There—the passing of an owl, mouse in talon, the slow yield of blood to the gapes of owlets. Deep beneath the walls the roots burrowed mole-like down to rock. Inside, the *rusbank* in the hall, the clock, the Aga with its shifting coals, stood in place. Outside was the great, cold, moving space of air and cloud and star.

Somewhere in the blacklands, just beyond the reaches of the *vlei* the dogs, hunting, stopped as one and listened. And then they barked—short, staccato, angry.

Someone waited in the dark. He heard the dogs, the sound of their approach. Quietly, deftly, he retraced his steps. He

79

scaled the fence, reached the road and crossed it, climbing up into the thorn scrub growing on the western flank of Oom Jaap Koen's abandoned farm.

# ❧ 5 ❧

Jan sat in the bar, newly-showered. His face and arms had been burnt by the sun that bounced all day off the shallow water of the cofferdams. He wore a white, short-sleeved shirt and his old school tie. He was too big for the stool. He drank his beer, half-perched, leaning against the counter.

It was a seedy bar, crammed with people: construction workers still dressed in overalls, their safety helmets tucked under their chairs. Kobie and Andrew were there, farmers' faces among the shopkeepers, clerks and site crew. Jan watched. He ordered another beer. He splashed some down his tie, wiped his mouth roughly with his wrist and drank more.

Kobie and Andrew, taking it more slowly, were going on about blowfly in their sheep. They talked loudly at each other, sweating above their buttoned collars.

They had not been on the dam wall that morning. Jan had. He had walked down from the site office, the white heat glaring from the acres of concrete. Ahead of him a man was directing a work gang, dragging a cable. He stood, his hands in his overall pockets, shouting directions above the wind. The work gang moved off. The cable rasped across the rough ground behind them. The man reached into his pocket for a packet of cigarettes. He lit one, crouching his hand around the flame. Jan strolled past. As he did the man looked up —a furtive glance before he turned away. Jan stopped. It was Freek Koen, Oom Jaap's elder son.

'Hello Freek,' said Jan.

Freek shook his hand briefly. All around the wind blew. Below, the workers waited, turned from the gusts.

'I didn't expect to see you here,' said Freek Koen. He glanced at Jan's overalls. Their issue was the same.

'The drought's been bad for all of us,' said Jan.

Freek held his cigarette tentatively in his hand. It burned down slowly between his fingers. He twisted his mouth and said, 'It seems as if I'll lose my farm thanks to you de Villiers.' He looked at Jan then, hostile. 'This time I wish you lose too. I hope the drought will finish all of you.' He spoke thick, deliberate English.

'What do you mean?' said Jan, defensive in his turn.

'You know well,' said Freek. The light was stark on the sallow planes of his face, his small moustache. He put his cigarette to his lips. The ash fell down; shreds of grey, they scattered on the ground. 'Your Uncle and Adrian.'

He pronounced the name in his own language, as it should have been spoken: Ad-ri-aan, underscoring it, reminding Jan that though the de Villiers might have forgotten their provenance, he hadn't.

'My father is an old man,' said Freek Koen. 'He has to take what he can get. There is nothing for him to fight with.'

'Listen Freek, it's got nothing to do with me.'

Freek Koen stepped back and threw his butt down into the maw of the wall. 'Your Uncle and brother have made an offer on Brakkloof. It's the most ridiculous thing I ever heard of. This drought finished us and they know it. They offered my father nothing—but he'll take it. It's like giving bones to a kaffir dog. It's hungry for anything.' He looked out across the gorge and then he said, 'Brakkloof's been in our family for a hundred and fifty years. You de Villiers,' he said, 'you don't give a damn for anyone. You never have.'

He walked down to where the work gang sat and waited. Freek Koen in his orange helmet, the nape of his neck red where his anger and the sun had caught him. Jan stood alone, the blood beating at his temples. Freek Koen in overalls— a man like himself, a man compromised by drought.

Jan did not follow him for there was nothing to say: I am a farmer too Freek, a man with goats, a worker on the wall like you? Would Freek turn and look at him distantly as he had when a boy, riding his horse along the *spruit*, aloof, secure on Brakkloof lands from the taunts of the bully Adrian? There was something incongruous about Freek standing in his orange helmet, a work gang to command. Adrian had always mocked the old mill at Brakkloof, the chaos of the yard, the ducks, the geese, pigs, dogs that roamed unchecked, at Freek Koen and his sisters terrorizing mousebirds in the orchard.

But now Adrian and Uncle Cedric were going to buy that farm—order it, knock it into shape, make it work their way with their machines and their vast bank loans. Brakkloof as Freek had known it would simply die.

Jan walked away fighting with the wind. He went into the pre-fab. site office and sat at his desk. The walls shook, pounded by the grit that was flung in gusts against its sides. Sweat ran down his legs, his neck, his back. A calendar picturing a vineyard and a purple row of mountains skidded back and forth on its nail. Jan swore at the wind, the dust, the noise, at Freek Koen with his sallow face and his hatred. At Cedric. At Adrian. In the end it always came back to Adrian. Whatever price was exacted, for whatever reason— Jan had always paid it. For Adrian.

He kicked the door shut, smashing his boot against the frame. Later he went out with Kobie and Andrew to the hotel in town. He had not phoned home. He had longed too much for the smell of the house, the mustiness of the gun cupboard under the stairs, the scent of stocks in the hall. Elsa.

Some young girls walked in, clinging close to each other, laughing among themselves. They perched on the stools nearby. Jan recognized two of them. They worked in the Building Society in the town where he went to deposit his weekly wage. He always watched their hands flit across the notes, checking them, careful fingers poised with the small, rubber stamp, entering the date in his savings book.

He took another sip of his drink. His eyes rested on the nearest. She had, he thought, an amazing bum. She wore white slacks. The material was thin. Her waist was small but her hips were strong. She was big, with long thighs and that firm arse.

He ordered another beer and watched. Jan licked his bottom lip, sucked it slightly, drank more. Her hair was blond, a little bushy, cut in layers. She had a small mole on her neck.

83

The gold chain she wore moved across it every now and then.

'A coon got squashed by a truck this afternoon,' said one of the site crew to the girls.

'Oh shame!'

'Silly *hout* fell off the back.'

'They drive too fast on bad roads,' said Jan quietly.

The girl in the white slacks turned to him, swivelling on her seat. Her front, diagonally striped, ploughed round through smoke. Lovely tits. He gazed at them then looked at the site foreman.

The man shrugged. 'Thank God it was a *hout*, that's all I can say.'

'He's also human, you know,' said the girl in white slacks. 'Shame!' she added. 'He's also got feelings.' Her voice was a little shrill.

The foreman passed round his cigarettes. A plastic lighter flared as each bent to the flame.

'Hello,' said Jan to the girl.

She glanced up at him, a brief appraisal. 'Oh yes,' she said, recognizing him. 'Seen you at work.' She smiled. 'How you?'

'Would you like a drink?'

'Thank you,' she said.

'You are Yvonne.'

'How d'you know?'

'I always see that thing on your necklace.' He put out his finger slowly to touch the gold-plated name suspended on a chain at her throat. Yvonne.

'A ginger square please.' She sat back on her stool.

'Yvonne,' he said carefully, 'is a pretty name.' He began again, enunciating. 'So,' he said, 'how long have you been working here, Yvonne?'

The tedium of preliminaries. All he wanted to do with Yvonne was to take her to his pre-fabricated hut, his iron bed, drag off her tight white slacks, get at those huge, imprisoned tits and drive Freek Koen from his head. No talking. No tenderness.

But Yvonne was not that kind of girl. Yvonne was nice. She had a fiancé in Graaff-Reinet, working in a garage while she saved up her salary from the Building Society.

84

'It's OK working there,' she said. 'You can go places. Only trouble is some of the other girls can get on your nerves after a while.'

Yvonne wore a diamond solitaire on her left hand. She was proud of it. So Jan talked to her about her plans and then he talked about her family.

'The trouble with my Mom,' she confided, 'is she still treats me like a kid. That's why I moved into a flat with my friend.'

Jan did not want to hear about her mother or her friend.

'It's better that way,' Yvonne was saying. 'Fanie and my Mom don't get on very well.'

Fanie—some great brute who played with those tits. 'No Fanie! Don't!' he could hear her squeal.

He ordered another round of drinks, and another. He slipped his arm along the bar behind her. She did not move away. She complained just a little more plaintively about Fanie.

He did not notice Kobie and Andrew any more. He drank drink for drink with Yvonne. He leaned back on the vinyl-padded bar and stared at her—at all of her—the way she flicked her tongue into the corner of her mouth like a little meerkat grooming its whiskers. He watched as she slowly crossed her legs. The slacks creased, puckered at the zip. She wriggled slightly on the stool. He watched her shift and stretch and settle. Her knee brushed his.

He moved away abruptly, took his safety helmet and tucked it under his arm. 'Got to go,' he said. 'Late.' He made a gesture with his hand—it was difficult to speak, he'd drunk too much. 'Nice talking to you, Yvonne.'

He turned on his heel and left the bar.

He saw her in the café a few evenings later as he was returning from the site. She was flipping through the publications on a stand trying to choose between a photo romance and a fashion magazine. She still wore her work tunic, prim to the neck.

Jan picked up an evening paper, paid for it and went over to her.

'Hello Yvonne,' he said.

85

She looked up, startled.

'Hello.' She did not use his name. 'How you? What you doing here?'

'Getting a paper. And you?'

'Looking for something to read.' She twisted the magazine in her hands. 'Nothing much.'

'By the way,' he said, feeling the silence, 'I need to transfer some money to a special savings account at home. Have you got any suggestions?'

Relieved to have something to talk about she put on her bright Building Society voice and said, 'Come in tomorrow and I'll sort it out for you. OK?'

'Thanks very much, Yvonne.'

'Any time,' she said. 'Well,' she hesitated, 'see you then.'

Jan watched her walk out into the street. She glanced back, gave him a pert smile. Then she was gone.

He did not mean to watch for her. He never went out of his way to find her. He did not always join her queue at the Building Society but he said to Andrew as they drove back to their house one Friday evening, 'It's time to go home. I'm getting *bossies* in this place.'

Andrew laughed ruefully. 'Like the army.'

'You didn't see any women when we were in the army. There seems to be one on every corner here.'

Andrew looked sceptically at the empty street. 'Can't say I noticed. By the way, Jan. Stop off at the bottle store. We must buy some beers. The boys are having a *braai* at the caravan park tonight. It's Oosthuizen's birthday or something. He told me to tell you.'

'Thought I'd go to the movies.'

'Count me out for that double feature at the bughouse!'

'OK. I'll come with you then,' said Jan, parking outside the hotel Off-Sales and searching his pockets for some change to pay towards the beer.

She was there. She and her friends, the site crew and the girl from the hotel reception. She was sitting cross-legged on the grass with a shandy in her hand. She wore a pink anorak with the collar turned up.

86

The men stood at the *braai*, sending up shouts of laughter. Freek Koen was cooking the *boerewors* and chops, turning them with a wire prong.

'Come join us, girls.' said Jaco Oosthuizen. He took Yvonne's hand and dragged her up off the grass and put his arm around her. 'Hell, this is only a nice chick, this. And Fanie's such a rough *oke*, hey Yvonne?'

'Fanie's got nothing on you for being rough,' she said, giving him a playful shove.

'No man,' said Jaco, 'you should see this Fanie! Huge guy! At school we used to call him Bok-Bok Prinsloo—no one could jump further than him when we used to play *bok-bok* at the hostel!'

Jan watched her, the fire lighting her face from below. She looked across at him—just a glance—and took a sip of her drink, holding it with two hands as though her mug were filled with something hot. She blew at the froth on the top. There—the small grooming action of her tongue.

He kept his arms folded, reaching out every now and then for his beer. The wind was cold at his back, blowing in across the dam. He laughed at the raucous jokes, told a few himself and found another fork. From the other side of the fire, and avoiding conversation, he cooked the meat with Freek.

And all the time he watched her and she, bantering with Jaco Oosthuizen, was aware—she did not show it—of his hands holding the fork and turning the steaks, this way and that.

Jaco started to sing old rugby songs. The others joined in. Jan, Kobie and Andrew squatted next to each other with their beers and their food. Freek sat a little apart, always morose. The tip of his cigarette glowed, a small counterpoint of light in the darkness.

Yvonne ate a sausage, nibbling round its edges, then wiping her fingers delicately on the grass. After a while she got up and picked her way towards the dark ablution block.

Jan stood, stretched. 'I'm off,' he said to Kobie and Andrew.

'Stay man,' said Kobie. 'There's crates of beer to get through.'

'No. I'm buggered.'

'Are you going to movies after all?' asked Andrew.

'Not tonight.'

He sauntered away, his hands thrust deep in the pockets of his jeans. He looked up at the stars, familiar in their winter brightness. The air was raw with the dry bite of frost.

His truck was parked near the ablution block. He walked around it, as though appraising it. He did not hurry. He heard the lavatory chain, the splash of water in the basin. He opened the door of the *bakkie* and stood hesitant, leaning his arms on the roof of the cab. Yvonne came out, saw him and stopped.

'Where are you going?' she said.

'Home.'

''Night.' It sounded offhand.

'Yvonne.'

'Ja.'

'Are you coming?'

'Why?'

He inclined his head slightly, looked at her.

She glanced towards the people at the fire. They were huddled close together for warmth and Jaco was still singing his rugby songs. She turned back to him. He could not see her face clearly in the darkness.

He leaned over and opened the door on the passenger side. She slid into the cab next to him. He started the engine and they drove away.

Kobie looked up as they passed, a piece of meat half-way to his mouth. He gaped. '*Yirra* Andrew!' he said. 'Now I've seen it all! *Bliksem!*'

Andrew followed Kobie's stare and shifted uncomfortably. No one else had noticed—except for Freek.

Jan took her to the prefab. house. He parked the truck, turned in his seat and looked at her. She hesitated a moment, as though she wanted to say something. Just briefly she touched his arm and then she opened the door and climbed out.

He followed her into the house. She looked round at the emptiness of his room, the narrow bed, the cubicle, the

88

cupboard. Jan switched on the one-bar heater, slung his jacket on the chair.

She turned to him then, waiting. He bent and kissed her —her neck, her ears, her mouth. She smelt of shandy and of talcum powder. He slid his hands inside her anorak. She shivered, laughed slightly, warmed his fingers with her own, restraining him but he tugged at her blouse, hurrying now.

'Hey,' she said, pulling back to look at him. 'Not so fast.'

She ran her hands up under his shirt to his shoulders, and along his collarbones. She explored his chest, his spine, the small of his back—slowly, so slowly, savouring it. Her fingers traced lightly across his thigh, lingered, came to rest at the belt of his jeans.

She stopped, stood quite still, drew away.

'Come on,' he said, 'don't mess around.' He pulled her back to him and slipped his hand down the front of her slacks between the cool silky panties and her skin. Down. The breath caught in her throat as his fingers found her. Small, urgent words against his mouth, she backed towards the bed.

The flat fluorescent glow of the compound lights spread across the floor and up the wall. Clothes abandoned on the bare linoleum, their shadows loomed across the ceiling.

She stretched up to him, guiding him. Somewhere out in the dark, the curfew siren wailed in the black part of town.

After that he could not leave her alone. He went to the Building Society on the pretext of drawing money. 'Would you like to come out to lunch?' he would say.

She would blush, hardly look at him with the other girls around—she with her solitaire diamond gleaming on her finger.

'OK, I'll meet you at the Road-House. The girls here go to the café for takeaways. I . . .'

'Fine, I'll be there at a quarter to one.'

He would go out then in the sunshine, take his turn to drive the workers back to the compound after their shift, the wheel dusty in his hands, the sweat budding at his hairline. He would drive along above the little town with its flat, straight roads, iron-rooved houses, hedged gardens. Behind an old bungalow stood a windmill, a reservoir, a row of peach trees. The school was squat and impersonal by the brown rugby field.

In the cold, dry dustiness of the site Jan did his work. He kept at bay all guilt. He quelled his rage, his impotence against the drought in Yvonne. And there, the dam waited, it waited to suck him in, keep him captive in the network of the great, greedy wall. A stickman pumping, pushing, hauling chains, bulking concrete—up, down, levers, lights, labour gangs, huge trucks spewing out the flesh of one more road.

At twelve forty-five he ate. At one fifteen he worked again. At three his tea was brought, dumped, tilting to the rim, redolent with boiled milk fat. Machinery rumbled, men shouted. Blasts, roars, the grind of concrete mixers in the road and crushers pounding rock to sand. Five thirty, knock off time.

He would drive the work gangs home again, across the dirt tracks to the tin houses blossoming like fungus in the *veld*. One day all that would be left would be the artefacts of men who had lived there once: tins, blades, pieces of cloth, a soggy place where the hole of the latrine had been, filled now, grass sprouting. Shower, dress, drive out in the *bakkie*. Stop off at the hotel. He was familiar with the call box under the stairs. He knew all the graffiti: Delia loves Marius; get pissed; *poes is koning*; the directory hanging on a chain.

He would phone home. Elsa's voice would be distant, momentary, far from the maelstrom of the wall. And then she was gone. Gone. Blackheath gone. Nella gone. Elsa gone. Jan de Villiers gone. So he would go out in the heat and the dust and the ugliness and meet Yvonne.

They would drive to the caravan park where caravaners never came. The cement tables, the benches and the rubbish bins stood under the willow trees where newspapers and rotting chip packets and chicken bones lay scattered in the wind.

At last they would make their way to her flat, second floor above the café, when the other girls were out. Eight forty-five, the coffee cups still warm, a record left revolving on the turntable—the last action of the day, the door locked against intrusion.

The gate on the road between Blackheath and Melvynside had been left open during the night. Angoras had strayed through into Cedric de Villiers' land. They were scattered in among his sheep. Cedric's stockman, checking the camps in the morning, returned to the big house and reported what he had found.

'Bloody goats!' snorted Cedric. He telephoned Elsa. 'Elsa,' he said peremptorily. 'There's a troop of goats got through into my place!'

'Oh?' said Elsa. 'I'm sorry, Uncle Cedric. I wonder how it happened? The fences have been seen to recently.'

'Some bloody fool left the gate open. I've said it once and I'll say it again, I'll break the neck of anyone I catch being so careless, mark my words.'

'I'll send Petrus over at once to round them up,' said Elsa apologetically.

Petrus and two others were sent to Melvynside to muster the vagrants and bring them home. Elsa went down to the camp and latched the gate herself. She and Petrus counted the animals together.

Elsa had returned to the house to listen to the weather report when Cedric de Villiers arrived. He strode down the passage.

'What is it Uncle Cedric?' She rose, a little startled.

'A sheep has gone missing. It's the second I've lost in three weeks.'

'Come and sit down,' said Elsa, turning from him, avoiding his eyes, remembering the shelter and the skin hanging in the doorway.

'Did that boy of yours bring a sheep in with the goats, do you suppose?'

'I doubt it—but I'll ask him,' said Elsa. 'Would you like some coffee? I'll get Chrissie to make it while I find Petrus.' She hurried towards the door, summoning Chrissie.

'In a moment, in a moment,' said Uncle Cedric, following her to the kitchen. 'Two sheep in three weeks is ridiculous.

You must get those *munts* of yours to be more careful with the gate.'

'Maybe it was one of yours.'

'Never! They know I'd thrash the daylights out of them if they did.'

They went to the shed where Petrus was repairing the generator. Nella and Tombizodwa were rolling ball bearings to each other across the floor, sitting in the dusty gloom, dishevelled and absorbed.

Petrus stood up and touched his hat. 'Good morning, Sir.'

'Petrus,' said Elsa quietly. 'One of Mr de Villiers' sheep is missing from the camp where you went to fetch the goats. You didn't see it perhaps, or bring it back by mistake?'

Petrus shook his head. 'We brought back twenty goats, that is all.'

'It might have strayed through the open gate in the night,' suggested Elsa.

'Two in three weeks! Two in three weeks is ridiculous!' Cedric turned to Petrus. 'You check this side.'

Petrus hesitated. He put down his spanner slowly and glanced at Elsa, a faint inquiry in his eyes. She shook her head imperceptibly. She slid her hands into her pockets— they had begun to sweat. 'Please could you send someone to look,' she said.

'Yes, *Nkosazan'*.' He put his hat back on his head. 'Perhaps it was a *rooikat*. There are many at this time.' He went down the steps and whistled to a man chopping logs behind the house.

'Those sheep have been stolen,' said Cedric. '*Rooikat* be damned!' He looked after Petrus. 'That native's too cocky by half, you mark my words.'

Chrissie had laid the tea tray with the best china. She always did when the older members of the family visited—a quaint respect for the past. She carried it through to the living room.

'I'm going to Grahamstown tomorrow,' said Uncle Cedric. 'After that I'm off to Kromme with the Clarkes. I haven't been fishing for ages.'

'How long will you be away?'

'A fortnight,' he said. 'I'll be seeing Adrian. I have a few things to sort out with him about Koen's land.'

'Has Oom Jaap accepted your offer?'

'He will! He will!' Cedric held the small fluted cup to his mouth and sucked in the coffee noisily. He licked his lips and lit another cigarette. 'Freek's the problem. He's holding it all up. Did you know he was at the dam with Jan?'

'Yes,' she said. 'Jan told me. Freek is very upset about the farm.'

Cedric waved the remark aside impatiently. 'We'll make something out of Brakkloof my girlie, you wait and see. You'll be glad of it. Right.' He stood abruptly. 'Got a lot to do before I leave tomorrow.'

'We'll look for your sheep, don't worry.'

'Goodbye, my girlie. You get Jan home as soon as you can.' He glanced out of the window into the yard. 'He's needed here, I can tell. This sort of thing is just the limit, mark my words.'

Elsa bit back her retort and walked with him to the car. 'Have a nice break at Kromme, Uncle Cedric,' she said.

'Yes, I intend to do a lot of fishing. If anything goes wrong at Melvynside give Adrian a ring.' He kissed her on the cheek, settled his hat and drove away.

Elsa stood undecided. Petrus was back in the shed. She could hear the soft chink of the spanner and the rasp of the ball bearings as the children rolled them back and forth across the floor. She went into the room and said, 'Do you think it was they that took the sheep, Petrus? Do you think it was the people of the road?'

He turned the spanner in his hands and examined it. 'Who can know this thing?' he said. 'Perhaps it is they. *Kanti*— and yet—the *rooikat* are many at this time.'

'Perhaps I should find out, don't you think Petrus?' she said.

He looked at her, not knowing how to answer.

'I will think,' she said as she turned away and hurried back to the house.

The decision to say nothing about the treks had been hers. It was not for Petrus to decide what she should do. She would speak to Uncle Cedric after all. But before she had finished ringing his signal on the party line she returned the receiver to its cradle. She sat on the stairs, resting her chin on her knee. She would wait for evening, for Jan to phone. He would know what to do.

But Jan did not phone. She waited—seven, eight, nine o'clock. She went to bed that night feeling abandoned for the first time since he'd left.

Petrus went out in the early morning in the cold. He left his house, speaking first in quiet words to Chrissie so as not to disturb their sleeping children. She looked apprehensive.

'I must stop them from taking Somandla's sheep,' he insisted. 'Somandla will catch them—then there will be trouble.' Somandla—Cedric: the powerful one.

'It is not your business,' said Chrissie. 'It is not you who took Somandla's sheep. Let Somandla catch them—it is their affair.'

'And then?' He looked at her. 'When Somandla sends the police? If the boy is there, what then?'

'How do we know the boy is there? It is only Alzina who says that she saw him in the road. If it was he, he would have greeted her.'

'How can he come home after he has stolen the gun?' he said.

Chrissie shook her head. '*They* will be glad when he is back. The *makoti* is always worrying about where he is—that I can tell. "Where is Abedingo?" she says. "Where is Nontinti?" Let her go and tell those people to leave the sheep herself.'

'*She* may be glad if Abedingo is there,' said Petrus, 'but not Somandla and not Adrian. What is *she* when they are here? Adrian can say anything to her. Do this. Do that—and she must do it. It is better if the *makoti* doesn't know. I must see these people myself.'

The baby started to cry and Chrissie picked it up from the bed and hushed it. 'What about Mama?' said Chrissie. 'She should not have gone on the train either.'

'We all thought he was in Port Elizabeth,' said Petrus. 'It was the only place to look.'

'There are stories from this place. There are stories from

that place. Everyone brings a story about Abedingo,' said Chrissie.

'I will speak to those people anyway,' said Petrus. 'Then we can decide.'

He took his hat and closed the door behind him. The frost spiked the yellow grass, making it crack and break underfoot. He left a trail across the ground. When the sun rose the prints melted out. Only a tuft of mohair fluttered on a barb of the fence where he had passed. He went down towards the road. He hurried, for the sun was rising, melting out along the crests and ridges.

Above him, where the track breasted the slope and branched off to Melvynside, Cedric de Villiers stood by his car in flannels and a blazer. He often stopped at this point to look across at his camps, his dams, reservoirs and pastures. To the east lay Brakkloof's scrufulous lands where the shearing shed guarded the hill. He was about to continue his journey when he noticed Petrus Ngubane hurrying up the road.

He put his hands to his mouth to hail him, to ask him what he wanted, when he saw Petrus clamber through the fence on Jaap Koen's boundary and disappear. Looking closely, his eyes narrowed against the early light, he saw a faint drift of smoke hanging in the morning sky.

A woman too, squatting by her cooking fire before the small house, heard Petrus pushing his way through the brush. She started up apprehensively and went down to see who was coming. She trod lightly against the iron cold of the ground, her feet as bloodless as the stones.

Petrus stopped and raised a hand in greeting. '*Ewe*,' he said.

'*Ewe*,' replied the woman cautiously.

'I wish to speak to Abedingo Ngubane,' he said, obviating denial. There was no time to waste.

She did not reply.

'I am his cousin. I come from the farm' He gestured towards Blackheath. 'I will say nothing,' he added, repeating it, for the woman looked apprehensive. 'I have also come to warn you not to take the *mlungu*'s sheep. He is very angry and he is looking for it.'

Petrus pushed past her into the clearing in front of the house. Near the wall lay the skin of the sheep stolen two nights before.

'Where is Abedingo?' he said again.

'He has gone with my husband.' She indicated the hillside above.

'Where are you from?'

'Gcashe,' she said. 'We have been looking for a place. Sometimes my husband did piecework for Koen. This time, that time—when there was need. He has gone now and we have nothing.'

Petrus went to the skin and turned it over, looking for the branding mark. 'You better get rid of this,' he said. 'Somandla may send someone. Where is the meat?'

'In the house.'

The woman stood with the tips of her fingers to her lips watching him.

'You must tell Abedingo Ngubane to come and speak to me,' said Petrus.

The woman shook her head. 'He is afraid.'

'Nothing will happen to him. Tell him. His grandmother has gone to Port Elizabeth to look for him. It is not right. She is old. I must find a way to bring her back. These things take time.'

'I will tell him,' she said. Her child wailed somewhere in the house, holding still to its thread of life. 'Will you wait to speak with him?'

'How long will he be?' He glanced up the slope.

Petrus and the woman did not hear the car coasting slowly down the hill. It was only when the door slammed that they turned and saw Cedric de Villiers striding through the bush towards them.

Petrus wiped his hands slowly on his overall. Already the sweat oozed at his temples, his lip. The woman backed away. Far up the hillside a dog barked, its call ending in a yelp, silenced by a fist.

'Whose sheep is that?' said Cedric, undoing his belt. He drew it out, uncoiling it. Petrus stood silent, watching Cedric's fingers.

96

'Whose sheep is that?' he snarled.

'Yours Baas.'

'My sheep!' He lunged at Petrus. The belt whipped across Petrus's cheek, tearing open the flesh. The woman cried out as though she had taken the blow for him.

'You bloody liar!' shouted Cedric. 'It was you who stole my sheep! I'll break your bloody neck!' He stood before Petrus, panting. Then he turned on the woman. 'What are you doing here?'

She crouched at the threshold of the house. He strode to the door, thrust her aside and shouldered his way in. The baby screamed—terrified, ululating wails. There was a stench of newly-butchered meat.

Cedric stood over the woman, breathing heavily. She shrank from him as though her skin smarted. 'You get out of here,' he said. 'I'm on my way to town and I'm sending the police. Do you hear?' He turned to Petrus. 'You,' he said. 'Take the skin to the car.'

The blood oozed from Petrus's cheek, pooled in the hollow of his ear. A fly hovered at his face, trying to settle. He dragged the sheepskin to the car.

Cedric followed him. 'Get in,' he said as he went round to the driver's seat and wrenched open the door. He started the engine, revving it as Petrus eased himself into the back. He drove off, tires spinning.

'Where are we going Baas?' asked Petrus tentatively.

'We are going to the police station!' snapped Cedric. 'So you'd better not try anything!'

Cedric phoned Elsa from town. 'I've got this boy of yours,' he said.

'What?' Elsa was uncomprehending.

'Listen, my girlie,' he said. 'I caught your bloody bossboy red-handed! I always knew he was a liar. Red-handed I tell you! Found him with my sheep in the bush on Jaap Koen's place. Him and some others. I knew he'd stolen my sheep and thank God I found him out. I wouldn't like to think of the lying bastard being on Blackheath with you while Jan's away.'

'Where is he?' Elsa's voice was shaking.

'Caught him red-handed, mark my words! Now listen my girlie. I've got him here at the police station. I've charged him with stock theft so if you're short of boys go over to Melvynside and speak to Bheki. He'll lend you someone in the meantime.'

'Hang on! Just hang on a moment!'

'There's no need to worry, my girlie. Koos Olivier has it all under control. There's far more to this than meets the eye, you mark my words! It's not just a matter of a stolen sheep, believe me! I can smell a rat a mile away! Captain Olivier will get to the bottom of it, you can be sure. He's sending out someone to clear the rabble at Koen's. No one's getting away with stealing my sheep!'

'But Uncle Cedric,' said Elsa. 'What makes you think it was Petrus? I know he didn't take it . . .'

'Don't concern yourself with it any more. I'm going to see Adrian just as soon as I get to Grahamstown. He'll deal with everything. I must be on my way, my girlie. This business has delayed me dreadfully.'

Elsa let him go without further argument. She held the receiver in her hand waiting for him to finish. When he had, she hurried out into the yard to find Chrissie.

Chrissie was feeding the chickens with Nella and Tombizodwa. *'Yintoni?'* she said sharply as she looked up and saw Elsa's face.

'My Uncle found Petrus on Koen's farm with his sheep. He says that Petrus stole it. He has taken him to the police station.'

'It is not he who has stolen the sheep,' cried Chrissie.

'I know that,' said Elsa. 'I'm sorry Chrissie. I'll go in and fetch him at once. I'll tell the police the mistake. I won't be long.'

Chrissie nodded. She picked up the bag of chicken feed resignedly.

'Do you know why he went to Koen's farm?' said Elsa.

'To find out about the sheep,' said Chrissie. 'To make sure. That is all.'

'Why didn't he tell me?'

98

'It is something you can know yourself,' said Chrissie. 'Sometimes we do not speak of these things. Why, I do not know. The people of the road were not his business,' she said, without accusation but with a slight reproof. Elsa sensed that Chrissie laid the responsibility for what had happened before her. Elsa had said nothing of the treks to Cedric, Petrus had followed where she'd led.

'He will not be thrown away,' said Elsa.

'You will not throw him away,' Chrissie echoed. 'And yet ...' It hung there between them. Chrissie lowered her eyes.

There were boundaries of privacy between Elsa and Chrissie, very clearly defined. They had been laid the day Elsa had gone away to senior school in Grahamstown. Their lives had been separated then. Elsa had preferred to bring home school friends for the holidays or to go over to Blackheath and ride horses with Jannie. But when they were small she and Chrissie had built shelters, cooked *ngqush*', played endlessly at hospitals. Then, Chrissie had been in charge, the matron's cap fashioned from a paper doily, clipped up on her head.

But when Elsa had been sent to boarding school, Chrissie had returned to the huts by the *spruit*. Their games were set aside. Chrissie had looked after her younger siblings, done her mother's housework. She had retreated, walking upright, head angled delicately—poised to carry wood, buckets, pumpkins.

Since then her relationship with Elsa had been constrained. The things that they could share were limited to the range of tasks within Elsa's household. Beyond they did not venture any more. Now their daughters played the same games. Both Chrissie and Elsa watched, knowing what would happen, unable to speak about it or to change it in any way.

The old jail was built of ironstone blocks like the outhouses on Blackheath. A pomegranate tree stood by the entrance. The husks of shrivelled fruit hung among the dry leaves. Small lizards darted up and over the parapet, plying between the secret interior and the sunlight of the outer walls.

Elsa parked in the street and went through the gate, across the yard and into the charge office. No one was there. The old wooden counter barricaded her from the desk in the room. A sergeant's hat lay upturned on the table. A row of African violets crouched in their plastic pots on the window ledge. There was an air of a room suddenly deserted, of a chair pushed back in haste.

Elsa rang the bell. It rasped, barely tinkling. She waited. She could hear a voice down the passage, and, impatient for attention, she went towards the sound. She stopped outside a door and tapped discreetly. The angry words went on, a strident, accusing monotone. There were brisk steps across the linoleum then, quite clearly, Petrus's voice raised in denial. She knew it was Petrus—there was no doubt in her. A thud, the dull shock of fist on flesh, furniture reeling back. A cry.

She hammered at the door. 'Let me in!' she shouted. 'Let me in!' But the key had been turned.

From the end of the passage Captain Olivier emerged from his room. 'Excuse me lady. Can I help you?'

Elsa rounded on him. 'They're beating a man in there! Stop them! It's Petrus Ngubane. Open this door!'

Captain Olivier came towards her. 'Come this way,' he said politely. 'I'll see what's going on.'

'Open the door.'

'Listen lady . . .' Elsa shrank from him as he took her elbow, moving her away. He put his other hand to the door knob. 'Smit,' he said peremptorily. '*Wag net*. Wait till I come.'

She shook his hand from her arm. 'What the hell's going on?' she demanded.

'Lady, this is not your business.'

'It is my business. I know you've got my stockman in that room.'

'If you'll just come this way, lady.'

'I won't go anywhere until you open the door.'

'Listen lady, this isn't the place for you,' he said. 'Come to my office. The corporal will make coffee.'

'I don't want your bloody coffee! I want Petrus released at once.'

'Who is Petrus?'

'The man in there.'

'How do you know what man's in there? We've had more than one case today.'

'It's to do with a sheep.'

'There's been a Bantu charged with stock theft this morning. I can't release him before he's been to court. Now listen lady . . .'

'You listen to me,' said Elsa. 'I don't care about court. I'm taking him with me now.'

'You can't do that, lady. Let me explain . . .'

A black corporal slipped out of the room, sidled down the passage to the front office.

'Ask him!' Elsa cried. 'Ask him if he wasn't beating Petrus?'

'It has nothing to do with Corporal Djantjes,' said the Captain evasively. 'This is Sergeant Smit's case. I expect there is certain information the prisoner is reluctant to give.'

'What information?'

'About who are his accomplices.'

'He doesn't have accomplices.'

'Lady,' Captain Olivier rubbed his small moustache patiently with a stained forefinger. 'I don't know who the sergeant has in there but the matter is for the sergeant to decide.'

'And this is how he decides, is it?' said Elsa. 'By beating him?'

'Lady . . .'

'What's the bail?' demanded Elsa.

'The Magistrate must decide that tomorrow. We cannot release this Bantu yet.'

'Why not?'

'It's not me who makes the laws, lady,' said the Captain. 'You can come to court in the morning.'

'If Sergeant Smit touches him again you won't hear the end of it.'

'Listen lady, it's not for you to order the police around, do you see?' His tone had changed. She could feel his aggression as he stood above her. His uniform with its epaulettes, its ribbon of rank, its shining buttons were very close. She stepped back from him, intimidated, and as her anger and bravado faded her jaw began to tremble as though from the cold.

Corporal Djantjes was back at his desk filling out a form, sitting very straight. He raised his eyes as she passed, lowered them again, admitting no communication. His business was not with her.

She stood on the step a moment, trying to still the spasm of shaking. She put her hand to her jaw, pressed her fingers tight against it and drew a deep breath. The air was warm and calm. The shadow of the pomegranate—a deep, shifting mauve— moved back and forth across the wall. Behind her the prison was silent. There were no voices, no cries. She walked away from the gates to her car parked in the road. The street was deserted. A white cat was stretched out on a verandah step, its belly turned up to the sun. Way down by the goods shed she could hear the slow panting hiss of a train.

The next morning Elsa waited in the court for Petrus. She sat alone on a bench watching the people come and go. Somewhere in an outer office a telephone rang incessantly.

When Petrus appeared with Corporal Djantjes Elsa half-rose, pulling her jacket close around her, her fingers tightening into the cloth. She stared at Petrus across the court.

His cheek was swollen, his lip grotesque in its distortion. His right arm rested in a sling, the plaster stark and white in contrast to his filthy, sweat-stained overall. His voice was muffled as though it took an effort to form the words.

The proceedings were brief. A first offender, employed and resident in the district for all his life, bail was granted and the case remanded. A trial date was set and Petrus was instructed to report to the police station weekly. The next case was called.

Elsa went down to the outer offices, paid the bail through a brass grille to a clerk who wrote a receipt and then hurried to the back of the court, looking for Corporal Djantjes. But he was already backing the van out of the yard, returning to the police station. Beside him sat another black constable, his cap pulled down over his eyes. They spun out into the road—two youngsters possessed of all the trappings of authority.

A third policeman, a sergeant, was standing in a doorway with his back to her, talking to the prosecutor. He straddled the threshold, legs astride. The stance suggested a rugby lineout.

'Someone to see you Smit,' said the other man.

The policeman turned to Elsa. His hair was thick and blonde, his moustache drooping at the corners, sideburns grown down, almost to meet it. A powerful young man, he had the nose, the fists, the neck of a boxer.

'I've come for Petrus Ngubane,' she said, holding out the receipt.

He leaned against the doorframe, took the slip and examined it. When he looked up at her, his gaze lingered— an insolent appraisal. She could smell him there: open, vigorous sweat. And had he been a dog he'd have smelt her too. Perhaps he could. Perhaps he knew about her fear. Perhaps this was how they worked—hunting, sniffing out those who were afraid.

He returned the receipt to her, offering it just beyond reach, waiting for her to take it from him. His fingers were hard, tufted with blonde hairs. His thumb had been crushed recently. The nail was bulging and black. The skin had been bitten away at the edges.

He walked round the building towards the cells. He went ahead of her in that bow-legged way that some men have, as though solicitous of too ample genitals. He seemed to carry them before him, nudging them with the hard curves of his thighs. He glanced back at her. 'Wait,' he said. Elsa stood in the shadow of the wall. The place smelt of open drains and urine.

Sergeant Smit returned, swinging his keys. 'You better see this boy reports every week. You bring him yourself, hey?' Again the insolent appraisal.

She dropped her eyes, turned to Petrus. Moving towards him, she put out her hand and touched the plaster on his arm. 'How did this happen?'

Petrus shuffled slightly.

'How did he break it, Sergeant?' she persisted.

'Maybe he slipped,' said the sergeant. 'It's his bad luck.'

'Don't give me that rubbish! You assaulted him! I heard you!'

'Prove it!'

His eyes met hers. Held them. She turned her head away, feeling the pulse beating in the hollow of her throat. His face, when he'd spoken, had been quite expressionless—a chilling innocence.

'Who set it?' she said.

'District Surgeon.'

'Where?'

'At the hospital,' he replied, flipping his keys and catching them. He took a piece of gum from a packet in his pocket and put it in his mouth. His teeth crunched at the sugar coating.

'Come Petrus,' Elsa said. 'Let's go.' She looked back briefly. The sergeant was leaning against the prison door, watching her, his arms folded.

They travelled in silence for a little way, Elsa driving cautiously so as not to jar Petrus's arm. Petrus seemed to doze, his breath rasping through his swollen lips. Then he stirred and looked over at her.

'What happened, Petrus?' Elsa said.

'I went to tell those people.' His voice croaked. He began again. 'I told them not to take the sheep.'

'Those treks that we saw in the bush at Brakkloof?'

'Those same.' He was silent a moment. 'It was they that took the sheep. That I could tell.'

'It's my fault,' said Elsa. 'If I'd said something to Uncle Cedric this wouldn't have happened. I know that it is my fault.'

Petrus looked down at his hand. He did not reply. The dried blood was black on his cheek.

'Did you tell my Uncle why you had gone there?'

'I did not get the chance. He said it was I who stole the sheep—that is all. He hit me then.'

'And the police? Why did they beat you?'

'They say I took the sheep. I said no. They say—why was I there with those people. They ask why I didn't report to Somandla'—he hesitated—'to Baas Cedric. That is what they say.'

'And your arm?'

'The sergeant held it. He twisted it round very fast. Then I fell. They took me to the hospital.'

'What did you tell the doctor?'

'He did not speak to me. They told him I was fighting.'

'And what did he say?'

'He must see the arm in five weeks. There is nothing else.'

Elsa felt a great weariness. It seemed that Petrus had no anger, no resentment for what had happened. All the recrimination belonged to her. Perhaps his detachment was his means of survival. What he felt he kept to himself. She had failed to understand his restraint before.

Chrissie was waiting on the back steps when they got home. Elsa stayed in the car, allowing Petrus and Chrissie their greeting alone. They stood close, their voices soft. Elsa could not guess their words. So private, so reserved—even as children they had watched each other quietly, saying little. Their lives were separate and in their own way secret from Elsa's and Jan's. What joy, what anguish, what love they shared was unrevealed. She would have done anything to break that barrier, to go to Chrissie and Petrus, to put her hands in theirs as she had as a child. Instead she watched them from a distance.

Jan phoned that night. Before Elsa could speak, could tell him all the things she had to say, he told her he was not returning for the weekend. He was going to work overtime. He would rather do that now than later, he said. The rains would come, and when they did he must be ready to come back at once. The line crackled and faded. 'What news have you?' he asked.

'Nothing,' she said resentfully, clenching her teeth against the rising tears. She could not explain about Petrus or the treks now that he was staying at the dam.

'This line's bloody awful,' he yelled. 'Can you hear me? Shall I try again tomorrow?'

'Jannie.'

'What did you say?'

'It doesn't matter.'

The seconds fell away.

'Has there been any sign of rain?'

'There's nothing. I don't think it will ever rain again.'

'I'll phone day after tomorrow,' he said briskly. 'Look after yourself.'

She said, 'Jannie . . .'

The call box signal bleeped out, 'Bye Els,' he said. Then he was gone. The line buzzed in Elsa's ear.

'Jan?' she said. 'Jannie?'

She put her head against the side of the dresser and cried.

'What's wrong Mama?' Nella ran to her and flung her arms around Elsa's neck. 'Mama, what's wrong?'

'Why doesn't it bloody well rain?'

She picked Nella up and held her, rocking her back and forward in her arms.

Jan went to the pre-fab. house in search of Andrew. He had to talk to someone. Everything was wrong. He could sense it. The line had not been good but still, he could feel Elsa's defensiveness. He had known that she'd been close to tears. When he'd asked if all was well she'd insisted there was nothing wrong but she'd been abrupt when he'd explained about the overtime. She was angry with him, he could tell. Nor did he deceive himself—he knew he did not want to go home and take his guilt in there for Elsa to discover.

Andrew was not in his room and Kobie was playing poker with some of the construction crew. Freek Koen was among them. They sat around a table, beer cans open before them.

'Join us, Jan,' said Kobie.

'Where's Andrew?'

'Gone home. Kid's on the way. Joy sent a message to tell him to come.'

'Hope he makes it in time.'

'He was only in a flap!' Kobie laughed. 'Real old woman sometimes!' Jan said nothing. 'Sit man! Freek, deal for Jan.'
Freek glanced up. He made no invitation.
Jan shook his head. 'Poker's not my scene. I'll be back later. See you.'
'Ag Jan, be sociable. Where you going now?' said Kobie.
'No prize for guessing,' said Freek but Jan had already gone, banging the door behind him.
He went to find Yvonne. The lights were on in the flat above the shop. He parked his truck and climbed out. He was crossing the road when he saw Yvonne standing in the doorway of the café, dark against the bright fluorescence of the interior.
Behind her a man was paying for cigarettes at the till. Jan saw him turn to her and put his arm around her, casually steering her towards a white Cortina by the kerb. He was a big man in a lumber jacket buttoned with silver studs, dark hair, long at the collar, a moustache. It was Fanie.
'Jump in, *poppie*,' Jan heard him say. Music blared from the radio as Fanie started the engine of his car and made a U-turn in the road.
Yvonne saw Jan as he stepped onto the pavement. Her face, illuminated briefly by the street lamp, looked back at him. He sent her a small, rueful smile in salute.
He lingered at the café window, looking at the cardboard boxes of tired green peppers and tomatoes propped on the shelves and then he went to his truck and drove into the town.
He bought a ticket at the cinema. A Western was showing. He found a place and sat with his legs stretched out into the aisle. At the interval he left, before the main feature had begun, and returned to the site, restless and dissatisfied. He thought of Andrew driving home to his wife, for the birth of his son. Jan knew it was a son. It was what Andrew had always wanted. It was what he would get. He thought of Elsa and of Nella but he could not find their faces, nor hold them clear.
He parked his truck outside the house and slammed the door. Kobie, Freek and the others were still playing cards.

107

'Jesus Jan,' said Kobie as he came in. 'We thought you'd knock the bloody walls down with the *bakkie*. You speed testing it or something?'

Jan jerked a chair away from the table and sat down. 'I'll play,' he said.

'Deal him Freek,' said Kobie.

Jan reached for a beer can and dug the opener into the rim. It fizzed out over his fingers.

'She stand you up or something?' said Freek, glancing at Jan's face.

Jan made no angry retort. He did not trust his voice.

# 🌿 6 🌿

Dorothy Southey phoned Blackheath. It was seven thirty and Elsa was out in the lands. Chrissie answered, and Nella, still in her pyjamas, clamoured to speak to Grandma.

Dorothy Southey was exasperated. Elsa was always unavailable. She did not return phone calls. She seldom visited. She had not been to a Women's Institute meeting in weeks. She had contributed nothing to the church fête. She ran as wild as a *tollie* on the hills.

When Flo Harcourt came to tea, Dorothy said, 'I wouldn't be surprised if Jan doesn't have to take a firm hand with the staff when he comes home. It's as well that Nella goes to school next year. I do believe she's forgotten how to speak English. They all jabber on in Xhosa like a flock of magpies!'

'I can't understand why Jan went to the dam in the first place,' said Flo Harcourt delicately. 'We all know how well-off Adrian is.'

'Jan likes to be independent. I can understand that. Adrian underestimates Jan.' Dorothy took up her tea cup. 'I think we all do. I think that we've been wrong.'

Flo Harcourt said no more. She sipped her tea. In all the years she had known Dorothy she had never heard her criticize her daughters while defending her sons-in-law. It was an interesting departure.

When Elsa returned to the house for breakfast Chrissie told her that her mother had phoned. Elsa cranked the Kleinfontein call and waited.

'Elsa, where have you been?' cried her mother. 'Joy's had a baby boy!'

'Oh Ma! That's wonderful!' exlaimed Elsa, delighted, but finding somewhere a sharp pang of jealousy that it was not her own. 'When was he born?'

'Last night.'

'It's rather early,' said Elsa. 'Is he all right?'

'Only ten days early, Yes, he's fine. So's Joy. It all went very smoothly.'

'What about Andrew?'

'He got back from the dam in time. Isn't it nice that they have a son at last?'

'Annatjie's going to be so envious, what with three daughters.'

'Yes, she will. Listen darling,' said Dorothy. 'We must go and see Joy. Will you take me to the hospital?'

'Tomorrow?'

'This afternoon. I knitted a blue jacket—will you believe it? I must have known!'

'Mum, I'm busy at the moment. I'm building a new dip.'

'What nonsense Elsa! What's the matter with that bossboy of yours?'

'Petrus's arm is broken,' said Elsa shortly. 'I have to do everything myself.'

'Then Jan will have to fix it when he comes home for the weekend.'

'He isn't coming home.'

'Oh,' said Dorothy Southey again.' Well, darling,' she recovered herself, 'will you pick me up at one? I'd like to do a bit of shopping in town before we go to the hospital.'

'All right,' said Elsa resignedly. 'I'll be there. Anyway, I might as well take Petrus to report at the police station. He was due to go tomorrow. By the way—have you got some booties or a jersey for me to give Joy? I haven't made anything.'

'No I haven't. You should have thought of that before now.'

After lunch Elsa drove out in the car, Petrus beside her, Nella perched in the back, a bunch of marigolds for Joy in her lap. Elsa slowed near the gate for the workers' children. They were playing with their wire cars. The small wheels squealed and bucked over the gravel. The children scattered as she approached, ran along beside the car. Nella waved and shouted from the window.

Just beyond the gates of the farm where the drive joined the district road and the sign for the drovers' resting place marked the meeting of flocks and the stop for the Mpumalanga bus, a young man sat at the edge of a *donga*, shoulders hunched, his arms around his knees. He waited until the car had turned into the road, had gathered speed and driven on. Then he rose and walked towards the stone gates of the farm.

Joy's room in the hospital was already full of flowers. A stork-like strelitzia held a small doll suspended on a ribbon as though from its beak. A bee, made from coloured pipe cleaners, sat in the prim petals of a carnation. Chocolates and fruit were arranged on the bedside cubicle. Nella's sad little posy of marigolds had been forgotten in the car.

'Hello, Auntie Dot!' cried Joy.

'Well done, darling,' said Dorothy Southey, kissing her niece on both cheeks. 'We're all so glad you have your son at last. I phoned Carol in Cape Town and she sends lots of love and congratulations.'

Elsa hugged her. 'How is he, Joy?' she whispered, her face close.

Joy squeezed her hand. 'He's beautiful Elsie.'

Nella peered over the edge of the bed and said earnestly, 'What's his name?'

'We're still arguing about a name,' laughed Joy. 'There'll have to be a William in it somewhere to please Grandpa!'

She settled back among her pillows. 'You can all see him in a moment.' She looked down at Nella. 'Would you like to tell the nurse to bring him, Nellie?'

Petra gave up her chair for Dorothy Southey and engaged them in a commentary on every stage of the labour.

Joy shook out the crocheted matinee jacket Dorothy had made. Everyone gathered round to admire it.

'I'm sorry I haven't brought anything Joy,' said Elsa. 'You took me by surprise.'

'That's OK, Els.'

'I'll find something special for him. I think I've forgotten how to knit.'

'So we've noticed,' said Annatjie. 'Not a single set of dolls clothes for the fête!'

Joy told the story of Andrew's arrival home, their dash to town, the waiting, the stitches, the baby.

'Where's Andrew now, Joy?' asked Elsa.

'He's just checking up on things at home and then he'll be here. It's so nice to have him back—even if it's only for a few days.'

'Is he well?' asked Elsa, a little wistfully.

'He's fine. He's got quite thin—if nothing else, the dam's been good for his figure! He said he'd try and make it back every weekend.'

'Lucky you,' said Elsa. 'I haven't seen Jan for more than a month. He's doing overtime. Apparently the pay is very good after hours.'

'Bugger overtime!' said Annatjie. 'I'd rather have him home.'

'Can we see the baby?' asked Dorothy Southey.

'Of course Antie Dot,' said Joy. 'Nell, go with Mum and tell the nurse to bring him.'

Elsa went down to the duty room, holding Nella's hand.

'Can we have a baby?' said Nella.

'Wouldn't that be lovely.'

Nella considered. 'Yes, but only if it's a girl.'

When they had admired Joy's son and analysed the provenance of each feature, whether Southey or Fraser, Elsa said, 'Mum, it's time to go. We still have to take Petrus to the police station.' She stopped, not wanting to explain about Petrus to the others and remembering her mother's irritation at Petrus's intrusion on their outing. Dorothy rose reluctantly.

'There's more Southey in this little man than in any of your girls, Joy,' she declared. 'He's just like Bruce when he was a baby!'

After they had gone Petra said, 'I'm really worried about Elsa, man. She's taken being on her own really badly. She's been most peculiar since Jan's been away. I mean, for example, she didn't even knit anything! That's not like her.'

'I'll tell you why,' said Annatjie. 'I know I shouldn't say anything. Kobie made me promise, but honestly, everyone's going to know sooner or later and I keep wondering what to do.' She glanced round at the others.

Petra lit a cigarette, intrigued.

'Jan's having an affair!' said Annatjie.

'Affair, my foot!' snorted Petra. 'I'd like to see that! Jan adores Elsa! He's been besotted with her all his life!'

'It's true!' said Annatjie. 'Kobie should know.'

'Who is she?' asked Petra.

'He met her in a bar. She's only about twenty. She works in a bank or something.'

'It's not possible,' said Joy. 'Kobie's got it wrong.'

'Something must have driven him to it. Look at Hannah, she was driven to it!' said Petra.

'Rubbish!' interrupted Joy impatiently.

'Ag shame! Poor Elsie,' said Annatjie. 'I think she must have some idea—that's why she's been so odd.'

'You mustn't tell her, Annatjie,' said Joy, putting out her hand in restraint. 'It wouldn't help at all. I know Jan— it must be something else.' She looked at the others, trying to find reassurance. 'Can you imagine what happens to a man in a place like the dam? He must be depressed, or worried or something. Do you blame him? So don't say anything Annatjie . . .'

'I'd like to get my hands on that Jan!' retorted Annatjie. 'I'd give him a piece of my mind!'

'You don't know the facts,' persisted Joy. 'It was probably a one-off thing. How can you judge? It might just as easily have been Kobie or Andrew.'

'No man, not them!' said Petra, a little tactlessly. 'But I wouldn't say no to a guy like Jan, that's for sure!' She laughed. 'And after all, he's only human.'

'Yirra!' said Annatjie. 'Men are such bastards! If I ever find Kobie's been having an affair I'll kill him, s'trues God!'

Petra suppressed a giggle. Joy hastily rang the bell for the sister to take the baby back to the nursery.

Elsa left her mother and Nella in the main street to shop while she took Petrus to report to the police. Nella bounced up and down, dragging at Grandma's hand and begging for a milkshake. They disappeared into the café as Elsa drove away.

Petrus went into the charge office alone. Elsa waited for him in the car. She turned on the radio. A mid-afternoon drama in Afrikaans was playing—a strident heroine, atmospheric violins. She changed the station, searched for music. She opened her bag and sorted idly through the contents.

Petrus was gone a long time. Elsa got out of the car impatiently and walked around the yard, looking up at the high stone walls and the pomegranate tree. At last he appeared. He came down the steps towards her, followed by Sergeant Smit.

Sergeant Smit sauntered by. Again the bold glance. He looked away in his own time and Elsa could feel the flush rising up her neck.

He got into a car and revved it noisily. He seemed to launch it through the gates. Elsa could hear him changing down —fourth, third, second as he approached a stop street, the exhaust snorting.

'Arsehole'' she said under he breath. Petrus did not indicate that he had heard.

The sun was low when they turned in at Blackheath. Nella had fallen asleep on the back seat. Petrus looked out at the *veld*. He fingered the scar on his cheek every now and then, exploring its contour.

Elsa dropped him off at the dairy to check on the milking. He touched his hat to her in thanks then went through the gate, walking with his light, swinging step across the paddock. He saluted a man at the water trough, raised his good arm. The worker replied, a greeting, a ribaldry. Petrus laughed and disappeared through the door of the milking shed.

Elsa woke Nella and led her sleepily down to the house. The back door was closed. The yard was silent. At the place where she had been building the dip with the workers, spades lay about. She went into the kitchen. The dogs, without greeting her, pushed past into the yard. They ran here and there, sniffing. The sheepdog stood at the gate and barked.

'Chrissie?' Elsa called apprehensively. 'Chrissie, why did

you lock the dogs in the kitchen?'

There was no reply. The house was empty. The kettle had been left to boil dry on the stove.

'Shall we go and find Chrissie, Nell?' Elsa said, keeping the alarm from her voice. She called the dogs. They ran just ahead on the path leading to the workers' houses.

'Carry me,' cried Nella. 'I'm tired.'

'Walk Nellie,' said Elsa, hurrying along. She dragged Nella by the hand.

Nella complained all the way down the track, trying to keep up. 'Why's your hand all cold and sweaty,' she said crossly. 'Put me on your back.'

The yard around the workers' houses was deserted but for old Alzina folding washing in the doorway.

Elsa kept the dogs at heel. 'Chrissie!' she called, a little timidly. 'Chrissie?'

Chrissie came round the side of her house. She stopped abruptly when she saw Elsa.

'What's going on?' said Elsa. 'Where is everyone? When I came home I found the dogs shut in the house. The tools were lying around.'

'It is all right,' said Chrissie in English. 'Everything is quite all right.' Then she said in Xhosa, almost an apology, 'There was a man here asking for Petrus. I told him Petrus was at the police station. He has gone now.'

She did not look at Elsa as she spoke. Her expression was deferential but closed to scrutiny. Yet briefly, in that first moment, caught unawares, Elsa had seen the anguish in Chrissie's face. Then Chrissie had closed it in, denied it to her. She said, 'How's Auntie's baby, Nella? What's his name?' The familiarity of banter, to keep Elsa's questions in check.

When she had regained her composure Chrissie turned to Elsa and asked her about Joy. She clucked and exclaimed and jogged her own child on her back unnecessarily for it was quite content and gazed sleepily over the rim of the blanket.

At last Elsa said, 'Chrissie, is something wrong?'

'*Akukhonto*. There is nothing.' She said it gently, in reassurance. And then she smiled and remarked reprovingly, 'We have not made rusks for a long time and Nkos' is coming home soon.'

'He won't be back for three weeks but let's make some anyway. We will do it together.'

They stood in the late afternoon light, in the dim kitchen at either side of the table, the pastry board and the bowl of dough between them. Chrissie's small face was shadowed by the silky edges of her black *doek*. Her eyelids were delicate and moist. Her small hoop earrings winked at her lobes. She glanced at Elsa, then turned away to set the dough near the stove. They worked in silence, at this the ritual of their womanhood.

Chrissie had suggested that they bake rusks to appease her, Elsa knew, but it was the same as if she'd put out her hand and touched her. A mute gesture of regard.

When they had finished, Chrissie went home, carrying a can of milk from the dairy. Elsa, sitting on the sill of Nella's window, as Nella searched for a bedtime book in the cupboard, watched her moving down the road. She was singing. More imagined than heard, Elsa knew which song she sang: *bayeza kusasa*, *bayeza*. Tomorrow, tomorrow they come.

For the first time in all her years on Blackheath Elsa locked the doors before she went to bed.

Bushpigs came in the night—down from the ravines on the *bult* and from the bush of Rooikloof. Driven by hunger they attacked some young goats in a camp. They herded them and tore the skin from them in carniverous frenzy. Some of the goats had been eaten and nothing was left but a skeleton festooned with cobwebs of gristle, sinew and hair. Gone were the yellow, vacant eyes, gone the soft-downed roundness of a groin.

Standing in the *veld* beside the remains, a carnage, Elsa remembered the cold bleakness of the night before: how far, how aloof the stars. Beyond the lights of the farmhouse and the yard the night remained unchallenged.

Once eagle owls, *mazimuzimu*, spirits, thudded down the *bult* and waited for her. Now it was bushpigs. Elsa kneeled appalled besides an injured goat examining the great oozing wounds in its skin.

'Shall we kill it?' she said to the worker who had come with her.

'No, we must take it to the pens.' He lifted it to the back of the truck. It cried pitifully. A third he killed for it lay eviscerated. Only the heart beat on.

She stood and looked around, alert and apprehensive. The bush on the *bult* was bland with midday light—just bush, just stones, just grass. But as the night drew on, as shadows grew, she sensed how it would change, unfold.

Predators are born in darkness, they hunt the *bult* and the circles of their range draw in—closer, always closer to the old house with its fragile hedge of quince.

Andrew Fraser and Kobie de Jager went home for the weekend. They left in the late dustiness of a Friday afternoon. Jan stayed behind. He should have been with them.

Kobie said shortly, '*Lekker bly*, Jan. Is there anything you want from home?'

'Don't need anything at the moment.'

'See you then.'

'Cheers.'

Kobie had gone out to the truck. Andrew had stayed behind a moment. Andrew with his ram's wool hair and his friendly florid face had said to Jan, 'Jannie man, come home with us. What about the farm?'

'The farm's all right. I'd rather work overtime and get more money to send back.'

'And Elsa?'

'Elsa manages. She does things her way. You don't need to worry about her.'

'That's bullshit, Jan,' said Andrew. 'You're not fooling anyone.'

'Don't give me a hard time,' said Jan. He pushed past and went out onto the site. He left Andrew standing in the doorway of the office. Andrew, his oldest friend, team-mate in the first fifteen, his best man, Andrew with his slow, regional speech who laughed at his own jokes and worked single-mindedly at his farming. Jan had shut him out in his anger and his guilt, knowing that Andrew was justified in judging him and knowing that Andrew had always resented somewhere that Elsa had chosen Jan and excluded him when, as a small fat boy, he had loved her unequivocally. Now, good-natured, honest Andrew was there to see what Jan had done and hold the hurt for Elsa, shielding her.

Jan had turned back to Andrew, to say—Wait, I'll come with you. Why don't we just leave this place altogether and to hell with the drought? But already Andrew had gone with Kobie. Jan could see the *bakkie* heading along the road, going south.

The site office was empty. Jan threw his papers into a drawer and walked out. He did not go back to his house to change. He went to town in his overall and boots.

He stopped at the café where a dark-haired woman presided in a sweaty arnel dress dispensing tepid pies and polony across the counter. He bought Yvonne some cigarettes and climbed the stairs, his boots clattering on the scuffed, black-painted steps.

She opened the door. 'So?' she said, looking him up and down. 'Why you here? I thought you were going home?'

'I'm working overtime.'

'Overtime?' she cocked a brow at him. 'Why aren't you on site then?'

'This is part of the overtime.'

'Is it?' She flicked her hair back. 'How much d'you get an hour for overtime?'

Jan leaned against the doorframe and smiled at her. 'How much do you charge?'

'Too expensive for you, my boy!'

He followed her in, threw the cigarettes on the table, put out his hand to take her arm. She slipped from his grasp.

'Uh, uh—you too greedy, mister.' Then she said, 'Hettie's away for the weekend.' Her words hung in the room, a little hesitant. 'Do you want to stay over?'

'And . . .' He stopped. 'And Fanie?'

She flushed. 'Fanie's not coming.'

'There's nothing wrong?' Jan sounded dismayed.

She turned to him. 'It's not your business Jan, is it?'

She went into the kitchenette. 'Will you have some wine?

I bought a bottle of red this afternoon. I even got a chicken loaf from the Greek shop and some rolls. They're nice and fresh. I saw the van come in with the bread.'

'Were you expecting someone?'

'Ja.'

'Who?'

'You.'

'How come?'

'Ag, I could see it sticking out a mile!' Then she said softly, 'You better think what we doing one of these days, Jan.'

Jan did not reply. He wasn't sure how to answer. Whatever he said would be a rationalization. What had started in anger and despondency at the drought, at his own isolation, at Freek Koen, had become an obsession. He did not want it to end. Nor did she, he knew.

There was something in Yvonne that sparked a wonderful, adolescent lust like the one when he'd been seventeen and had gone to stay with his friend Errol in a small town during the Easter holidays. They'd hung around the dam in the afternoon with the Constable's daughter Annelize and her friend Noleen and kissed under the tired old willow trees.

Tanned girls, broad-faced with strong teeth and big, laughing mouths. Their bosoms bulged under their blouses in a way that those of the other girls he knew never did—they were too small, too prim, too confined and were never to be touched. All joyless and frustrating.

Noleen and Annelize had been different. They didn't mind taking their clothes off to swim in their bras and pants, jumping, shrieking, their flesh bouncing, strong legs, strong backs, shrill voices. Those girls could kiss by the hour and if only their bosoms could be explored they held enough promise for Jan to be hopeful of more. But just as he was making headway, just when he got to being allowed to feel Annelize with her pants still on, the holidays had ended and the willow trees had stood deserted by the muddy dam, and the windmill in the back garden of Errol's house had sent its crazy shadow round and round, and the boys had said they'd write and never did.

Yvonne had all the promise of an Annelize under the willow

trees. Annelize had grown up into an Yvonne. She did not insist that the light was turned out before he touched her. She did not tell him that he was unromantic. She had never expected him to say, 'I love you'. He had Yvonne with the kind of urgency with which he'd fantacized about Annelize when he was seventeen. The fantasy had come true, been consumated. He didn't want to give it up.

And yet, within Yvonne, holding out, he knew, against the time when he would go, there was a tenderness they dared not recognize. He had sometimes caught her watching him intently but when he looked at her she would drop her eyes, say something trite. She protected him from his own guilt, pretending none herself. In a strangely generous way she took responsibility for what had happened. He wondered what the price for her would be.

Yvonne opened the kitchen cupboard and knelt down to look for glasses. Jan nudged playfully at her bottom with the toe of his boot. She slapped at his foot and laughed, but as she took the glasses she clenched her fingers round them, held her breath a moment—she had no intention of crying. Why should she in front of him? What did he know of her thoughts? Her moments of regret? 'Get the wine out of the fridge,' she said.

'Why'd you put it in the fridge? It's red!'

'What's the difference?' she replied crossly. 'I like it cold.'

He laughed. 'OK, so you like it cold.' He took the glasses from her and poured the wine.

She went through to the living room and put a record on the turntable, recovering herself. Jan brought in the drinks.

Yvonne drank the first glass so fast the wine lay heavy in her joints and the emotion she had felt ebbed away. 'D'you like the record?'

'I like it,' said Jan, who never listened to music. 'It's great for teenyboppers.'

'Old man!' she said, tucking her legs up beneath her.

'Come off it.'

'Well, I know how old you are.'

'How come?'

'You told me the year you left school.'

'So?'

'So you were eighteen in sixty-six. You're twenty-nine now!'

'Brilliant deduction,' said Jan drily.

A lorry sped by in the street. The net curtains, grimy with Karoo dust, rustled dry as insect wings against the pot plants on the sill. Jan leant back and closed his eyes. Kobie and Andrew's truck would be heading out across the farmlands. Where would they be? Burgersdorp? Hofmeyr? Perhaps they had stopped at the café in Steynsburg to have a cup of coffee and talk to fat Koos Venter before they went on to Cradock. After that they would climb Daggaboersnek, sliding down towards the place where the *witgat* trees stood moon-white in the darkness. Daggaboersnek, the Baviaans and home.

He shook his head and drank more wine. Yvonne lit a cigarette. Her ring flashed.

'What happened to you today?' he said.

'Weeell,' she drew out the word. 'I made a mistake when we were cashing up so I had to stay back to sort it out. And we had a kitchen tea at lunch time for Barbara. She's leaving at the end of the month to get married. She's going to live in Molteno—I ask you! And she's pregnant and feeling awful. I'd die if that happened to me.'

'If you were pregnant?'

'No man, if I had to live in Molteno.'

'Where will you live?'

'I don't know,' she said, visualizing sharply a small house behind a garage somewhere, a windy-drier sailing round in a dusty gale.

She put her cigarette down in the ashtray and sat on Jan's lap. She was heavy with abundant flesh and bone. She held her glass for him to sip and then she drank herself and gazed at him over the rim. 'Shall we eat,' she said.

'No!' He undid her belt, her zip. She stretched—she always did—a prelude. She would draw him on then, minute by minute, the things she said a little brittle, a little bantering. An accomplice—she played the game well. She spoke no word in tenderness. She did not dare.

Much later she cleared away the glasses and the plates from

their abandoned supper, speaking little, closing him out of the kitchen as she washed the dishes. Jan stood alone at the window looking down into the street, at the cars parked outside the café. The girders of the wall thrust up against the sky. Beyond the site a train was passing, a small thread of lights flickering now and then like a wind-blown candle flame. It moved out, finding its way in the huge blackness of the plains. It reminded him of Elsa.

He turned away. Yvonne was standing in the doorway, a cup of coffee in her hand. 'Here,' she said. She held it out. It rattled slightly in the saucer and she steadied it with careful fingers. 'I suppose you'll go now,' she said. She had seen his face, his preoccupation.

'Do you want me to?'

'Whatever you like, Jan.' She handed him the coffee.

She chose a record and hummed to herself, avoiding his eyes. She went through to the bathroom and turned on the taps. When she came back to the living room he was still standing there. 'So?'

'I don't think I'll stay,' he said. 'But,' he smiled, a little hesitantly, 'I won't be working all the time. We can do things...'

'If you want it that way.'

'It wouldn't seem...'

'Right staying here,' she finished it for him, adding briskly, 'that's fine by me.' She went to the bathroom again and fiddled in the wall cupboard, looking for bath salts. She splashed half the contents of the jar into the water, her hand unsteady. He came to the door.

'Would you like to go into town tomorrow evening? We could see a movie, have dinner at the hotel perhaps.'

'Yes.' She trailed her hand around the tub, stirring up the bubbles. 'Thank you, Jan. See you then.'

He took her arm. 'Yvonne,' he said. 'I stayed because of you...'

She bit the corner of her bottom lip, half-smiled. Still she did not look at him. 'I'm flattered, hey Jan,' she said lightly. 'Really I am.'

# ❦ 7 ❦

There is a township by mud flats where salt grass grows.
People go with old tins on Sundays and dig for pencil-bait.
A bridge, high above the estuary, pumps traffic from the
city to the hinterland. The place smells: sulphur, offal, carbon
waste. There is a municipal graveyard. The headstones are
grimed with decades of smut. Among the mounds grow the
small, tough, wiry bushes of a primitive vegetation.

Way along the coast is a salt factory with its pans, toned
pink, indigo, grey, teal-blue. Beyond, in a break in the dunes
—a place where the south-easter shrieks—is a small, rocky
island, home of sea birds.

Behind the flats where the waders flock and where the skeins
of cormorants fly out across the bay, the township lies guarded
by the power station, its great chimneys smoking in the sky.

Along Daku Road are houses, shoulder to shoulder, faded
and cracked. A picket fence, a hedge of *tecoma*, so choked
with smoke it is dying slowly over years. There is a church
with a small, flat-topped tower, arched windows and a grey
asbestos roof. A school bell leans on stilts. Further down
the road is the squatters' market where, on Fridays, women
gather. There is a grandmother with a skinned cow's head
in an enamel basin. Only the nose still glistens black and
moist. The cheeks are livid, the eyes turned up towards the
sky.

Beyond are the Welfare Offices. Behind, a stretch of ground
with a rash of scrub leaning with prevailing winds. It is a
place where boys hunt rats and mice. The news of weeks,
of months, of years is wrapped around the bushes. Here mules
graze, one a wild albino. Donkeys copulate when the sun
is warm.

Up Daku Road the cream and orange buses toil: Centenary

123

Centre, Njoli Road, Kwa-Ford and on into town. A funeral van—Easy Terms—painted blue, clatters down towards the Police Station. There are boys at the corner, women at the bus stop, a dead dog bloats in an empty lot. Billboards— drink Golden Mustang—a cowboy, a cactus, a canyon. Here is White Location. Here Red Location—all in corrugated iron.

Down the road, walking carefully, for the way is long, goes Nontinti Ngubane, matriarch of vagabonds. She has been searching for her grandson Abedingo, from Cookhouse to Alicedale to Port Elizabeth.

He has been here. He has been there. Once he too had stayed with Ngubane, but he had run away with the money the *makoti* had given him to buy her bread and sugar. They had not seen him since. He was gone — *dlakadlaka*—a child of the road.

The Community worker at Centenary Centre says she must see the man at the Welfare Offices. So she goes—an old woman and waits on the steps, afraid to enter the polished linoleum passage with the many doors leading off.

At last she is beckoned in in her long skirts and her turban —a country woman among the billboards and buses—to wait in a room with a bench and fly spots on the window.

'Abedingo Ngubane?' No one has heard that name here. 'You should ask the police.'

She shakes her head.

'When did he go?'

'It is eight months, maybe nine.'

'Why did he go?'

She cannot tell his reasons.

'Have you heard from him?'

'No.'

'Why do you think he came to Port Elizabeth?'

'His mother is here, somewhere.'

'Do you know where she lives?'

'No, I do not.' Nontinti does not look at the Welfare Officer. What would he know of the girl who walked away long ago, down to the bus at Melkbos Siding, returning only twice to leave her sons? What could this man know of her

124

face looking for the last time at those children? These are the things Nontinti has carried all her life.

The Welfare Officer will enquire from the police and from the Place of Safety. He will send a letter if he hears. She is out in the open ground.

She walks—down Daku Road, down Avenue A, past Sali's Store. There is no money for bread, no money for tobacco. She must keep what she has for the journey home. Down Red Location. Down White. She turns in at a gate. Here lives the son of Ngubane from the farm across at Klein-fontein. He has found a corner for her to sleep in. He knows what she is saying. She may stay until the letter comes. Then she will decide.

But when the letter does come it is not from the Welfare Officer. It is from her niece Chrissie and it says: you must come home Mama, for the boy Abedingo is here going up and down from Gcashe to Mpumalanga. It is time for your return. And so she starts again. Another journey—so many tickets, so many stations, so many hours without food or rest. Coega, Addo, Paterson, Groenheuwels. On and on.

And so it was with Abedingo: who can know his days. There was nowhere to go but Gcashe and Mpumalanga where the doors of households were closed against him. What could he know of Captain Olivier's file in the Police Station? He went here. He went there. He slept where the darkness found him. He caught rats. He caught mice. He sat in the grass, hour after hour, enticing them. He snapped the backbone between thumb and forefinger—a quick movement, a small grating sound, bone on bone. The rodent lay inert, its toes pink and tender, curled in against death. Abedingo cooked, ate and hunted again.

He had hidden the gun. He had wrapped it in a piece of plastic he'd found in the road. He had climbed up across the hills, up beyond the homesteads of Gcashe to the edges of the farmlands. He had found a cave, rancid with the smell of *dassie* droppings. He had slept there, gathering trails of dried grass and twigs and made a tiny fire, no more than a handful of smouldering tinder to roast his catch.

He had been afraid. Afraid of the deep murmuring of the night, of the jackal's yelp, of his hunger, of the rock shelter with its strange dark drawings of figures and animals. Like the eyes of the ancestors they watched him, a parade of ghosts, uncompanionable and beyond reach. He feared them and so he went away, leaving the gun hidden under stones. He made his way to Gcashe.

Dogs barked, women shouted, the gardens were empty. It was winter still. The dirt bins behind the store yielded little—only cockroaches, flat and treacle-coloured. There was nothing else to eat.

He headed for Port Elizabeth. He went on foot to Cookhouse. From there he hitched a lift in the back of a truck delivering cabbages. He huddled among the vegetables in the cold. The driver bought him bread and left him on the road near Uitenhage. He walked the rest of the way.

He knew of Ngubane in White Location. He went there, looking for a place to stay, for news of his mother. But Ngubane had not seen his mother since she was a child on Blackheath. There was no one else to ask. He begged for work at Sali's Store. At Yeko's. He did not have a pass so there was nothing he could do. He walked the streets, keeping away from Ngubane's wife who did not want him in the house. He loitered where the hawkers sold ginger beer. He scavenged in the bins behind the Municipal Market where the white man in the short-sleeved safari suit kept a sharp eye out for those who picked up the leavings.

He saw the boys in the streets—those that went about together and pilfered what they could. He watched when some of them were crammed into the police van that patrolled the roads. Six, seven, eight people, all in the wire cage at the back: fathers, grandfathers, sons—those that worked and those that didn't, those who had left their passes at home and those who had none.

The van skidded round the bend in Daku Road, through the gate into the prison yard. It closed, was locked. Final. For an hour the streets were empty and then the people filtered back.

Abedingo spoke to Ngubane of the van.

'You have no *dompas*, *mfo'wethu*,' Ngubane said. 'Keep

126

away. You know what they may do with you if they catch you without your reference?'

Abedingo shook his head.

'They will send you home—or they will make you go to *mazambane*.'

'*Mazambane?*'

'The prison farm. Far away. You will work till the heat of the sun boils your blood.'

*Mazambane*. The potato farms. Hard labour. It was a word in the mouths of those who knew each alley, each backyard, the hiding places in the open lots.

Ngubane's wife said, 'You must go home *mfan'am*. They will catch you one day. You are not supposed to be here. The *mazambane* is a place where a child can die.'

One day he went to Sali's Store. The *makoti*, tired of his idleness, sent him to buy bread and sugar. The sun was bright, the wind warming and far off, beyond the shanties, the low hills were blue. There were children singing in a school playground. There were women in the street. A radio was playing in the shop and old Sali presided at the counter in his white overjacket.

The van came suddenly. Abedingo did not see it but he sensed the voices of the women falter, continue then—softer, more subdued.

A policeman got out and sauntered across the bare ground before the store, scanning the change he had taken from his pocket. A fear took Abedingo as though it were fingers gripping at his throat. He ran. The policeman turned, surprised. '*Yima!* Stop!' he shouted. But Abedingo did not stop. He went on running. He hid at last in a ditch, fighting for his breath. There was no one. There was nothing. Only a dog hunted in the open ground.

He went on walking, across the *veld*, past the shacks of squatters, along the railway line. At nightfall a goods train came by. He chased along beside it, put his hand out, caught the edge of the door of a cattle truck, swung himself up. He wrenched his shoulder as he rolled into the darkness of the empty car. He lay on the floor, cradling it.

The train passed the reaches of the town, the outlying sidings, toiled on towards the hills, out into the night.

He returned to Gcashe. He found a bird-cage in a dump. The yellow paint had peeled off the wire. The base was buckled and rusted. He baited it with a scrap of sodden mealie cob and waited. He caught a rat, grizzled and verminous. He caught another. He wandered about with the bird-cage—up and down the open lands of Gcashe and Mpumalanga.

Then one day he smelt beans boiling. He followed the scent from down among the brush where he waited with his cage. He crept to the edge of a clearing, like a rat himself, and watched a woman at a cooking fire.

The woman had a baby on her back. It was very small, its fuzz of hair sticking up above the blanket. Her dwelling was no more than a shelter—sacks, paraffin tins, a piece of iron leant against a bush. She stirred her beans with a stick. The old pot was charred and dented beyond a shape.

Then a dog growled. It came at Abedingo from behind. Abedingo shouted, thrust his bird-cage at its head and broke into the clearing. The woman backed away, alarmed. She called the dog to her.

'Please Mama'—his voice was meek, Nontinti had taught him well—'I am hungry, I have nothing but this cage for catching rats.' Abedingo put the cage at his feet—a gesture of submission.

'Where are you from?' said the woman.

'From the farm. The people have thrown me away.'

The woman said warily. 'Why is that?'

Abedingo did not reply. He turned his head, drew his sleeve across his eyes, forcing back the tears of hunger and despair.

The woman took a tin and filled it with a portion of beans. She handed it to Abedingo. He dug his hand into it, burning himself. He licked the juice from his fingers.

The woman came closer. The baby stirred against her back. She looked at Abedingo: he was only a boy, there was no harm in him.

Later her man had come. He was angry. The dog growled again, baring its teeth.

'What are you doing here?' the man said, pulling him up. He could see the fear in Abedingo's eyes. His wrist was frail and slack beneath his grip.

'I am from the farm. The family has thrown me away.'

'Why have they thrown you away?'

'It is for the boy. It is for Sipho.' The words were wrenched from him.

'Are you by yourself?'

Abedingo nodded.

The man let him sit by the fire. He took some bread from the bag he was carrying and gave it to the woman. She broke off a corner and handed it to Abedingo. He ate it as they watched him.

'So tell me now,' the man said. 'Tell me about the boy Sipho.'

He stayed with them, trapping mice, birds, whatever he could find. He found a sack in a ditch and dragged it within the shelter.

By day the man went out, returning each time with something to eat, at other times with wine, methylated spirits or a carton of sorghum beer. He drank it by himself. Then he would lie in the sun while Abedingo went off with the cage to look for rat tunnels in the grass.

And then one night the man took Abedingo with him. They robbed a trader's house on Mpumalanga. The man killed the dog that guarded it by ramming a stone down its throat. He broke a window and Abedingo was sent through to unbolt the door. The house was empty but he left the stench of his fear in every room.

They took a radio, clothes, food and liquor. They slunk away in the night, past the dog lying in the sand, its mouth locked in a snarl around the suffocating stone.

That night Abedingo drank too: brandy to burn away the horror. It subsided as he drank and he began to speak. In the background the radio played. The woman hummed with the tunes. Abedingo talked. He talked of the farm, of Nontinti, of Sipho and then—a moment of defiance—he spoke of the gun. The man was still and then he leaned forward and said, 'The gun, *mfo'wethu?*'

The next day the man made Abedingo take him to the shelter high above the farmlands to fetch the gun. Abedingo went, shivering within his blazer, sick with the acid bite of the drink.

The man took the rifle and the bag of ammunition and

examined them. He smiled and carried them back to the shelter. Then he hid them where Abedingo could not find them.

They moved on—from Mpumalanga to Gcashe, from Gcashe to Mpumalanga—just ahead of retribution. They pilfered from houses and gardens, from trading stores. They set snares.

Spring was over. Summer came and wilted the bushes. Autumn slipped away. Winter returned. The nights were full of the thin threads of the child's cry.

There was fighting on Gcashe and the police had been about —cruising where the roads allowed, aerials bobbing.

Abedingo, the man, the woman and the child went back to the hills, to the cave where the figures watched from the rock face. Then they moved further into the farmland, looking for warmth. They followed the crests of the ridges or the *poorts* where stockmen rarely came. They saw *bakkies*, cars, bicycles travelling sporadically along the district road far below. They kept away.

They went to Brakkloof where the man once did piecework in the season. There was no one there. They walked around the house. It was deserted. An old chamber pot lay on the back *stoep*. The man kicked it with his foot. It rolled across the stones and the handle broke.

Once, when Abedingo was hunting, trapping on the *krantzes*, he went further than he usually did, to the boundary of Blackheath farm. Beyond the *poort* where the *bult* slid down, he could see the Rooikloof and the house among the pepper trees, the tractor in the yard, the workers' huts like a row of river pebbles near the *spruit*.

So far away. He could not go there now—a vagabond, a thief. The man with the gun would surely follow him and silence him. A weapon, like a white man, is a powerful thing.

One night they stole a sheep. It lay vacant-eyed where they had slaughtered it. They dragged it back into the bush where the woman waited.

The next time they were hungry the man sent him alone. He gave him a knife to slit its throat. He made his way down to Blackheath and watched in the dusk among the thorn scrub as the children played between the houses. Approaching the gate to Melvynside he glanced up and saw old Alzina in the road, wood on her head. She turned as though peering through the twilight. Abedingo slid silently behind a bush and she walked on.

He went down towards the gate and fumbled with the loop. He opened it. Alzina, further down the path in the gathering dark, stopped again to stare at him. He hurried on swiftly, without securing the chain.

He took a sheep from Somandla's flock. He killed it and hoisted it to his shoulders. The blood from the slaughtering crawled like moist fingers down his neck.

And then, two mornings after, Petrus Ngubane came to the hut. He spoke to the woman, telling her to send Abedingo home. But then Somandla had come, like a whirlwind picking up the dust, and struck Petrus Ngubane with his belt. Abedingo had seen him crumple over and had heard the woman crying.

He went to Blackheath but his Grandmother and Petrus Ngubane were not there. The people—his people—were afraid to talk. They said that he should speak to Petrus. It was Petrus who was having trouble with the police. He had gone away—but not before he had seen, below the *bult*, the grave of his only brother Sipho, marked with white-washed stones around its small perimeter.

He returned to the man and he said, 'Tell me how to use the gun.'

The man brought it out and they wiped it clean. Slowly and with care he showed him how to shoot.

He and the people of the road moved on, back to Gcashe, back to Mpumalanga. Then in time, retracing, they returned to Brakkloof. They had learnt, with an instinct as sure as a *rooikat*'s, to double back, to circle, from bush to bush within its territory, always beyond the hunter's reach. That it is pursued is its defence against complacency for it is wary, cunning, devious, found where least expected. And so it had become with Abedingo.

131

# 🌿 8 🌿

The weeks went slowly. With each day the windmill pumped less. The dam was empty. Its surface had cracked into jagged fragments of mud. There was a tidemark at its rim where once the water lapped and wildfowl had gathered in the evening light.

Elsa and Nella watched an old tick-ridden tortoise making his way across the dam floor. He was born of that dam it seemed, for the shields of his shell were as dry and brown as the scales of mud. He was the only living thing among the sapless bushes.

The scars made by the sun had crept nearer and nearer to the homestead. The skin of earth was blistering back. The trees, the plants, the buildings seemed to hold their places tenuously. Only the *bult*, thrusting rock on rock, was unchanged—and the deep, long gash of the Rooikloof, cleaving down through stone.

Chrissie was busy in the kitchen making bread. This time Elsa did not help her for she was checking records, fences and machinery with Petrus. Jan was coming home for the weekend and everything must be perfect. Somehow, with more inspiration than hope she concocted an arrangement of leaves for the mantelpiece and a few bedraggled spikes of stocks were salvaged from a bed. They would smell good in a dark corner even if the petals were faded and edged with brown.

The salt bushes needed water but Petrus had gone to the hospital to have the plaster removed from his arm. He had taken the *bakkie* and a companion to collect the post and rations. Elsa went to supervise the work alone.

A driver and a team of women had taken the water tank into the land. The tractor trundled up and down between the rows. At each salt bush a woman tilted the thick hose to the base of a plant. Another sprinkled a handful of fertilizer. So they went—up and down, up and down—taking turns for the hose was heavy, the wind strong and the work tiring and dirty.

Elsa returned to the house when the workers knocked off for lunch. Nella had found a young brown-hooded kingfisher in the hedge. Its leg was injured. She and Tombizodwa had put it in a shoe box sprinkled with grass. The bird sat in a corner, its back feathers turquoise as Indian silk. They fed it *mealie* rice. 'Why won't it eat?' asked Nella anxiously.

'I don't think it knows that sort of food, darling,' said Elsa. 'And perhaps it's frightened.'

She heard the truck returning and the thud of sacks as meal and grain were unloaded. She went down to the yard. Petrus came across to her. 'Let's see,' she indicated his arm.

He held it out, glanced at its thinness critically, his lips pursed.

'What did the doctor say?'

'There is a letter.' He took an envelope from his pocket. 'I must see another man in Grahamstown.'

Elsa read the roneoed form and the attached note: Petrus Ngubane's bones had knitted imperfectly. Corrective surgery was necessary. He would have to consult an orthopaedic surgeon in Grahamstown. A tentative appointment had been made. It remained for Elsa to confirm it.

Elsa went inside. The kitchen smelt of freshly-baked bread and Chrissie was setting the loaves out on a wire rack.

Nella was sitting on the landing, the box with the kingfisher on her lap. 'It's dead,' she wailed. 'It wouldn't eat and now it's dead.'

Elsa bent to take the box, to divert Nella, but she clutched it to her. 'Don't!' she said crossly. 'I want to bury it like they buried Sipho. In a box with flowers.' She ran off with Tombizodwa to rummage for cottonwool to line the coffin.

Later Elsa saw them standing by the hedge. They had made a cross of twigs tied with grass. Seedy marigolds and a tuft of golden shower were stuck in the sand around the grave. Tombizodwa stared around, anxious to be off, but—always

133

compliant—she waited while Nella sang in a solemn monotone, Elsa's gilt-edged recipe folder clasped like a prayer book
between her hands.

The afternoon dragged on. Nella was fractious, Elsa impatient. Only Chrissie continued with her work undisturbed.

At five Andrew, Kobie and Jan left for home. They stopped
off at the café to buy cold drinks for the journey. Jan glanced
up at the window of Yvonne's flat. It was open. The thin
net curtain hung limp in the still evening air. He did not
inspect the cars parked in the street: he knew that amongst
them would be Fanie's white Cortina with the miniature pair
of boxing gloves dangling from the rear-view mirror.

Andrew returned to the truck with Cokes and a stick of
*biltong*. Kobie took the wheel and they drove out of town,
away from the huge rent of the dam, into the quiet dusk,
turning south-east.

It was a long drive. They talked the talk of farmers, leaving
the site behind them—the strings of lights, the girders in
the sky, the water damming up and up, slowly drowning
the old lands. A shepherd's bush hunched against the twilight,
sheep resting in its lea. A windmill loomed. The scab of bushes
stretched across the plains, each making its own small dusk.
A house lay below a ridge, a clump of cypresses desolate
beside it. Jan sat, eyes half-closed, watching the darkness.
The headlights caught the startled eyes of a springhare. Later,
an owl, which had settled in the warm dust of the road, turned
at their approach, raised its wings and rose out of sight. They
paused at a crossing, looking for a train, but the railway tracks
were empty. They levelled out equidistant in the night.

They took turns to drive—on and on until at last their
own district road led east into the hills and they reached the
gates of Blackheath farm.

Far below them was the tall house, the head of the palm,
black against the sky. The top half of the front door stood
open. There—a shadow. Elsa. She stood in the hall, framed
with light.

Elsa. Jan wished he could have left behind in the concrete
greyness of the barbarous damsite all the feelings of guilt
that had stalked him since the night he had taken Yvonne

to the pre-fabricated hut. They followed him here where they did not belong.

Kobie drove into the yard and Jan got out, stiff from the ride. Elsa ran to him, jumped at him, held his head close to hers. When Kobie and Andrew had gone they walked in through the front porch. Elsa turned to Jan, took his weekend case, set it down and went up on tiptoe to kiss him, to hold him round the neck.

Jan put out his hand to close the door, to bolt it against the thing that dogged him. To keep it out. The faint smell of stocks hovered in the hall. He held her very close. She seemed so small.

'I got a message from Adrian when I was at the dam,' said Jan at breakfast. 'He's at Uncle Cedric's this weekend.'

'Oh God!' Elsa groaned. 'I purposely didn't tell Uncle Cedric you were coming home because I knew he'd be over here bothering you as soon as you arrived.'

'Uncle Cedric won't take no for an answer. I can't convince him I'm not interested in Koen's land.'

'Daddy! Daddy! Come and see where I buried the kingfisher!' cried Nella, running in. 'Come and see, Dad.'

'Just now. I'm going to eat my breakfast first.'

Nella took an apple from the fruit basket and gazed at him reproachfully.

'Come here, you funny little person!' Jan said, pulling her towards him. She sat on his lap and inspected his breakfast, helping herself to some of the bacon.

'Nella! Fingers out of the food!' said Elsa, irritated. 'If you want some I'll give you your own.'

Jan worked at his breakfast, relishing it. 'I must speak to Petrus and see what he's buggered up since I was last here,' he said conversationally. He looked across at Elsa. Her face was tense, unsmiling. She watched him with dark eyes. 'What's the matter Els?' he said, half-laughing.

'Nothing.' Somehow she could not acknowledge what she and Petrus had done together.

'OK Nellie,' said Jan as he pushed away his plate. 'Show me your kingfisher.'

'Come Dad. It's in the flowerbed and we made a cross and everything.'

'Jan,' said Elsa, putting out a restraining hand, 'I must speak to you before you find Petrus. It's very important.'

'Daddy!' said Nella imperiously.

'I'll be right back, Els,' he said.

Elsa sat at the table, her teacup warming her hands. Opposite, Jan's place was empty, his table napkin crumpled by his plate. She looked at it, reached across and folded it mechanically, over and over. The steam from her tea drifted against her cheek.

She had run to him the night before, held him to her. He had hugged her, kissed her warmly, stroked her hair, whispered all the endearments she had wanted to hear so much.

She had cooked him bacon and eggs and he had sat at the kitchen table and asked about the farm. She had brought the lamp and told him everything—farmer to farmer. But she had not mentioned Petrus's arm. That could wait till morning. She had not wanted contention at his homecoming. She had sat with him instead, the old familiarity settling back. He had glanced through the post and the accounts as he drank his coffee.

She had bathed with him, washed his back. She had laid her cheek against its dampness and said to him, 'You've got so thin and muscly.'

'So have you!' She had been pleased with that.

They had gone and looked at Nella sleeping. Jan had bent and kissed her head, smiled at Elsa.

She had prepared for him like a lover. There were flowers on the table and she had made a nightie, sprigged cotton and lace. He had noticed neither. He had got into bed and turned out the light before he'd taken her into his arms.

He'd loved her as he always had, knowing her so well. He had been so tender, but somehow, he seemed to lack the longing she had felt. He had been protective—husbandly. And after, he had held her gently, his fingers closed round hers.

'Jannie,' she had whispered but he had merely grunted slee-

136

pily and not replied. And yet she knew he was awake. She knew it by the feel of his fingers, the tenseness in his arms. She'd slept beside him far too long to be mistaken. She had lain, eyes open in the dark, bewildered.

Elsa went upstairs. She dumped the contents of Jan's case on the floor and sorted through the clothes. She took his washing to the bathroom. She stood a moment, the lid of the laundry basket in her hands, feeling empty in a way she could not explain.

She heard a car. She glanced through the window. It was Cedric and Adrian. 'Why can't you bloody well leave us alone!' she said loudly to herself.

She looked down and saw them walk across the yard. Uncle Cedric wore his dark green hat, pulled low over his eyes. His ears stuck out as though they supported the brim. Adrian followed him.

Adrian had been rakish when he was young. His hair had been thick and had flopped across his forehead. Now it was thinning and grey showed through at the edges. He held himself upright but his waist was undefined, his face slack. He was no longer rakish. He just looked middle-aged and prosperous.

He did not see Elsa watching in the shadow of the window. She tramped downstairs, treading deliberately on the fourth step. It snapped loudly.

Jan had gone no further than the hedge where he was inspecting the flowers scattered over the kingfisher's grave. He came to greet Adrian and Cedric and Adrian put his hand on Jan's shoulder and guided him towards the house.

Tombizodwa hovered at the gate, a tin can balanced on her head, staring expectantly after Nella. But Nella took no notice. She followed her father up the verandah steps.

'Just come with us and have a look,' Uncle Cedric was saying when Elsa entered the living room. 'It's dirt cheap, it could be very productive land.'

Jan sat in the armchair. He crossed his legs, leaning his calf on his knee. He ran his hand up and down the ribbing of his sock.

Uncle Cedric had forgotten to remove his hat. Today, with

137

it still on his head, he reminded Elsa of a *koringkriek*, for he sat with his hands on his knees, his elbows stuck out, his shoulders hunched, his head thrust forward. His face was red and his jaws worked constantly, to keep—it seemed —his teeth in place. In his short-sleeved shirt and trousers, despite the cold, he was bristly and hard.

Adrian took Elsa's hand a moment and said, 'Hello, love, it's good to see you.' He always spoke to her like that. He seemed to listen to himself as he said it, impressed with his own affability.

'You must go over the farm yourself, Jan,' insisted Uncle Cedric.

'Look,' said Jan. 'I'm already working my arse off at the damsite to keep this place going. How the hell do you expect me to fork out for more land?'

'But it's a giveaway!' said Cedric.

'I'll put up money for you,' said Adrian blandly.

Elsa turned away:—You can have my marbles Jannie, I don't like them any more.

—Here, I don't need this old fishing tackle. Take it.

—Have the jaloppy. You won't want much else living here.

—You can run the farm half shares. I'll pay you every quarter for the labour. Ha, ha, ha.

'Keep your money,' said Jan levelly. 'I'm not adding to my problems.'

'I don't understand your thinking Jan,' said Cedric.

'I'll lend you the cash interest-free,'—an afterthought from Adrian.

'No.'

Adrian shrugged. He glanced at Elsa and said, 'I thought that I might convert Koen's old *pondok* into a holiday cottage but Liz wants to build a new house altogether. Anyway,' he stood up, 'I'd like to look at it now. At least come with us Jan and tell us what you think. You too Elsa.'

Elsa turned to Jan. 'There'll be too many of us in the car,' she said. 'I'll stay.'

She wanted to find Petrus, to tell him to keep out of the way until Adrian and Cedric were gone.

Jan said, 'Please come, *kleintjie*.'

'Oh, incidentally, Elsa,' interrupted Adrian. 'Liz is over at Melvynside making something special for dinner tonight. You'll join us, won't you? We're expecting you.' Elsa glanced plaintively at Jan. 'And Liz wondered,' continued Adrian, 'if you have any of that marvellous peach pickle we had last time we were here? Could you spare a jar?'

'There might be some. I'll have a look. I haven't made anything for ages.'

'Too busy chasing after angoras to bother with housekeeping,' said Cedric. He laughed and cocked his head and looked at her with his hard, locust eyes.

She took her chance to hurry through to the kitchen to find Petrus. He was already waiting for Jan in the backyard. She indicated Adrian's car in the drive and sent him home until they returned from Brakkloof. She did not want Uncle Cedric to see him.

Adrian took the road to Jaap Koen's farm. Nella sat in the back of the car on Jan's lap, her head leaning on his arm, her rough little fingers entwined in his.

They crawled out towards the railway line and the small rutted tracks which webbed the base of Mpumalanga Mountain. Elsa hardly listened to the conversation. She watched the sky, the barren roadsides. They drove past huts and goat pens, past Langa Store where a small boy sat on the step and beat a cardboard box like a drum.

Adrian turned in at the gates of Brakkloof. The cypress trees clustered together round the old house, scab-barked and tired. Adrian parked on the causeway over the dry riverbed and he and Cedric got out and sauntered along the bank. Elsa and Jan followed with Nella between them.

'Jan,' said Elsa, taking his arm and holding him back. 'What is it? What's wrong?'

'There's something off about capitalizing on people like Oom Jaap,' he said, avoiding her eyes and the real meaning of her question. He stood, his arms folded, his legs astride. 'Adrian and Uncle Cedric are like vultures. If it was Blackheath . . . Besides that,' he said, not wanting to think of the possibility, 'I'll have none of Adrian's bloody condescension.

Come,' he put his arm around her. 'Talk to me *kleintjie*. Tell me what else you've been doing. Why haven't you been playing tennis and why haven't you been eating?'

She did not want to speak of the farm, nor of Petrus with Cedric and Adrian striding about not far away. She turned the conversation to the dam instead. But Jan was non-committal and so they wandered up and down the empty riverbed and played with Nella, gathering pebbles and piling them up—a little citadel beside the watercourse.

Above them the old house stood with its shutters closed. An ornate chamber pot, decorated with rosebuds and blue rococo ribbons lay on the steps. It was stained with a season of red dust, sticky with cobwebs, its handle broken.

Well beyond the huts the workers' houses stood on the bare earth behind a barrier of *garingbome*. The windows were boarded up. Scrufulous brush grew where the woodpile had been.

Elsa listened to the wind fretting in the thatch above a doorway. It plucked the grass stems like a plectrum tapping at the string of a Xhosa harp. Laughing doves moved here and there in the quiet, searching for forgotten grains.

She had loved the unobtrusive doves ever since Nontinti had told her the meaning of the colours in her bead necklace: blue is for the feather of the dove that picks the seeds scattered at your mother's door, red the clay with which I adorn my body and the colour of my eyes that have watched for you so long; green is for the hillsides on which your father's cattle graze, white the long, long road leading north.

Restlessly Elsa climbed up towards the farm garden, wishing that Adrian and Cedric would hurry so that she and Jan could go home and be alone. Standing at the edge where once Mrs Koen had grown purple irises, contained within the sandy confines of a brick-marked bed, she gazed down towards the workers' houses. An unlatched door grated back and forth in the wind. A dog, a yellow dog, emaciated as a meerkat, ceased its watching and lay down, too weak to explore the sound of people by the river. Elsa did not see it as it slept. Nor did she see a young man, still as the shadow of a *garingboom*, standing in the lea of the wall.

140

Adrian and Cedric were back at the drift where Adrian's big grey car sparked light from shining hubcaps. Cedric said —how many times he had said it— 'I'll tell you what Adrian, if you decide to knock down this place, the new house could be built there,' he pointed to where the land rose gently to the east, 'and then you'd have a marvellous site with a view towards Melvynside. All you need is a few natives to keep an eye on things. I'll help Jan run it. Mark my words, Adrian —Jan will come round. He always does.'

When they returned to Blackheath, Elsa insisted on being dropped at the end of the long drive, resisting any suggestion that Cedric and Adrian might come in for tea. She and Jan walked up towards the house, Nella running before.

'Jan, Petrus is waiting for you,' Elsa said. 'But there's something I must tell you.'

'What's wrong? Has he been playing up?'

'The police assaulted him, Jan. He had a broken arm and a messed-up face. The doctor doesn't know if he's going to get full use of his hand again. He wants him to see an orthopaedic surgeon.'

Jan stopped. 'Christ!' he cried. 'Why didn't you tell me before?'

They stood in the drive under the old poplar trees and Elsa spoke slowly, deliberately, leaving out nothing. She told him about the gate that had been left open, the police station, the sergeant. She told him about the treks and of how she had not mentioned them to Cedric.

'That was irresponsible Elsa,' interrupted Jan. 'If they'd been on our land what would you have done?'

'They weren't on our land or Uncle Cedric's. They were on Brakkloof.'

'That's not the point.'

She shook her head. 'You had to see them to understand.' She hesitated. 'It was something about the woman, Jan. So hopeless—just holding on. I couldn't send her away. I suppose it's all my fault that this has happened. How could I have known what would come of it?'

Jan looked across the lands, beyond the poplars to where the salt bushes grew. He could see how the drought had eaten into the old farm garden, the terrifying greyness of the *veld*. The windmill screeched in the wind, pumping its plunger into a dry socket.

'Cedric told me to fire Petrus. I didn't, of course,' said Elsa. 'Adrian was always going on about it on the phone. I was vague with him. I expect he thought I'd done what he told me like I always have. I'm sorry Jannie,' she said, putting out her arms for him. 'Please don't be angry.'

'It will rain,' he said, as if that would solve it all. 'We'll manage somehow.' He patted her absently. 'I'm going to speak to Petrus now. Are you coming?'

'No.' She would not intrude between them. 'I must see to lunch. Hurry back. I don't feel like sharing you.'

Jan found Petrus in the workshop directing another worker. He turned abruptly as Jan entered. Jan saw the jagged blue-black scar against the high, even contour of his cheek. Petrus grinned and came forward with a quick step. The man at the workbench greeted Jan cheerfully, standing with some pride at his handiwork—a skill acquired unexpectedly because of Petrus's injury.

'*Ewe*, Ngubane!' Jan said. He slapped him on the shoulder. 'What am I to do with a cockrel with one leg, hey?' He glanced at Petrus's arm. 'You have been fighting?'

He admired the other worker's progress, complimenting him on what he'd done. He looked round the old room, smelled the scent of oil, grease, dip, wood shavings, the cold damp of the stone floor. Then he went outside with Petrus, leading the way to the goat *kraal*.

As boys they had often sat on the wall and tried to shoot stones across the enclosure and over the other side with their catapults. Now they leant against the gate. Petrus, his apprehension dispelled, took out his pipe and slowly filled it from his cloth pouch. He lit it and puffed quietly, waiting for Jan to speak.

'So Ngubane,' said Jan. 'It has come to this?' He indicated his arm. 'Tell me.'

Petrus had been his friend from the time he was a small, rough-haired child with a skin burned as brown as a *boerboon* seed. They'd fished in the dam, penned tortoises in *kraals* of thorn twigs and called them goats, shot mice and transported them on the backs of their wire cars, had races with those same cars up and down the roads they'd made on the slope behind the shed. They'd shot birds with their catapults and roasted them, charring off the feathers and eating them by the fire made on the *bult*, well away from the house.

Then Jan had been given a gun, a .22, and Petrus had not been allowed to touch it. That had been the moment when the sharing had ended, that the friendship as it had been had drawn quietly to a close.

Jan had carried the gun. He had used it and Petrus had retrieved the booty: a guineafowl, a rock pigeon, a francolin. Once he had shot a cobra the colour of iron, of rock and earth, its mouth gaping—so delicate and white inside, the texture of a petal. They had examined the fangs, squeezed the poison out, drop by drop. They had cut it open to inspect the contents of its stomach. Jan had decided to boil it and reconstruct the skeleton, each tendril of bone slotting into the spine. He had emptied old Alzina's beans from their pot on the stove and left the snake to simmer.

Glutinous and grey, it had been found by Alzina when she came to stir her lunch. She had screamed and screamed and the gardener had been called to dispose of it.

Then there had been the years between when Petrus had gone to the Transkei to school, sent to relations far away. He had worked in a town after his initiation. It was a time he never spoke of with Jan.

When his father died Petrus had returned to Blackheath to take his place, head of the family. By the time Jan had finished Agricultural College Petrus was already married to Chrissie, the father of a son, understockman. He called Jan '*nkosan*'—the days of their boyhood were over.

As he walked back to the house Jan remembered these things. Disjointed, they overlapped in his thoughts: cobras, catapults, wire cars. It was more than that. Much more. Somewhere, undefined as yet, Jan knew that he would have to make a choice—as Elsa had the day that she had seen the treks on Jaap Koen's land. He was glad when Nella pounced on him from the orchard wall where she and Tombi-

143

zodwa had been lying in wait for him. It deferred decisions for the moment.

Elizabeth de Villiers flew to the door of Cedric's house when Jan and Elsa arrived for dinner that evening. She was a-jingle with bracelets. She hugged Jan and called him a handsome boy. 'So thin Jannie!' she exclaimed. 'You're unrecognizable! Hi Els!' Elizabeth kissed Nella who stood, thumb in mouth, wrapped against the cold in a pink woolly dressing gown, her favourite pillow clutched in her arms. 'Your cousins are along the passage Nellie. Go and say hello.'

Uncle Cedric leaned on the mantel. Adrian stood opposite, drink in hand. Above them on the chimneypiece, a mounted buffalo head glared down with unaligned glass eyes which gave it a wild, angry look. A decade of dust lay on its horns. Small spider webs festooned its nostrils.

'It's simply lovely to see you all!' cried Elizabeth, twirling her wine glass. Her nails were beautifully manicured, painted translucent pink. She moved her hands with grace—they were an adornment—they did not work. She said, 'You've both got so thin and brown. Guess what, Jannie?' she turned to him.

'What?'

'Adrian bought a new car! It's gorgeous! It's really divine!'

Adrian said, 'Oh come on, darling, don't exaggerate.'

'Straight out of the box!' said Elizabeth gaily. 'A Merc sports in pale blue. Aidie's given me the grey car. The sports is dreadfully impractical of course—I mean, where would I fit the three kids? But it's lovely and he lets me drive round town in it. I'm terrified I'll prang it—it cost a fortune!'

Elizabeth chattered on, the coals fell through the grate. Adrian threw on a log and prodded it with a poker. Jan helped himself to a beer and stood at the edge of the group, his foot on the fender. Cedric's old labrador lay dreaming by the pile of wood. Elsa curled into a big black leather chair and drifted. The wine was heavy. She was tired and disturbed.

She looked up at Jan. His dark hair was rough, his face gaunt, burnt deep brown. His eyes seemed pale and preoccupied. He stood quite detached from all of them. It seemed, suddenly, that there was no more Jannie in the man who stood there with his brother. No more Jannie with the round face, Jannie with the big hands and feet. He stood remote from the person she had known all her life: Jannie with a catapult, Jannie making clay oxen down by the *spruit*, Jannie the wing in the College rugby team; Jannie at their first dance with the tuft of hair on the top of his head suitably flattened with a dab of Brylcreem; Jannie who had fished with her in the Bushmans River, ridden bikes, horses, donkeys— remote even from Jan who'd made love in the Rooikloof or in the loft or on the big bed in the house, secretly and with a grin. The man who stood there in front of the fire had been born on a damsite.

A bell rang loudly.

'Grub's up!' cried Cedric. 'Chin-chin!' he said, raising his glass. He winked at the buffalo head on the wall. 'Here's to you, you silly old bugger!'

The dining room was spartan, filled with heavy furniture, carved chairs with creaky leather seats. In the centre of the table stood a vase on a crocheted doily.

A leg of lamb surrounded by onions, spiced pumpkin and roast potatoes squatted before Cedric's place. The maid stood waiting, a forgotten greasy dish cloth slung across her shoulder. Adrian took charge of the wine, Cedric of the carving knife.

'Well,' said Cedric. 'Let's get on with it. Oh . . .' he stopped, put down his knife and fork. 'The grace! Of course! An old man on his own tends to overlook these things. Adrian,' he said, 'will you do the honours?'

Elizabeth giggled and whispered to Elsa in an undertone, 'The old heathen's never said grace in his life before.'

Cedric de Villiers sat with his hands folded, his big head bowed, while Adrian said a Latin prayer that no one had heard before. Elsa peeped at him. His round face was pink and pious in the candlelight.

'What do you think of our plan to build a retreat at Koen's farm?' said Elizabeth.

'It all sounds very nice, my girlie,' said Uncle Cedric.

'I thought of something Sardinian—nothing fancy, but

clean, elegant lines. Don't you think that would be perfect in the setting? White walls, flat roof, lots of exotic plants?'

'It's supposed to be a rustic retreat!' said Adrian. 'She says she won't go there if it's not Sardinian—I ask you!'

· 'Silly Aidie!' pouted Elizabeth. 'You have no sense of design and never will have!'

'When are you building this?' asked Elsa.

'We've got to wait for the sale to go through first,' said Adrian. 'It shouldn't take too long now.'

'Beggars can't be choosers, that's what I say,' said Cedric.

'Freek Koen is making a fuss and holding out for a better price,' interrupted Adrian. 'He won't get it. If he doesn't let us have it, he'll have to give it away in the end. The land's in shocking condition.'

'We'll wear him down soon enough, mark my words,' added Cedric.

'Who'll run it?' asked Elsa suspiciously.

'Jan will,' said Adrian. 'Once he's back from the dam.'

Jan put down his knife and fork and looked over at Adrian —changed his mind, took up his wine glass and drained it.

Elsa said, 'What about the Koens?'

'What about them?'

'Well, what'll they do? It doesn't seem right to use the drought to exploit people.'

'Elsa love,' said Adrian with a patient smile. 'What do you know about these things? We must take a chance when the market's down. It's tough I know, but I really can't be responsible for the Koens and their failures.'

'There's something greedy about making a deal out of someone else's bad luck.'

Adrian laughed. His voice was like butter. 'My love,' he said. 'That's life.'

'Imagine if it was us?' she cried. 'I don't know how you can do it! Jan will never go in with you. My father would have scorned using another man's misfortunes the way you have.'

'Your father,' said Cedric de Villiers, 'didn't have the reputation of being a shrewd farmer.'

Elsa banged down her wine glass. 'Uncle Cedric . . .'

'Hang on Els!' said Jan warningly.

'I will not be quiet!' retorted Elsa angrily. 'Why should I? Here they all sit discussing a holiday cottage and they don't give a damn about the Koens, or anyone for that matter. They just do as they please! Look at what Uncle Cedric did to Petrus!'

'That's got nothing to do with it,' said Cedric. 'You're speaking out of turn, my girlie.'

'Love,' said Adrian soothingly, 'you're very sweet but you're being sentimental.'

'For Christ's sake Adrian, don't tell me I'm being sentimental! I'm buggered if I'll keep on making excuses to everyone for you de Villiers! Don't talk to me about sentiment! You've got no scruples—neither you nor Uncle Cedric!'

For a moment no one spoke, no one moved. And then Adrian started to laugh. 'Elsa,' he said. 'You're really quite a little hellcat! There—say sorry to Uncle Cedric and let's forget it.'

'Why should I say sorry for anything? Besides all this business about Brakkloof, Uncle Cedric took it into his head to arrest Petrus without any evidence. It's he who should say sorry!'

'Elsa.' Adrian's voice held a warning.

'Elsa is right,' said Jan suddenly.

'You absolutely amaze me, *kleinboet*,' said Adrian. He picked up his wine glass, held it to the light and sniffed the contents, his long nostrils dilating.

Jan thrust his leg out under the narrow table. He jerked his foot up at the crossbar of Adrian's chair. 'Piss off Adrian!' he said.

With a crash Adrian fell backwards onto the floor.

'Aidie!' shrieked Elizabeth, flying from her seat.

Adrian struggled up, flapping fat hands at the wine splashed on his jacket. 'My God!' He shouldered Elizabeth out of the way. 'My God, Jan!'

Elsa laughed out loud.

'You bitch!' shouted Elizabeth, turning on her. 'It's your fault!'

'Get out Jan!' Cedric rose grimly.

Jan did not look at him. He guided Elsa from the room, strode down the passage to the bed where Nella was asleep and took her in his arms. He carried her out to the car, banging the front door behind him.

The night was bright with moonlight and with stars. The squat trees were thorn-white by the *spruit*. The lands of Black-heath stretched out towards the *bult*, the cobwebs of their fences and their gates dividing them. A reedbuck whistled in alarm somewhere in the *vlei* and on the lawn the *dikkops* ran crying.

'See the *dikkops* Elsa,' said Jan. 'There were always so many on Blackheath.'

She smiled. 'So many more than on Kleinfontein.'

He stopped the car before the old white house and put his arms around her. 'I'll come home *kleintjie*, don't worry.' He stroked her hair. 'I'll come home soon and bugger Adrian and everything else. It will be all right.'

They took Nella in, closed the door and climbed the stairs. They missed the fourth together and Jan grinned. 'Shall we steal sweets from the spare room cupboard?'

'No Jannie,' whispered Elsa. 'Let's make love in the big bed instead.'

They went to the Rooikloof the next day. They climbed below where the waterfall had been, away from the left bank where the child had died. There was no water in the *poort*. No pool. The rocks stood bare in the bed of the *spruit*. The sand was loose and dry and gave beneath their feet. The small body of a frog, dried and brittle as bark, lay in the lea of a rock. There was a place where some creature had dug for water in vain.

Nella, hot from the climb, stripped to her panties and ran, small and pale, up and down the watercourse.

'She needs friends,' said Jan, watching her. 'She'll make them when she starts school, I suppose.'

'She has a friend,' said Elsa. 'She plays with Tombizodwa all the time. It's just sad it's going to end one day in the kind of mess we're landed with.' She looked up at him.

'What's going to happen with you and Adrian?'

'Scratch my back Elsie and forget about Adrian. I don't care what happens to him right now.'

'Seriously Jan.'

He shrugged. Elsa sat silent. The big trees shook in the wind. Nella trailed back, asking for a drink.

'Do you think you'll be able to work with him after this?'

'All I know is that I'll run the farm the way I want to and to hell with Adrian and Uncle Cedric.'

'And Petrus?'

'We'll see what the surgeon says. He was born on Blackheath. He belongs here too. Nothing will change that.'

His voice was tired. Elsa sat beside him and he held her fingers in his, but he did not speak again.

The sun was low when Jan said, 'It's time to go. I still have to pack. Andrew and Kobie will be here soon.'

Elsa, looking pensive, went to dress Nella. Nella put her arms up and said, 'Why's Daddy always going away?'

'Little *boklam*.' She caressed Nella's small, crooked ear, that stuck out of the cropped hair. 'He'll be home again with the rain.'

'But it never rains!' protested Nella.

Jan, still sitting on the rock with the picnic things, watched them walk up the river bed towards him. Not since he'd been a new boy at school, stoical in grey flannels, blazer and basher, had he felt such a dissonance as he felt now, returning to the dam.

The last Sunday tea before the start of school—one more slice of cake (compulsory because it had been specially baked and kept, a gesture against the hollowness), always unenjoyed because of what it signified: another parting, another term.

Jan knew as he left for the dam that day, just as he had known when he'd been driven out as a boy, that he would accept the inevitable the nearer he got to his destination. As a schoolboy he'd looked forward, in a grudging kind of way, to seeing his friends again even though he'd left behind a roomful of birds eggs, comics, sweet papers stuffed down the side of the bed, a half-made wire car and Petrus. And so today he knew that once he'd driven out with Kobie and with Andrew and they'd crossed the railway line at Melkbos Siding, turned north to Cradock and passed beyond the familiar farms, the empty dams, the ridges that were known, he would look—no possibility of escape—for the strings of lights, the girders, the small, squat town.

And then again, when the days had gone by and the dust and the grime and the endless noise and aloneness had sucked him in, he would go (he would not fight it any more) to the flats above the café—second floor on the end—and find Yvonne.

In the winter evening, the light going down below the jagged wall, the parquet cold beneath his feet, he'd undress her bit by bit. In the half dark of her small airless room she'd wait for him. He'd put aside all thoughts, the remnants of his guilt.

Above the bed the picture of an urchin crying would hang at an angle, always unadjusted from the morning's dusting.

# ❧ 9 ❧

The salt bushes needed to be watered again. They were withered and Elsa was afraid they would not recover. Petrus could not drive the tractor with his injured arm. The other driver had gone to Adelaide with the truck. Dorothy Southey was visiting relations in Port Elizabeth for a few days and no one could be spared from Kleinfontein. Elsa had lain awake most of the night wondering what to do. And so, apprehensive but determined, she called Petrus to the shed and climbed up onto the tractor. Painstakingly he explained the procedure to her. Then, a little nervous, with Petrus looking on, she backed it out of the shed. Nella stood by on the orchard wall with Tombizodwa, watching—half-delighted, half-afraid.

Up and down the lands went Elsa, the tractor belching and wheezing, the gears stiff. Her legs ached from pressing down on the pedals. Behind her trailed the women with their tins of fertilizer, dipping the hose, spouting out water, a bucketful a plant. Up and down, up and down, Petrus standing by the gate, his pipe clenched between his teeth.

Cedric de Villiers, driving down the district road from Melvynside on his way to town, stopped at the gate between his farm and Blackheath. He saw Elsa up on the tractor and Petrus Ngubane standing by the fence.

Elsa was turning the tractor back along the furrow when she noticed Cedric's car. She stopped the engine. The women following her laid down the hose, watched with interest as the old man climbed through the fence and walked across.

'Good morning, Uncle Cedric,' said Elsa from high on her perch. 'What is it?' As she got down she could feel that her hands had begun to sweat. Her breath felt short.

'Elsa!' said Uncle Cedric peremptorily, 'you should not

be driving that tractor! It's dangerous when you don't know how, you mark my words!'

'I'm perfectly all right.'

'Where's the tractor boy?'

'I have no driver since you took Petrus to the police and they broke his arm. The other man has gone to Adelaide.'

'Now listen my girlie, I can't allow it! Also,' he glanced over his shoulder at Petrus standing some way off. 'What's that bastard doing out of jail, you tell me? My God, but things have come to a pretty pass here. I've a good mind to insist Jan leaves that bloody damsite.'

'I bailed Petrus out,' said Elsa.

'My girlie,' Uncle Cedric took her arm firmly and marched her down the furrow away from the workers. 'He's a stock thief and a lying bastard!'

'Uncle Cedric'—Elsa shook him off—'Petrus is going to court in a few days as you well know. Then we'll see who's a stock thief!'

'I told you to get rid of him. I spoke to Adrian.'

'I am very tired of Adrian phoning and telling me what to do,' interrupted Elsa. 'Jan left me in charge and I do not choose to fire Petrus. I am quite happy driving this tractor, thank you.'

Cedric looked at her keenly. 'Listen to me, my girlie. By tonight that boy must be off this property, do you hear? After that we'll talk. I'll even give you one of my drivers. But first I want that native out!'

Elsa laughed scornfully. 'No Uncle Cedric,' she said. 'You seem to think workers are commodities to be bartered.'

Cedric de Villiers removed his hat and slapped his thigh slowly and rhythmically. Almost, Elsa backed in fear. He was very angry. 'If I were your father I'd put you over my knee and spank you.'

'You're not my father, thank God!'

Cedric's mouth twisted. His tongue edged along his lower lip. 'You're very like your father, my dear, as I've remarked before. Stubborn as hell—but soft. Soft. It doesn't fit in this family.'

Elsa smiled, her composure sure. 'I'll do what I think best,

Uncle Cedric.' She clambered back into the seat of the tractor. 'After that, we'll see who's soft.' She started the engine with a small flourish.

Uncle Cedric turned on his heel, walked to his car and drove away. Elsa watched him, knowing that the battle lines were drawn. There was no going back.

Elsa sat on her iron horse breathing in the dust and the warm moist smell of the reservoir water splashing on the ground. No longer afraid of the big machine she sang as she drove—just to herself, glancing back every now and then at the women following.

She ached so much the next day she hobbled as she walked. But she was back in the lands, back on the tractor. The sky was wide above her head, the dry wind blew, the sun beat down on her upturned face. From her perch, moving along the rows of plants it seemed she could see all of Blackheath. The noise and the dust filled her ears, her eyes, her hair. Still she sang. They would not harness her again. Not Cedric. Not Adrian. Blackheath belonged to Jan. It belonged to her.

Petrus Ngubane was convicted in the Magistrate's Court. On Cedric de Villiers' evidence it seemed indisputable that he had either stolen the sheep himself or been an accomplice. The treks had disappeared before the police could arrest them. There was no trace of them in the district and Petrus Ngubane was evasive when he spoke about them. He could give no plausible reason for his presence at the shelter. Elsa, sitting in the court with its high windows, could do nothing to defend him. Even if she had been called as a witness, she could have made no rational explanation for her own part in the affair.

The case took only twenty-five minutes to decide. Petrus was instructed to pay a compensatory fine of R200 to Cedric de Villiers in default of which he would serve a sixty day jail sentence. Elsa did not have enough money in her bank account. She was not going to ask for credit. She had done that too often in the weeks before.

She said to Petrus before Constable Djantjes took him away, 'I will bring the money tomorrow. I will go to *Nkosana* at the dam. I'm sorry that you have to spend the night in prison but I will be as quick as I can.'

She hurried from the building to her car. Her hands slipped on the wheel as she drove. Sweat ran down her palms. She glanced at her watch. It was already ten.

When she got home she ran upstairs, dragged an overnight case from the cupboard in the spare room and packed it for Nella. She left instructions with Chrissie and drove away with Nella, taking the road to the de Jagers' farm.

'Elsie!' cried Annatjie in surprise when she saw her coming up the steps to the front door. 'It's nice to see you, man. You haven't popped in for ages.'

Nella tore off round the house to find Annatjie's daughter Cheryl, her small suitcase banging against her side as she ran.

'Come in,' said Annatjie. 'I was about to make coffee for my Mom and me. You're just in time.'

'Annatjie,' said Elsa, restraining her a moment. 'I have to go to the dam to speak to Jan. It's very important.' Annatjie searched her face warily. 'Will you look after Nella? I don't want to take her with me and my mother is in Port Elizabeth.'

'No, no of course,' said Annatjie. She took Elsa's arm and gave it a squeeze, misinterpreting the reason for the journey. 'You'll have a lot to talk about. Do you want to stay over, hey? I'll have Nella as long as you like.'

'I must be back by the morning.'

'Be with Jan, man.' Annatjie glanced into Elsa's face again. 'Are you sure you'll be all right by yourself? You know, if you like, my Mom could easily manage the kids and I could come with you.'

'I'm fine, Annatjie,' said Elsa. 'I didn't think I'd told you . . .'

'Well, you see,' Annatjie began hesitantly. She reached into the pocket of her skirt, searching for cigarettes.

'News travels fast in this place!' said Elsa. 'The case was only heard this morning. I thought I hadn't mentioned it to anyone.'

'The case?' Annatjie was mystified. 'The case?'

'Petrus's stock theft case. I have to pay the fine or he'll be in jail for weeks. I don't want to ask the Bank for any more credit. I can't phone Jan and I can't guarantee he'll ring tonight. I'll just have to go and get the money from him myself.'

Annatjie struck a match and thrust it at the end of her cigarette. She coughed and shook the match vigorously, turned and flicked it away into a flowerbed, not looking at Elsa, alarmed at how nearly she'd let Jan's secret slip. She said, 'You never told me anything about stock theft Elsie, but surely you aren't going all that way just to get some money! No man, wait till Jan phones and tell him to send it. Why don't you ask Adrian for a loan? What about that, hey?'

'Adrian's the last person I'd ask! Anyway, he wouldn't give me a cent for Petrus!' Elsa laughed out loud at the idea. 'I want to see Jan, Annatjie,' she said.

'No man, it's madness! Come in and have some coffee and we'll talk about it. I'll see how much I've got to spare.'

'That's really good of you Annatjie, but you know I can't accept. I must be off—there's no time for coffee now. It's already quarter to eleven. Please could you keep Nella for the night? I'll be back so late it would be better to fetch her in the morning, if that's OK?'

'Els, listen man, it's such a long way.'

'Please Annatjie,' said Elsa. 'I've made up my mind. I haven't seen Jan for weeks. I want to go. Nella,' she called.

Nella ran down the steps of the *stoep*, Annatjie's small daughter following. Elsa put out her arms for Nella, held her close and kissed the upturned cheek, the warm neck. Nella did not protest at being left behind. She wriggled to be free, excited at the prospect of a friend.

'Would you like me to take anything for Kobie?' asked Elsa.

'Go on, man,' said Annatjie. 'There's no time to think of things like that. If you see him give him a hug from me and tell him to behave.' She said it with forced brightness. 'Don't worry about Nella, hey? She'll be fine.'

As Elsa drove away, Annatjie hurried into the house. She

rang Joy Fraser and she said, 'Joy? Listen man, can you think of how I can get a message to Kobie or Andrew?'

'You know there's no way of phoning, Annatjie. Why?'

'Elsa's gone to the dam to see Jan and he isn't expecting her. I tried to stop her but she wouldn't listen. I don't want her to find out about that bladdy girl, Joy. I don't want her hurt. *Yirra!* I could kill Jan!'

Elsa drove through the rest of the morning and into the afternoon. She sang to fill the hours. The road was empty but for the odd farm vehicle—lorries, *bakkies*, the occasional tractor. The winter sun was warm through the windscreen but outside the wind was sharp, the *veld* grey and endless, stretching away to the flat-topped *koppies*, the ridges and the empty sky.

At Colesberg she stopped at a garage for petrol. She went into the cloakroom and brushed her hair. She had brought some make-up and her special bottle of birthday perfume in her bag. She wished she could have had a bath and changed into something fresh. Her jeans and jersey were crumpled and hot. Her hair felt limp.

Jan was in the site office when Elsa arrived. She had begged the foreman to allow her to go down to the small prefab. hut. She found her way across the ground, rutted where trucks and earth-moving machines had passed. The wind lifted dust in sheets, ruffled back the pewter-grey water of the dam. Near the wall a bulldozer drove up and down, its engine strident, the voices of workers drowned in its erratic cadences.

Jan was alone. He was standing with his back to the door. He was looking through some files. Elsa watched him a moment before she spoke: Jan in his overalls, preoccupied with the papers in his hand, his dark head bent.

'Jan.'

He turned abruptly. She knew by his face—just an instant —before he came to her, his arms held out in welcome, that he had been appalled to see her there.

'Elsie!' he cried. He searched her eyes—for anger, for hurt, for accusation: he did not know.

'Aren't you pleased to see me?' she said.

He brought her closer, held her head against him. 'Of course I'm pleased. It's just so unexpected. What is it *kleintjie*? Has something happened? Where's Nella?'

'Nella's fine. It's Petrus. He's been convicted. He's in jail and I need to pay the fine to get him out. I came because I didn't want to ask for any more overdraft. I didn't know what else to do.'

Jan ran his hand through his hair. He glanced down to hide his relief. 'You came all this way ...' he half-laughed, his voice cracked unexpectedly, 'for that? God Elsie!' He sat down in the chair behind his desk, stood again. 'I think I've got enough in the Building Society,' he said.

The site foreman gave Jan the rest of the afternoon off. He stared after Elsa as she accompanied Jan to the car. He lit a cigarette as he watched her take Jan's arm, draw close, turning often to look up at him.

As they drove away Jan said, 'You should have written. I'd have had the money transferred.'

'It would have taken too long and I couldn't leave Petrus in jail. Anyway, I wanted to see you.'

'I don't like you driving so far alone—never mind the cost of the petrol. It was a rather rash thing to do, Els.' He turned down the main street.

'You've just gone past the Building Society,' she said.

'I thought you might prefer to wait at the hotel and have some tea while I draw the money?'

'I want to be with you.'

'Aren't you tired? I think you ought to put your feet up.'

'I came to see *you*,' she said. 'What's wrong Jan?'

He did a sharp U-turn. 'All right,' he said. 'Come with me then.' He put his hand out in reassurance. 'Tell me about Petrus's case.'

She told him and while she spoke she watched him, so out of context in his overall and boots, driving down a street so unfamiliar to her, so clearly known to him.

The Building Society was empty but for two tellers behind the counter. Both looked up as Jan and Elsa entered. Jan wrote his withdrawal slip and Elsa stood beside him, her hand on his arm. She followed him to the first teller.

The girl was searching for something among her papers. She greeted them without glancing up. She took Jan's savings book and flipped through the pages. Her engagement ring winked and flashed as she fumbled in the till drawer and counted the money. She slid the notes across with long, tapered fingers. Jan reached out his hand for them. 'Thank you,' he said hoarsely.

'Pleasure,' the girl replied, almost a whisper. She glanced at Elsa, half-smiled and then she turned from the counter and hurried away to a cubicle with a frosted glass partition. Jan and Elsa left the building. The door swung behind them.

Yvonne, standing in the small partitioned office, heard the door bounce back on its hinges. She returned to her place, her head held high. She could not hide the burning flush on her neck.

She had seen his wife. So had the other girls. They too had watched as she had held his arm while he wrote out the slip for the money that she needed for their home. His wife had been beautiful. And refined and assured, beyond reach.

Yvonne lit a cigarette, disobeying the restriction on smoking at the counter. Everyone was quiet. She knew that they were watching her—in judgement or in sympathy, she did not care.

After work she went to the café and phoned Fanie. She needed to belong—to be the first, the most important.

'Hello *poppie*,' Fanie yelled down the erratic line. 'This is a surprise. What's up, hey?'

'Just wanted to say Hi,' she said, groping for familiarity.

'There's a bikers' rally next weekend,' he said. 'Are you coming?'

She shifted the phone to the other ear. 'Yes Fanie, OK.'

'All the crew from here will be going. Can you fix up Boet with Hettie perhaps?'

'Yes Fanie, OK.' She gazed out of the café window at the street beyond, leaned against the shelf where the small packets of *biltong* and peanuts were displayed on steel spikes, the box of bubblegum, fly-spotted apples, bruised with handling. She picked at one with her nail. A bikers' rally. The crew from Graaff-Reinet in their lumber jackets and their boots. Boet and Hettie. Fanie. She took a tissue from her sleeve and blew her nose.

'What's that?' said Fanie.

'Nothing. I just blew my nose.'

'You got a cold?'

'No.'

'Is something wrong?'

'No.'

'Hey, *poppie*, I miss you. It's not so long now.'

'Yes Fanie, not so long.'

'*Vasbyt*, see?'

'Yes Fanie, OK.'

The café owner stood behind the counter. He was eating a *samoosa*, moving the bites round and round his mouth, his half-shaved jaw champing up and down as he watched her.

She paid for the phone call and a new packet of cigarettes.

'Trouble with your boyfriends again, hey Yvonne?' he said. He wiped his chin with the back of his hand.

'No one gives me trouble,' said Yvonne. She took a cigarette from the pack and lit it. As she exhaled the smoke she could feel the tightness in her jaw. 'No one gives me trouble Mr de Freitas,' she said. 'Not Fanie. Not anyone.'

'What shall we do now?' said Elsa as she put the money Jan had drawn into her purse. 'Shall we go to your room? I want to see where you live.'

'It's so cold and impersonal,' he said.

'Come on Jan. Just let me see. I want to be able to visualize you. You seem strange here.' She touched his overall. 'Not like Jannie at all.'

'Don't be silly! Of course I'm the same—it's this bloody awful dump that's the problem.'

He did not want her to go to his room with its bare walls and its bed with the rough grey blankets and the chipped shaving mirror and cold linoleum floor.

No one would be about but soon the men would return from the site and tramp along outside the thin board walls, barge in to invite him to the pub or to play poker or a round of darts. He would not touch her here. This was not her place, his wife. But she insisted, so they drove down to the living quarters and they went inside.

He stood in the doorway of his room, leaning against the frame. 'Like school?'

She nodded. 'I wish I could stay with you.' She sat on the bed. 'I think it's rather romantic!'

'You must go before it's dark Elsa. I don't want you on that road late at night. Let's have tea at the hotel. It's the best I can offer in the way of entertainment.'

'Jan.' She came to him. 'Forget about tea. Close the curtains.'

He put his hands on her shoulders. 'No Elsa. It's a sordid, ugly place. It's not for you.' With relief he heard a truck, the voices of the other men.

She put her arms around his neck, looked into his face, at each small feature, to see if they were still the same, when he himself seemed so different and so far away.

'I want you to come home soon,' she said, keeping her eyes on his.

'I want to come home myself. More than you know.' He looked away then. 'It won't be long Els.'

They went to the hotel. The paper napkin used as a cloth to disguise the bar tray was wet where the milk had slopped from the stainless steel jug. The waitress brought a saucer of commercial biscuits: lemon creams and pink, papery wafers. They did not eat them.

'You should have something,' said Jan. 'It's a long drive. I'll order a sandwich.'

'I'm not hungry.'

The tea was tepid and bitter with tannin. It left a reddish stain on the sides of the thick white cups.

'I have to take Petrus to an orthopaedic surgeon in Grahamstown,' she said.

'When?'

'Friday.'

'All this travelling.'

'Do you think I should go and see Nick Chase—you know that lawyer? Hannah Weaver's brother-in-law?'

'No Els. Leave it till I get back.'

'It'll be too late then.'

'For what?'

'To get him compensation.'

'Who from?'

'The police.'

Jan drained his cup. 'Don't play the big, brave mouse Elsie. You can't start pushing the police around.'

She was about to argue. She wanted his support, but he sat detached and she knew that it was not the time to ask it.

He took up the teapot and said, 'Have some more.' She shook her head. 'Time to go, Els.' The shadows were long in the lea of the verandah. The cold drought wind of early evening had got up. 'Four hours driving. Will you manage?'

'Why not?' She stood and gathered up her jersey. She put it on, pulling it over her head. She could hear the crackle of static in her hair. It stuck to her cheeks and forehead like cobwebs. She brushed it away, noting all these things minutely, denying the desolation that she felt until she was alone.

Jan took her hand and walked with her to the car. He made last minute enquiries about the angoras, the cows, his horse, the pump.

She turned to him. 'Give my love to Kobie and to Andrew. Tell them I'm sorry I didn't see them and that Annatjie and Joy and the children are all fine. Goodbye Jannie,' she said. 'I'm glad I came and saw where you live.'

She knew as she said it that she lied, that the Jannie who belonged to her had somehow changed, had gone. She would not find him here. She knew she had invaded—quite unwittingly—a part of Jannie's life he did not wish to share. Not because he did not love her but because it could never be appropriate for her to be there.

He hugged her, kissed her hair.

'I love you Jannie,' she said. 'I miss you so much.'

'Don't get upset,' he said and he kissed her again. He opened the car door and touched her fingers resting on the edge of the window. 'Drive carefully. Love to my Nellie. Take care of yourselves.'

She turned into the road, glanced back. He waved and she drove on, out into the cold of the late afternoon. The little town, the stretch of water, the wall were gone and Jan, standing on the pavement, seemed far away.

She thought instead of Jannie—long ago—a daydream retrospective to fill the miles, rejecting the memory of the prefab. office and the spartan bedroom. She needed Blackheath where Jan's belongings, his fisherman's-knit jersey, his hunting knife, his old red toothbrush in the slot in the bathroom would somehow bring him closer. Inanimate, these things at least were real and unchanging.

She wished she hadn't gone to find him, to feel the dislocation and aloneness. She knew he was unhappy but he would not tell her why. She could not reach him—not there, not in a place where neither he nor she belonged.

It was ten to ten and half an hour from home when Elsa realized she had a puncture. She stopped, sat a moment peering at the farmland on her left. To the right Mpumalanga Mountain rose up, brooding over the twisting district road.

She got out of the car into the cold. The night was very quiet. Far away she could see the lights of a farmhouse obscured now and then by the shift of branches stirring in the wind. She guessed it was the Pringles and she knew it was too far to walk to them for help. She opened the boot of the car and took out the spare tyre and the tools.

Her fingers were clumsy and stiff as she fitted the jack. She jerked off the hubcap. It clattered on the road. Dust and grit were clogged around the bolts of the wheel. She struggled to loosen them with the spanner but it only rasped on their unyielding edges. She tried again, ended by flinging down the spanner and kicking the tyre petulantly.

She climbed into the car and banged the door. Her hands were so cold she could barely flex her fingers. She listened. There was no sound but the night wind strumming faintly in the fencing wires at the side of the track. And then, in her rear-view mirror, reflected briefly, she saw headlights far up on Mpumalanga Mountain. A car was driving across the hill, going carefully. It seemed to creep through culverts until at last it reached the even surface of the road. A big car, squat, dark. It seemed ominous to Elsa.

The car stopped. The driver got out. Momentarily, within the lighted cab, Elsa could see the head of another black man turned towards her. She reached out to lock the doors, withdrew her hand again, ashamed of appearing distrustful and afraid. She wound down the window a little way. 'Molo,' she said. Her voice was high and hoarse.

'Good evening!' He was a big man, heavy-featured, wearing an overcoat and cap. It was too dark to see him clearly.

'I've got a puncture,' said Elsa unnecessarily for he had already bent to look at the front wheel.

'I can fix it for you,' he said. 'Where are the tools?'

Cautiously Elsa unclenched her fingers and opened the door. She could feel the sweat sliding down her sides despite the chill of the wind. The big man picked up the spanner she had discarded in frustration. He came towards her with it in his hand. She stepped back—a moment before flight —but the man squatted down beside the wheel.

She heard soft footsteps behind her. She swung round. The other man approached, holding a torch. His face was round, heavy at the jaw, his eyes slanted and prominent.

'Good evening,' said Elsa in a whisper.

You can tell a native by his face, Uncle Cedric had always insisted. Watch out for slanted eyes. They're a dead giveaway for a criminal type.

The notion had always infuriated Elsa. Now, standing there, she could feel the panic rising. The man greeted her, gave a small, transforming smile. He crouched by his companion and held the torch steady so they could see.

Elsa stood a little apart, feeling suffocated. She pushed her hair back from her eyes every now and then, brushing it away, aware of every movement that the others made.

The deflated tyre lay on the ground. The big man trundled the spare wheel nearer. The man with the slanted eyes stood suddenly, moved towards her. Elsa tensed, almost cried out, but he was only turning impatiently from the wind.

Then Elsa heard the sound of an approaching vehicle. Alert, the pulse beating at her throat, she listened, straining to hear.

From behind, taking the slope from the drift she had crossed just before she noticed the puncture, a car was approaching. The twin beams of its headlights arched up into the sky, levelled as it breasted the slope. The big man turned his head, blinked in the glare.

It was a van. It stopped abruptly. Both doors slammed. Two men were silhouetted against the lights. They moved with the authority of those unused to personal caution. Elsa saw the flash of buttons. It was Sergeant Smit and a black corporal.

She started towards the policeman, put out her hand as if to draw him to her, checked herself, appalled at her relief.

'Trouble?' he said.

'A puncture.' She had to stop for fear of betraying an unsteady voice.

Smit took in the wheel, the two men bending over it. The big man put the spanner down—a discretionary gesture. 'Evening Sir,' he said quietly.

'OK. I'll see to this,' said Sergeant Smit, pulling a torch from his belt and switching it on. Casually he ran the light over the faces of the watchers.

The man with the slanted eyes brushed his hands delicately against each other and turned on his heel.

'Thank you,' said Elsa, walking after him. 'It was very good of you to help.' She sounded apologetic, despised herself for it. She said to the big man. 'Thank you for stopping. I'm very grateful.'

'There's no trouble,' he replied. He touched the peak of his cap and went back to his car. He started it up and drove away. The wide red rear lights receded, the bodywork rattled as it disappeared over the rise.

Elsa went back to Sergeant Smit. The Corporal, careful of his uniform, laid his cap aside and stooped to bolt the wheel. Sergeant Smit held the torch. He did not assist.

'Didn't expect to find you here,' he said conversationally. 'What you doing out alone at this time of night, Mrs de Villiers?'

'I was going home.'

'This isn't your farm road.'

164

'No.'

'Your husband usually let you drive around in the dark?'

'No.' Elsa shivered, feeling the bite of the wind as her fear subsided.

'Dangerous you know. There could have been trouble.'

'Yes.'

Smit turned to the corporal, 'Move it hey!' he said. 'I'm getting bloody cold here!' He gestured with his head to Elsa. 'Come sit in the van.'

'I'm fine thanks,' said Elsa a little stiffly, remembering the reason for her journey, her handbag on the front seat with the money to pay Petrus's fine tucked into the pocket. 'Well,' she said, flustered and not wishing to appear ungrateful. 'What are you doing out yourself?'

'Superman you know'—he made a movement with his arms—'I'm everywhere!' He laughed. 'Want a smoke?'

She shook her head. He took a cigarette from a packet in his pocket, struck a match and bent his head to it: a practised mannerism, he had the stance just right. 'Trouble up on Mpumalanga,' he said. 'Another store got broken into. Didn't find anything. It's not easy to catch those bastards. They pilfer a few things and disappear. Nothing to go on. So,' he said, 'you were glad to see me, hey?'

'Those men would have sorted it out, I suppose,' she said. 'But you've been very helpful,' she added, knowing how priggish she sounded.

'Ja, sure,' said Smit. 'The guy who stopped was Nxumalo. He's an *induna* up at Gcashe. He's OK. But still, *you* didn't know that, did you?'

'No.'

'So I thought.'

'What do you mean?'

'Excuse the language but I never saw anyone so shit-scared in my life.'

'I was not.'

He looked at her, took his cigarette from his mouth, pinching it between forefinger and thumb. They both knew she lied.

★

The hospital in Grahamstown was set back on the hill. Petrus waited in the outpatients with his letter from the doctor. Chrissie, in her black shawl, sat beside him. She stared about, her hands twisted in her lap. Leaving them, Elsa drove down to the supermarket in the high street. At the shop's entrance black children hung about begging for cents. Beyond the town, visible above the rooves, Makanna's Kop rose up, crowned with its sentinel plantation of old stone pines. Pigeons turned across the sky, came in as one to rest along the spine of the great cathedral's roof.

Elsa was packing her groceries into the boot of her car when she saw Adrian. He was walking up the street with a colleague. The black children, huddled in a scrap of sunlight on the pavement, moved away imperceptibly. Authoritative, Adrian gave no leeway.

He noticed Elsa and stopped. 'This is a surprise,' he said. The colleague hurried on towards Advocates Chambers and Adrian stepped down beside Elsa's car. 'Liz didn't tell me you were coming. Did you speak to her? Mind you, she's been so busy with some garden club do, I expect she forgot. Why're you here?'

'I brought Petrus to see an orthopaedic surgeon.' Elsa could feel her face grow hot. She tucked her hair behind her ear and tugged at the ends.

'Petrus? Wait a minute Elsa, what's he doing out of jail?'

'I bailed him out.'

'I told you to fire him.'

'I know.'

'Well?'

'I didn't. Nor will I.'

'Listen my dear'—she had heard it all before—'I'm the major shareholder on Blackheath and you will do as you're told.'

'No.'

'I don't want another family row over this boy, do you see?'

'Of course Adrian.'

'Then just do as I tell you Elsa.' He almost patted her cheek then, thinking her compliant. 'You can easily find a replacement. It won't be difficult.' Magnanimous Adrian, taking control again.

'Sorry Adrian,' she said, opening the car door and putting it between herself and him. 'I've no intention of doing what you want.'

She slid into the seat and started the engine.

'Elsa . . .'

But she had backed the car. She drove away, leaving him standing in the road. A pair of ragged children had been hovering around her parking meter. They ventured to ask him for five cents but he swept them aside impatiently and strode up the street.

Elsa passed the Museum and cast a nostalgic glance at the white façade. Then she turned up beside the University, parked the car and went in through the big gates of the Botanic Gardens. She walked down the path past the Old Provost, dreaming under its gumtree. There was a small tea room in the gardens where she had often gone with her parents on outings from school. Discreet ladies, wives of the dean, a professor, the archdeacon perhaps, served tea and scones for charity. Their talk was low and gentle over the chink of crockery. An elderly couple sat by the window. A pair of young mothers attempted a cup of coffee and a conversation against the demands of two strident toddlers. They gave up, leaving the checked tablecloth strewn with mauled crumbs and spilt milk. Still, Elsa envied them their companionship as she sat alone on the bricked paving under the trellis, a pot of tea before her, dissatisfied, angry with Adrian and wondering what to do.

From the quiet of the Botanic Gardens with its gravel pathways and its ancient trees, the sounds of the town were far away, a murmuring in another place. Elsa closed her eyes. She was tired. She felt alone. The two young mothers were strolling back across the lawns, their babies going before, arms held out, legs set in the perilous momentum of children who have just learned to walk.

Elsa glanced at her watch. She had forty minutes before she had to meet Chrissie and Petrus. She finished her tea, bought a selection of one cent sweets from the glass jars on the counter to take home for Nella and hurried back to the car. She would go and see Nick Chase after all. There was nothing to be lost in speaking to him and no one else to ask for help. She did not consider what Jan might say. It did not concern him any more.

Nick Chase's rooms were in Advocates Chambers. They were functional and unpretentious. There were people waiting to see the Legal Aid attorneys. Most were black. They talked among themselves, voices subdued. The receptionist was speaking on the telephone. Elsa stood by her desk and looked about. She knew that Adrian's office with its familiar designer lamp, its glass and chrome furnishings and polished pot plants was on the floor above.

She imagined she could hear him walking softly up and down above her head on the thick fawn carpet, knowing she was there, listening, waiting to discredit her. She started each time there was a footfall on the stairs outside. She was relieved when the receptionist turned to her with a smile.

Nick Chase was out. He was in Court. He would not be back in Chambers until the morning. Elsa went away disappointed. She stood undecided in the street, then she crossed to the hotel and found a public telephone. She looked up Nick Chase's home address in the directory, noted it and drove back to the hospital.

Petrus and Chrissie were waiting for her, sitting aside from the patient queue. A date for a corrective operation had been set. Petrus showed the notice to Elsa then tucked it in his breast pocket and followed her outside.

'Would you like to shop?' Elsa asked. 'I will take you to town and I will meet you again at three o'clock by the big church.'

She left them where the winter sun was bright and the shadow of the cathedral spire did not reach. She went back up High Street towards the Drostdy Arch. Nick Chase, she had decided, would go home for lunch as the people of Grahamstown usually did. She turned into a quiet road, shaded by pines. A neighbourhood dog lifted itself lazily from the warm tarmac and waddled onto the verge. She passed Adrian's big house. The front door stood open. A tricycle lay on the steps. Elizabeth's grey Mercedes was parked in the garage.

It was strange to pass by the house with its formal garden and leaded panes where she had stayed so often. Somewhere inside were Elizabeth and the pretty children. Soon Adrian would be back and they would sit in the dining room while the maid brought the meal in Spode serving dishes. Her uniform would be white—it always was—and her *doek* intricately tied. Elizabeth insisted on standards.

Nick Chase lived in a pink-painted settler bungalow at the end of Harrismith Street. It had a long verandah and deep sash windows. Pushing the idea of her presumption aside, Elsa tapped at the brass knocker.

Helen Chase opened the door. 'Hello,' she said as though it were the most natural thing to see Elsa standing there. She had a face full of lightness. Her brown eyes crinkled when she smiled. Her hair was thick and humbug-coloured, bundled up on her head. Small bits trailed haphazardly at her neck and temples. She wore jeans and a red jersey. She was barefoot. She had kicked her shoes aside in the passage.

'Mrs Chase?' Elsa said. 'I'm so sorry to worry you. My name's Elsa de Villiers and I'm a friend of Hannah Weaver. We farm nearby—just over the hill, in fact. I wondered if I could see your husband? I'd like to speak to him about a farm worker who was assaulted. I know I shouldn't come barging in but I'm only in Grahamstown for the day and it's rather important.'

Helen Chase was used to supplicants. They found her all the time. 'Come in,' she said. 'By the way, are you any relation of Adrian and Liz de Villiers?'

'Adrian's my brother-in-law. Are they friends of yours?' Elsa's voice was wary.

'We know them,' said Helen Chase, offering nothing more. 'I was just about to make a cup of coffee—would you like some? Nick's not in at the moment but he'll be back for lunch. You know, there's something familiar about your face. Weren't you at school here?'

'I came to board in standard six.'

'What was your maiden name?'

'Southey.'

'That's right! You have a sister, Carol—quite a bit older than you I suppose? You're very alike.'

'Yes.'

'I remember Carol well. She was a year or two below me at school. Small world, isn't it? Is Carol still so pretty?'

'She is. She hasn't changed at all. She lives in Cape Town now. She's got two boys.'

'She was wild at school. Nick will remember her. I think he rather fancied her.'

'She was nearly expelled a couple of times. I could never live up to her reputation!'

Helen Chase led the way to the kitchen and switched off the kettle. She set out a tray and took it to the living room.

'Have you seen Hannah lately?' she asked. 'We haven't been up to the farm for ages, but things are a bit difficult for Hannah at the moment.'

'Yes,' said Elsa, 'I know. In fact, it was because of Hannah that I knew about your husband and the work he does. It was a chance remark at a party. I wouldn't have known what to do otherwise.'

'What's the problem? Would you like to tell me or would you rather leave it for Nick?' Helen drew aside the heavy green curtains and settled into the chintz sofa, her feet curled up under her.

Elsa had just begun her story when the front door was flung open and two boys came in. They wore their grey school jerseys, flannels and heavy black lace-ups. They both had straight-cut hair, rough small-boy hands. The uniform, the school bags stuffed with things, reminded Elsa of Jan when he'd first been sent to Grahamstown, to the same school as Helen's sons with its old stone buildings and its clock tower. Again she felt the familiar pang of regret that there was no other child—no son with an exclamation mark of hair, with grubby knees and big, new, white scalloped teeth and Jan's green eyes.

'You must stay for lunch Elsa,' said Helen Chase when Elsa had greeted the boys.

'No really, I don't want to disturb you. I'd just like to

ask if Petrus has a claim worth following up.'

'Don't be silly!' said Helen. 'You can't possibly leave before lunch.' She said it so simply, so naturally, Elsa could not refuse or even feel she had intruded. She wanted to curl into the chair, the way Helen had, as a gesture of friendship, and in relief that she had dared to come.

Nick Chase arrived just after one. He greeted Elsa warmly, as unperturbed by her sudden appearance as Helen had been. Their daughters in their green uniforms, blazers and boaters, followed, bringing a cold gusty wind with them. Three or four conversations began around the room at once.

'Ma, you'll never guess what Drak did in maths today!'

'Dad can we get a fishing rod? Clapham asked me to Bushman's for the weekend.'

'Who's Clapham?'

'Arse Clapham.'

'Ssshhh Stuart! His name's Tom.'

Everyone laughed.

'Helen, where's lunch? I have to be in court at half past two.'

'The man from Fingo Village brought back those forms this morning. They're on the hall table. Don't forget them.'

'About the school dance—Ma are you listening—the theme is Alley Cats. Can you draw a huge dustbin for me? I brought home some newsprint.'

They assembled in the dining room, the pale winter sun coming through the windows. Nick Chase sat at the head of the table, a big man in his grey suit. He ran his hand through his hair every now and then, pushing it aside. Elsa thought he had a wonderfully humorous face. He had a gap between his front teeth and he laughed often, bantering with the girls, listening with every appearance of enjoyment to his sons' schoolboy jokes.

It was a home where the children talked and the parents listened and talked back, where Karen's school dance was as important as the case Nick was taking on appeal, where Stuart's fall-out with Rooster Dodds was considered from every angle as were Lesley's speculations regarding who her

171

friend Natasha fancied now, where Campbell's discovery of parhassis caterpillars in the garden was as exciting as Helen's B-plus for her sociology assignment.

At ten to two the children flew out of the house like sprews migrating. The boys went off to sports in T-shirts and shorts, oblivious of the cold. The girls wound their long scarves round their necks and hurried away separately.

'Right,' said Nick Chase to Elsa, 'now that the rabble have gone, come and tell me all about this farm worker you're so concerned with.'

'Off you go,' said Helen. 'I'll bring you both some coffee. No, don't worry about clearing away Elsa. I've got lots of time. You talk to Nick.'

It was easy to explain about Petrus to someone like Nick Chase. He sat back in the huge chair by the fireplace, elbows resting on the arms, his hands arched finger to finger at his chin listening as Elsa talked.

She began with the treks, the woman, the child, the dog, Uncle Cedric, the police, Adrian. She ended with the letter from the orthopaedic surgeon that Petrus had shown her at the hospital.

'You know what it means making a claim against the police for assault?'

'Not really. But I'm prepared to give it a try.'

'It won't be easy.'

'Do you think I should leave it?'

'No. It's very interesting.' He smiled. 'Will you stand as a witness?'

'Of course.'

Helen brought two mugs and set them on a low table.

'There's one thing that's strange,' said Nick Chase, taking up his cup and stirring it. 'Why do you think Petrus Ngubane went back to speak to those treks. Why do you think they were suddenly so important?'

'I really can't say. Maybe he felt the same way about them as I did . . .'

'That's just speculation.'

'It's twenty past two Nick,' Helen interrupted. 'You'd better drink up and go.'

'I'll have to speak to Petrus Ngubane,' said Nick Chase.
'When's he coming back for the operation?'
'About ten days.'
'Bring him to see me then.' He stood, explored his pockets
for his keys. 'Where are the keys, Helen?'
'I don't know. You're always losing them.'
A search began around the room and hall. At last Helen
discovered them in the bathroom.
'This is the third time you've left them on the loo this week,
Nick,' she said.
'A great exaggeration!' Nick patted her bottom affectiona-
tely.
Helen and Elsa watched him drive off in his old grey Volks-
wagen. He scraped the sump on a hummock in the driveway.
'Hopeless!' said Helen. 'He's always doing that. The car's
going to die on him one day!'
'I'd better go too,' said Elsa. 'You've been wonderful. I
really had to talk myself into coming here but I'm so glad
I did. You've both been so welcoming.'
'Don't run away yet,' said Helen. 'I've hardly had a chance
to talk to you. Let's have another cup of coffee. You haven't
told me anything about you or your family yet.'
Helen led her back to the living room, sensing a need in
Elsa, guessing what it might have taken someone as reserved
and self-reliant as she appeared to be to come knocking on
a stranger's door. There was both defiance and vulnerability
in Elsa, a determination and a reticence.

Elsa drove out of Grahamstown in the late afternoon, Petrus
and Chrissie settled among their parcels, talking quietly
between themselves. She felt a strange lightness, an exhila-
ration. In Helen Chase's living room she had laughed and
talked and listened as she had not done for many months.
She no longer cared what Cedric or what Adrian might say.
She would not allow them to intimidate her. She had sought
the Chases out to still a restless conscience. She had been
afraid, unsure of how they might receive her but Helen and
Nick Chase had liked her, had affirmed her. They did not
question the validity of Petrus Ngubane's claim: they took

all that for granted. She had done what was right. For the first time she felt confident that it was so.

The twilight came on fast. They crossed the Great Fish River at Carlisle Bridge where an old farmhouse stood close to the road and *garingbome* grew in the open places. The river was almost empty, the dusk was thick and dusty, the sky a dull copper up above the hills.

The first stars were out when they reached the district road to Melkbos. It wound between the *koppies* and crossed at a causeway where no water flowed. Elsa drove slowly for the track veered sharply at the drift. There was a small grave half-hidden in the bush. Elsa had always meant to stop and see who it commemorated. They passed the store with the flat rocks before it, the church and the abandoned house built more than a century before. A track led to Melkbos Siding where some empty cattle trucks stood on the star-streaked rails.

The cattle grid rattled beneath the wheels as Elsa turned in at the entrance to Blackheath. Glancing in the rear-view mirror she could see that both Chrissie and Petrus were asleep. She did not wake them when she reached the next gate. She opened it herself, drove through, closed it again, hitching the ring across the wire hook.

She dropped Petrus and Chrissie at the path to the workers' houses. They got out in the cold, their breaths coming in small, frosty puffs. Sleepily Chrissie hoisted a parcel to her head. Soft greetings, thanks, a day well spent, they went off into the dark, trudging between the sweet-thorns.

Elsa turned the car to travel back the way she had come, to Nella and her mother waiting with a hot supper by the fire on Kleinfontein.

A hare squatted in the road at the crossing. Blinded by the headlights it gazed back at her and she smiled. It moved its huge ears, sensitive to each sound the night might bring. It jinked away into the bush, small and solitary.

She reached the gate again and stopped to open it. She stood in the cold and breathed in the air, looking up at the parade of stars.

She went to the gate to unlatch it, but it was open. She

174

glanced around, startled. Five minutes before she had closed it herself, securing the hook across the pin.

The gate, it always seemed to be the gate. The first time with the sheep and now again, unaccountably, it hung loose where someone must have passed—someone furtive and yet defiant, who had left it deliberately to swing.

Frightened, Elsa hurried to the car, drove through and then dragged the gate shut. She left the car to idle as she fumbled with the loop and chain. Her sweating fingers slipped on the cold metal. She peered into the bush hunched at either side of the track. But it was very dark and she could see nothing. Her arms were weak and it felt as though her blood had retreated, like a snail drawing into its shell, leaving her limp.

She hurried back to the car, slammed and locked the door. She went on alone, glancing from side to side at the places where the headlights caught the trees and brush. But there was nothing—only the darkness and the stillness of the winter night.

# ❧ 10 ❧

Late August and the sky had changed. The air was dense. Cold. A day went by. A night. At the pre-dawn the wind got up. Nella had climbed into Elsa's bed, frightened by a dream. Curled in the warmth, she did not stir. Elsa woke in a stillness heavier than any she had ever known. There was no light. No moon. No stars.

But then there was a sound born out somewhere on the hills and she lay, touching the smooth cold ruffle of the eiderdown and listened, feeling like a subterranean small creature with a world of tumult rising, far beyond comprehension, in the unknown light above.

She could hear it coming, like a train on course, from the highest uplands of the Winterberge—down, down—passing Brakkloof where the thorn tree stood divided by the shearing shed, down the deepest valley on the northern boundary, down Rooikloof. The old house creaked, bracing itself for the moment when the wind would strike.

It broke over Blackheath, twisted the rafters of the outbuildings, unlocked bolts long-soldered in the iron of rooves, scattered them, leaving gable stones exposed and gaping at the sky. Glass broke. Elsa sat up in bed in the thick vibrating dark. Nella stirred, put out her fingers to feel for Elsa's nightie and slept again. A strange turbulence seemed to shake the house, breached by the storm and open to the night.

Somewhere among the flocks brought in to the home camps on the day before there would be goats, frozen-flanked, that would die. She heard the tear of metal as the shed roof lifted and fell.

She knew the sheepdogs would be sheltering in the shed so she got out of bed, pulled on a jersey and shoes and went onto the landing. The rooms were breathless, the frenzy was outside. She hurried downstairs to the kitchen, found a torch and unlocked the back door. The wind surged at her. She shouted for the dogs but they could not hear her where they huddled beneath the tractor, bricks falling about them.

Elsa struggled across the yard as though through surf—it seemed as if there was no air to breathe. She screamed the names of the dogs. At last they detached themselves from their hiding places and, bellies close to the ground, they ran to her.

Elsa thrust open the back door. It slammed behind her. She leant against it in the numbing cold, fumbling with the bolt. Jan's old sheepdog nudged at her hand with its nose, seeking reassurance. She talked to it as Jan might have done, in the special way he kept for animals, for small children, for herself even—a little teasing, a little gruff, but always gentle—and the dog, responding, leaned against her leg, its muzzle resting in her palm.

Suddenly the wind died, arrested. The stillness was absolute. Elsa stood, poised. In the blackness she waited, the dogs at her feet. At last it came, streaming from the sky, thundering—the hooves of the rain trampling the earth. On and on and on. Slowly Elsa climbed the stairs with a frightened triumph.

And Jan—far away in the artificial light of the site houses, listened. The wind found no resistance in the pre-fabricated boards of the bungalows. With the old instinct of a farmer he heard the shift of wind, the striking rain. His pillow was cold from the air that crept up the walls from the jointed foundations and the concrete floor.

The time had come to go, to barter the orange helmet, the overall, the desk full of files for a wage packet and a discharge card. To leave. He lay rigid in the bed, a stickman in abeyance, with the frail house shuddering around him. He listened without triumph—for the rain had come, but there was so much unresolved.

And so it rained. For days it rained. Goats died, a horse slipped in a gulley and broke its leg. With shaking hands Elsa went out alone and shot it.

Trees unleashed their rooting. The river plundered them, rising to a torrent, dragging them beneath the water, casting them aside against the falling banks, chaining tree to tree, branch to branch, root to root. Saplings drowned, last year's nests. A meerkat had been washed into a mesh of branches: a grotesque dying.

The rain obliterated the thorny wastes of grey along the *bult*. There was no sound beyond the wildness of the sky — except the clock in the living room, the heartbeat of the house, a slow measured gonging.

The damsite was a wilderness of water. The earth that had been built up into banks by great machines dissolved in sticky quagmires of red and ochre ooze, trapping the bulldozers, steamrollers and trucks that had made them. The stretch of water damming up rose steadily. The engineers were down there, watching the levels, worrying.

Jan sat in his site office. The walls seemed to twist and shift with the movement of the wind. Like a sailor in a frail boat he felt he might slide away in the muddy sea.

Jaco Oosthuizen, the foreman, came to the door. Raindrops splashed from the rim of his safety helmet. 'Help us out de Villiers,' he said. 'We're trying to move a machine at the edge of the wall. We need some more boys to haul it off. Do us a favour and go to the compound and bring someone up to give a hand. It's mucky as hell where we are and I can't get the truck out.'

'Fine,' said Jan, reaching for his keys. 'How many chaps do you want?'

'Five or six. Thanks hey.'

Jan drove down the slippery track towards the compound. When he returned with the workers in the back he parked as close to the site as he could without sinking his wheels into the mud. His overalls were sodden and gritty against his skin. He went over to where the foreman and his gang waited in the lee of their stranded vehicle. Among them was Freek Koen. His helmet was pulled low over his eyes, his boots were thick with clods. Somehow, within the wind and rain, he had managed to keep his cigarette alight, a small,

178

damp glow cupped in his hand. He glanced at Jan, then stared off across the site.

'Right,' said Jaco Oosthuizen. 'Let's get on with it.'

The workers lashed the machine to a cable. A strange, dark pantomime of figures, they worked in the mist. In unison their voices rose, fell, ended as the metal would not budge, swelled again as they strained to move it.

Jan stood with Freek Koen. 'The rain has come at last, Freek,' he said.

'Ja, so I see,' said Freek. 'Bugger all good to me now the farm's sold.' He peered up at the sky, the rain tilting at his face. 'If it had come a month ago I'd have made my father throw the offer back', he moved his hand, a gesture of dismissal and contempt, 'and told your brother and your uncle to get stuffed.'

Jan looked down at his boots, shook his head. 'I'm sorry Freek. I don't want Brakkloof. I never did. I tried my best to stop them but they didn't care.'

'Only Koens have ever farmed that land. You guys will never make it work for you. I'm telling you, it won't belong. You'll leave it and it'll be just bush again like when Willem Koen first went there.'

'What will you do now, Freek?'

'That's my business.' He turned on his heel and went to the workers. He helped readjust the lashing of the cable and then he put his shoulder to the machine and pushed with the others. The chant was lost in the shrieking of the wind. It broke against the face of the wall like a wave breaking on rock. Jan joined the men, straining with them, head down. Boots holding, then slipping, they inched the machine away.

The lashing snapped. With a fierce tear it broke. The workers ducked as the cable whipped above them—lethal, black, it coiled out. The machine lurched as the cable struck across the ground. It caught Freek Koen. He stumbled and fell. He rose to his feet, arms outstretched towards the men crouching on the ground. The wind gusted suddenly. Jan, transfixed, saw Freek Koen fall again. He slid slowly backwards over the edge of the wall. His fingers clawed for the scaffolding, held it briefly—a small man suspended in space, weighted by the concrete bigness of his boots.

The wind loosed him. He dropped spreadeagled. Jan ran towards the edge, slithered on hands and knees, dashing rain from his eyes. There was nothing to see. Freek Koen had disappeared into the muddy torrent a hundred feet below.

All day they searched the river, the wall looming above them, black and evil in the rain. Jan trudged the bank. In places where the earth gave way the wind threatened to loose him too and send him hurtling to the rocks below.

It was already evening when they found Freek Koen. The rain was driving in again as they carried his body up on a stretcher. It was lifted into a waiting van by two attendants. A blanket was pulled across his face. Jan turned away and walked on alone, numb and shaking, oblivious of anything but the great hollow roaring of the wind.

Each feat of engineering, each bridge, tunnel, railway and dam had claimed its victims—sacrifices to the spirits of the mountain or the river or the sea. And so it was with Freek —a small figure, frozen an instant to the straight strong girder, falling, falling, into the chasm of the gorge. Jan walked on, unheeding of the wind and rain in his anger and despair.

He went to Yvonne, sodden still. He climbed the stairs, his boots leaving eddies of mud in the clear polished puddles in the passage.

She took his helmet. She took his boots. She ran a bath for him and hung his overall by the heater. Flung across a chair it steamed, the patches of mud baking dry. She made him coffee. He would not eat. She sat on the bathmat beside him but he did not speak.

At last he said, 'I've cocked it all up, Yvonne.'

She touched his hair—a small tenderness—then withdrew.

He said again, 'I've cocked it up for Elsa. Freek Koen. You.'

'At least I knew what I was doing.'

'Do we ever know what we are doing in these circumstances?'

She did not reply.

He took her hand and looked down at her ring. 'You were Fanie's.'

'I still am, I suppose.' She bit her lip to hold her tears. She smiled at him but her chin trembled. 'I knew I'd never have you.'

'Did you want me?'

'It doesn't matter if I did or not. I'm getting married at Christmas when Fanie qualifies. I'm glad!' The mascara blurred on her lashes. 'I did something wrong against Fanie and your wife. I must pay for it.' She hesitated. 'I do pay for it. Fanie's a good guy.' She could not go on.

He kissed her wrist gently. 'God I've been such a shit, Yvonne. It wasn't your fault. It was mine. And Yvonne...'

'I must see if your things are dry,' she interrupted him, her voice choked. She went through to the living room. She gripped the chair where his clothes lay, clenched her fingers on its edge, fighting for control. She knelt by the overall, turned it, laid her head against it, unable to hold out any longer. Jan found her there. He put his arms around her. She clung to him and wept—slow, shuddering sobs.

Still the wind moaned up and down the corridor of the dingy block of flats. Jan took her to the bedroom, turned out the light and held her, soothing her in the shaking dark.

She did not play with him with the trite, brittle banter they had used. She did not restrain herself, keeping him away. She went to him, crying still, knowing there would be no knowledge of each other, no word, no tenderness again, that from the moment that he left the bed, walked from the room, there would be nothing more. It would all be gone, as if it had never happened, the feelings of this night would die, or perhaps be left—a shadow of guilt at another time—to be regretted.

She said as she lay beside him, 'I never knew anyone like you in my life. I know I never will again. I loved you so much.'

He turned to her, struggling to say what he wanted her to hear and understand but she put out her hand to stop him. 'Leave it Jan. It has been enough. It doesn't matter.' She touched his face and said, 'Please go now.'

Jan dressed slowly in the damp overall and muddy boots. He took his helmet. She was sitting at the edge of the bed, very still. He put his hand on her shoulder. She covered it with hers.

He went then, out into the night. The wind had died and a sodden mist had drifted down across the town, the lights of the café were diffuse and distant. He walked out, shoulders hunched, hands thrust deep in his pockets. Alone, the mist closing in around him, Jan could also cry.

## ❧ II ❧

---

The rains had been good. There was snow on the Winterberge in the last week of August. All the stock was near the homestead. The camps were left to *rooikat* and to jackal. There was no need for vigilance. There was nothing to plunder.

Fires had been lit in the grates. There were meals to cook and jams to bottle. Chrissie had made three cakes in as many days. Jan had returned and Elsa, exhilarated at his homecoming, had been eager to show him all she'd done and to go with him round the farm. He had been resistant, preferring his old routine and wanting to reconstruct life as it had been before he went to the dam. He couldn't. So much had changed.

Elsa missed the farm. She missed driving up to the top camps to inspect the fences. She missed the dairy, the workshop, the shearing shed. She could go there still—but they were Jan's domain again. She was no longer free to move implements or send the workers out to do what she or Petrus had decided. Jan wanted it the way it had been. Without consciously wishing to offend her, he rearranged the workshop. Haphazard, it returned to its old disorder. Elsa said nothing. It was no longer her place. Petrus was polite, friendly even, but his allegiance had shifted. She could no longer stop and discuss things the way she had.

She got out her sewing machine and made Nella a dress. She went to have tea with Annatjie and Petra, she knitted Joy's baby a jumpsuit, played tennis on Tuesday mornings. She worked in the front garden, replanting beds that had died in the drought. Somehow the shadow of the palm tree chilled her and she dug the cold ground with chapped, fumbling fingers.

Only Nella was unequivocally happy. Elsa felt a pang when

she saw Tombizodwa, abandoned by Nella, sitting disconsolately in the small house where they had played through the long, dry winter. Nella rode jubilantly in the jeep with Jan, followed him round the yard, watched him at any task within her reach, returned to speaking English.

Elsa gave Tombizodwa a handful of sweets and told her to go home. Unable to change things or explain, she sent her away. She watched her walk obediently along the road, the dust puffing up around her feet. Elsa felt as alone, as excluded as Tombizodwa.

One night Adrian phoned. Elsa answered the call.

'Elsa?'

'Yes? Hello Adrian,' she replied cautiously.

'Is Jan there?' His voice was peremptory and cold.

'I'll call him.'

Jan was in the living room reading a farming journal while he drank his coffee. 'Jan,' said Elsa.

'Ja?'

'Adrian wants to speak to you.'

He got up abruptly and went through to the hall. 'How's it going Adrian?' she heard him say.

'What?' exclaimed Jan. He looked over at her in surprise and—she could see it — with some aggression. 'Don't know anything about it. Talk to her. What?' He listened for a moment. 'Bugger off Adrian! Don't start lecturing me,' he said.

He handed the receiver to Elsa without looking at her.

'Yes Adrian?' Her voice trembled. She knew why he had phoned.

'Have you gone off your head Elsa?' said Adrian.

'I don't believe I have—why?'

'Captain Olivier just rang and said he'd got a letter from Nick Chase's outfit demanding he pay damages for that fellow who worked for us, Petrus whatever his name is.'

'So?'

'How dare you go to a lawyer and bring a charge against the police without consulting me.'

'Why should I consult you? I didn't charge you with anything.'

184

'It's my farm too. My employee.'

'You don't run this farm Adrian. I sent you a statement last month. You still get your profits.' She stood very straight.

'The whole thing is totally ridiculous. You can't sue the police!'

'Why not?'

'Because it's an insane thing to do! Haven't you got any sense of family loyalty?'

'What's it got to do with family loyalty?'

'Captain Olivier did me a big favour once Elsa—a very big favour. I could have ended up in court over the business with that kid but he got me out of it. I can't allow you to bring charges against him for assault! It's all very embarrassing. I told him I'd see you made Nick Chase get off his back at once. Do you hear?'

'What about Petrus?'

'Bugger Petrus!'

'I'm prepared to give evidence for Petrus and support him if necessary,' said Elsa coolly.

'For Christ's sake Elsa,' Adrian was getting very angry. 'This is bloody preposterous! Put Jan back on the line.'

'It's got nothing to do with Jan,' said Elsa. 'I didn't even tell him. It was my decision to take Petrus to see Nick Chase and my decision to bring the case against the police.'

'I want to speak to Jan.'

'Leave him out of it Adrian.'

'If you bring this to court Elsa, I'll have no option but to act for the police. I'm warning you now, I'll make mincemeat out of you.'

'Fine Adrian. I'll take that chance.' She put the phone down, her hands shaking.

'What the hell's going on?' said Jan.

'I'm taking the police to court about Petrus. Adrian,' she said, 'is appearing for Captain Olivier's men.'

'You're not serious?'

'I am. I'll rub their noses in the shit too,' she said defiantly. She looked at him. 'Are you going to support me, Jan?'

He stood by the fire, facing her. Then he took up his farming journal and flipped through the pages. 'I'll think about it,' he said, noncommittally.

He had closed her out. He might as well have struck her. She went upstairs. She shut the bedroom door and undressed. She put on her pyjamas and climbed into bed. She switched off the light and pulled the blanket round her. She curled herself up small, turned away from Jan's side of the bed. He had rejected her. More bewildered than angry, she lay in the darkness, waiting.

Jan threw down the journal. The fire had died. The logs were furred with soft grey ash at their ends. He went out through the side door into the garden. The moon had risen full above the pepper trees. Ragged clouds drifted across the sky. The air was cold, but not with the chill of the wind that had shrieked across the damsite. It held the promise of a gentler rain, of summer.

He could hear the goats in the *kraal* beyond the shed. His old sheepdog came to him and licked his hand—a deferential greeting. The tousled crown of the palm tossed above, the windmill creaked. Jan looked back at the house. Their room was dark but he knew that Elsa would be awake, curled in the furthest corner of the bed, her back to his side, her arms locked around her chest, believing he would not notice and think she was asleep. What could he say to her? Don't close me out Elsa? Not knowing how to say it he had always withdrawn until she had recovered and put out her hand and pretended that nothing had happened.

Often on the damsite he had tried to think of ways to acknowledge what she had done on the farm. A gift? A letter? And yet, he had resisted it. Formal gestures of thanks seemed embarrassing. He had known her too long, too well to change his way of relating to her. It would be at variance with a lifetime of living together. And somewhere—he knew, ungenerous as it was—his resistance stemmed from an unease at her competence, at the independence, that he'd always known was there and that he'd hoped would not assert itself. But it had, and now, bewilderingly, warm, compliant Elsa was resentful, defiant even.

Briefly—he did not stop the impulse—he thought of

186

the anonymity of the dam. He had done as he pleased, been himself without compromise, even with Yvonne.

Perhaps being on Blackheath had been the same for Elsa. She too had lived alone, answered to no one. It had been a strange kind of freedom for both of them. She had asked no questions about the dam when he returned, leaving him to share what he chose. Instinctively she had not intruded in his experience, hoping perhaps that he, in turn, would respect hers.

She had welcomed him lovingly, and with relief, but her new self-reliance was evident to him. As he stood in the garden looking up at the tall palm tree he knew he had been wrong to resent it or to have expected that she would be the same when he himself had changed. He had always been her caretaker. Perhaps she did not want that any more—a caretaker might no longer be appropriate.

He squatted down on his haunches next to his dog and ran his fingers through its thick fur. He scratched its head, talking softly to it. Then he went inside and he took the stairs two at a time. He turned on the light in their bedroom. Elsa looked at him with dark, watchful eyes.

'I'm with you Els,' he said. 'It's OK. If you have to rub their noses in the shit, then you have to. But I'll be there, like always.'

Elsa sat up slowly and said, 'Do you mean it Jan?'

'Why not?'

She got out of the bed and came towards him. 'You really mean it, Jannie?'

'I mean it. I thought it through and it seems like a good idea.' He looked at her standing there in her old flannel pyjamas and laughed. 'You're a fierce little thing aren't you? No one ever dared take on Adrian before.'

'I'll take you on too.'

'Why don't you try?' he said, catching hold of her and pulling her close. 'I love you Els,' he said.

It was she who had always said it first, awaiting his affirmation. This time he asked for hers.

One Friday morning Elsa went to the shed and unlocked

187

the small room where the rations were kept. While Jan had been away it had been Chrissie's job to distribute meal, beans, sugar and milk. Elsa resumed the task. The women stood around waiting for her. She greeted them and sat down by the big corrugated tank that held the *mealies*. She took from each their tin *bhekile* and filled it.

Nonkitha, Nomatse and Griffisi with her tufty hair and wide pale face, stood about talking. Old Alzina shuffled in, complaining loudly about her rheumatism. The grains rushed down the scoop into the tins. Tombizodwa was last. Hanging back until the others had finished, she presented Chrissie's tin. She took it from Elsa with downcast eyes, balanced it on her head and went away, as small and unobtrusive as the sparrows that flitted back and forth through the shed doors.

Elsa sat alone, running the *mealies* through her fingers. The midmorning hush returned. The old press stood in the corner. It glowed yellow, smoothed by the constant rubbing of mohair and wool. As a baby Nella had been placed inside it. She had peeped through the slats at the shearers working in the heat, out of harm's way.

The dogs barked, the pepper trees stirred. Elsa could hear Chrissie shouting in the yard, her clear voice raised in excitement.

Elsa locked the door of the storeroom. She put her keys in her pocket, turned, then looked up startled. In the entrance to the shed, shadow stark across the cobbled floor, stood Nontinti Ngubane. Very small, very thin—but upright—she waited at the threshold.

Elsa ran to her. 'Nontinti!' she cried. 'You are home!' Surprised at her relief in seeing the old woman she took her hand in hers. Nontinti's fingers were so frail, so fleshless. Her face was a fine-boned skull from which the old eyes peered, pupils ringed with the blue of age. Chrissie stood nearby, touching Nontinti every now and then to reassure herself.

'It was a long journey?' said Elsa.

'Indeed it was so.'

'You have not found him?'

'I have not found him but I have followed him always

188

—to this place, to that,' she said. 'Ngubane sent a letter that he is here.'

'Abedingo?'

'Abedingo.'

'How does Petrus know?' said Elsa.

'It is said. That is all.'

'Chrissie, is this true?'

'It is said.' Chrissie echoed Nontinti's words.

'Where is he?'

'We do not know,' said Chrissie. 'He only came once, looking for Mama—but she was away then. Petrus was in town.'

'Why didn't you tell me?'

'Because . . .'

'Why Chrissie?'

Chrissie did not reply. Elsa looked at her, suddenly comprehending the reason for Petrus's visit to the treks, his silence, the silence of the other workers. 'You should have told me Chrissie.'

'*Kanti*,' she said, — and even yet—'he feared there would be trouble.'

'That's nonsense Chrissie! Nothing will happen to him—you know that. He must come home. The matter of the gun is finished. He must bring it back, that is all.'

'His heart is very black,' said Nontinti. 'That is why he has not come.' She looked down at her fingers. 'His heart is very black, I can tell. That is a bad thing for a boy.'

Elsa looked into her face. Nontinti, she knew instinctively, had suffered far beyond the telling. 'Chrissie will make you food,' she said. 'When you have rested we will talk together, you and I. We are glad you are home. We greet you Grandmother.'

They walked slowly towards the house. Nontinti looked about, up the hillside to where the workers' houses clustered in the scrub. Her feet faltered, Elsa took her arm, led her gently.

When Nontinti had eaten, Chrissie accompanied her back to her house, calling the farm women as she went. Elsa returned to her sewing corner in the spare room. She laid out the dress she had been making for Nella—gingham,

189

smocked at the yoke and trimmed with lace. She sat a long time turning the handle of the old machine round and round, seeing beyond the sentinel silhouette of the cotton reel, the whole of the farmlands, the curve of the *spruit*, Rooikloof, the place below the *bult* where the boy Sipho had been buried. Nontinti Ngubane was back. Abedingo was somewhere in the hills and still the matter of the child was unresolved. She remembered the gate that had been left, unchained and hanging on its hinges—a gesture of defiance—the night she had returned from Grahamstown.

'Listen,' said Annatjie as she popped tomatoes into a plastic bag to be weighed, in the café in town, 'why don't we have a big party, hey Elsie? I mean,' she scratched under the pile looking for riper ones, 'it's been so bladdy boring with Kobie and them away—don't you think? God, I'm glad they back! I was getting so sick of having my Mom staying all the time. Shame!' she said, 'I mean it's not that there's anything wrong with my Mom, but she only gets on my nerves after a while! Still, you wouldn't catch me staying alone like you did. Didn't you get scared in that big house all by yourself?'

'What sort of party?' said Elsa, knowing Annatjie well enough not to be diverted.

'A *braai* at our place. Kobie says a sheep-on-the-spit. Everyone can bring something—you know, salads, puds and things. Hey Elsie, I must tell you,' she glanced about to make sure no one was near. The shopkeeper's wife was serving fried fish and cold drinks to a group of black road workers, her voice strident as she urged them to hurry despite the fact that no one else was waiting for attention. 'Elsie,' whispered Annatjie, 'I'm almost sure I've got a bun in the oven!'

'Annatjie!' Elsa cried. The woman at the counter glanced over at them curiously.

'Ssshhh man!' said Annatjie.

'That's wonderful!' said Elsa, squeezing her arm.

'*Yirra*, I've only been feeling grim these last few days! I just know I'm pregnant—anyway *Ouma*'s at least a month late! I'm going to the doctor now for a test.'

'Four children!'

'This one better be a boy or Kobie will kill me!'

'Kobie must be thrilled.'

'Kobie says he's been saving up for a boy all the time he's been at the dam. Man, I must tell you Elsie, he's been driving me mad! He won't leave me alone!' She giggled and then she asked curiously, 'How's Jan?'

'Oh, he's fine. Busy planting more salt bushes and repairing where the storm caught us.' Elsa knew that was not what Annatjie had meant.

'You should see a doctor Els,' said Annatjie. 'You've waited far too long.' She touched her hand, not meaning to offend.

'I've got Nella,' said Elsa, turning to the mound of tomatoes and selecting a handful. 'We were talking about the party, Annatjie.'

'Ja, the party. We'll have it at our place, OK? We'll ask everyone. Why must we only have fun at Christmas?'

'How many people?'

'About seventy? Eighty?'

'What would you like me to make?'

'Why don't you come over tomorrow morning? I'll ask Joy and Petra and we can plan the whole thing? We'll paint a nice welcome home banner for Kobie and them.'

'Are you up to it—feeling like you do?'

'No problem. I want to let my hair down while I can!' Annatjie looked at her watch. 'I must fly or I'll be late for the doc! Hold thumbs hey?' She hurried to the counter and paid for the tomatoes. 'Tata Elsie,' she called. She went by the window, her earrings bobbing, her heels tap-tapping on the paving. Elsa collected her box of groceries and followed Annatjie into the street.

An old black man came out of the butchery on the corner. The fly screen banged behind him. He clutched a packet of chicken feet under his arm—yellow, scaley, gristle-palmed, they stuck up from the mouth of the bag. Slowly he counted his change into his handkerchief, twisted it, returned it to his pocket. He shuffled past her, hollow-cheeked, his coat flapping in the wind.

Oddly disconsolate, Elsa watched him go. She went to her truck and drove away from the town, hurrying home.

She passed the station where once she'd played with Jannie among the *mealie* sacks, nervously watching the tracks in case the train to Doringbult arrived and there was no escape.

She realized as she drove alone along the empty district road that the feeling of displacement within her own community—the *ithinzi*—that she had felt while Jan had been away was with her still. It caught her at moments like this, always feared, always anticipated like the train that, as a child, she'd believed would take her off to Doringbult. It dogged her like a guilt, secretly admitted but always unabsolved. She thought that it would go with Jan's return, that when he was there she would no longer notice the inconsistencies or brood on things that had happened since Sipho Ngubane's death. She had been wrong. The dissonance, the *ithinzi* followed her, unwanted. She did not tell Jan about it in case he scoffed. She was unaware that he would recognize the feeling and find relief in sharing it.

Nor did she know why Annatjie's 'How's Jan?'—a puzzled, anxious expression on her face—should have disturbed her so much, made her want to fly home, find Jan, fling her arms around him, hold him close and say 'It must be all right, Jannie. Nothing will change, will it?' knowing he could no longer offer her such reassurance.

When she got back to Blackheath Jan was walking up and down between the salt bushes with Petrus and another worker —Nella trotting behind—getting on with the business of farming as they always had.

'Hello Els,' Jan called. 'Did you collect the plants from the depot?' He came over to where she had stopped at the grid. He inspected the bagged saplings in the back of the truck. 'Bloody miserable looking things!' he said. His hair was spikey with sweat, his face streaked with dust. He wiped it on his sleeve. His socks hung around his boots. 'What have you been doing in town all this time?' he asked.

'Gossiping with Annatjie.'

'What has Annatjie got to say?'

'She wants to have a big party. Sheep-on-the-spit and everything.'

'I could do with a good thrash! When?'

'Soon. A welcome home for the chaps from the dam!'

Jan looked momentarily at his boots. The dam. He kicked at a stone. 'Great,' he said, glancing at her, his face defensive.

'What is it Jan?'

'Great I said.' He turned and shouted. 'Petrus!' He gestured with his arm. '*Yiza!* Come.' He swung himself up into the truck and waited to toss down the plants. 'I'll be home for tea just now Els,' he said.

'You know what?' said Elsa, when he'd climbed down.

'What?'

'Annatjie's pregnant.'

'That's nice.' He was matter-of-fact.

He was standing at the window, leaning his arm on the roof of the cab. She looked up at him. 'I wish it was me.'

Again he glanced away. Then he gave her a rueful grin. 'Hang in there Els—it's us next. We're going to do something about it. It'll be OK. I know it.' He tapped the door. 'Right,' he said briskly. 'I must get moving.'

He climbed through the fence and went across the land. He walked, head down, to where Petrus and Nella waited for him among the salt bushes.

— We'll have six children Els.

— Six!

— Why not? Three of each! A whole de Villiers span! He'd been over the conversation so many times in his head.

Kobie was very jovial. He had been drinking beer all afternoon as he'd directed the erection of the spit. He slapped Jan on the back so hard in greeting that he spilled his drink. He trod on Elsa's toes when he kissed her hello. He dispensed beer haphazardly, handed round plates of fatty meat and shouted at the two small farm boys that manned the fire.

'Elsa!' Andrew Fraser came to her and kissed her cheek. 'How are you, girl? Haven't seen you for a long time. Jan told me how well you ran the farm while we were away.'

'Did he?' Elsa was surprised.

'Yes he did. He said you'd given him some good ideas. He used to boast about you!' He laughed. 'Didn't surprise me!'

Elsa gave him a hug. 'It's nice to see you home, Andrew. Your little boy looks just like you though Mum insists he's a Southey!'

'Southey be damned!' said Andrew. 'Fraser genes always dominate.' His eyes were warm behind the thick lenses of his glasses. 'Let me get you some wine Elsie. Kobie's a real barbarian. He doesn't have a clue about how to serve his guests!'

Annatjie hurried in with a tray of snacks.

'Hello Elsie!' she said gaily.

'You're looking very grand and beautiful, Annatjie,' said Elsa, admiring Annatjie's long red dress, bugle beads and all.

'Never mind that it's a *braai*!' exclaimed Annatjie. 'I got dressed up because I'm going to dance!' She glanced at herself in the mirror above the mantelpiece. Her blonde fringe was straight, her hair teased up into a flossy bouffant on the top of her head. 'I'll have to be careful about my weight, Els,' she said conspiratorily, smoothing the red material. 'I'll be fat as a sow if I don't watch it. God, I wish I could have a cigarette—I really miss that!' She looked round the room. 'Where's Jannie Els? I want to book a dance before all the others get him.'

Andrew returned with Elsa's wine. 'Come and sit and tell me all about how you became a farmer.'

'It wasn't a big deal, Andrew!' she said. 'I had Petrus there.'

They sat on the verandah steps, Elsa curled against the wall in her velvety green jumpsuit, Andrew with a beer in his fist, elbows resting on his knees.

Elsa always remembered Andrew in his school rugby jersey. Invariably he had got the worst of the tackling for his jersey was stretched in fistfuls and hung below his shorts. In the line-out he had been big and ponderous. He had roared when he got the ball, bellowing as he thrust his way through the defence.

The senior girls had been allowed to attend rugby matches at the boys' College. Two by two in their blazers and bashers and dull green uniforms they'd sat on open benches by the small pavilion and watched.

Elsa had only been aware of Jan, tall and lithe then, fast on the wing. After the match when the girls had waited to file back to their school they had stood in a close group and laughed and talked self-consciously while the team members crowded round in their navy and blue jerseys, wringing with young male sweat.

Andrew had always come up to Elsa, his face puce from his efforts, his hair curled tighter than a karakul lamb's and grinned. 'Hello Elsie,' he'd say.

She'd liked him far too much to be brittle or to tease as the others were inclined to do. She knew that with Andrew it would hurt. The look in his eyes had always been too hopeful and direct. He would talk, a little awkwardly in front of the others, then go away, turn and wave as he went into the changing rooms. Jan would linger on, claiming her—his right—fingers brushing secretively, his face close to hers a moment. Then he would be gone too, too self-assured for a backward glance.

'What was it like at the dam, Andrew?' said Elsa as she sipped her wine. 'Jan doesn't talk about it at all.'

Andrew took a long draw from his beer mug, smacked his lips and looked down. 'Not so bad girl! Freek Koen's death upset Jan a lot. I don't think he likes to be reminded.'

She nodded, knowing. She did not wish to talk about it either. It brought too many painful issues to the surface. 'What did you do in your spare time?'

'Went to the pub,' said Andrew. 'Never had so many hangovers in my life, I can promise you!' He laughed and scratched his head. 'Played cards or darts. Bullshitted with the other chaps. Went to movies in the bughouse in town sometimes. It was a terrible place. The flick always broke down in the middle. The chaps used to boo and throw ice cream tubs around. It was pandemonium! There were some really tough types there, you know. I kept out of their way.'

'And no girls!' she teased. 'Poor Andrew!'

He glanced at her apprehensively and cleared his throat. 'No!' he said. 'Absolutely no girls.'

'I was only joking, Andrew,' she said, patting his knee.

'Ja, ja of course,' he grinned. 'Listen Elsie, aren't you starving? Let me get you some lamb.'

'You help yourself,' she said. 'I must check if Nella's asleep. Those kids have been rampaging around and it's time for bed.'

As the evening wore on the party became more raucous. Kobie and his friends stood by the *braai*, shouting with laughter, the flowerbed beside them filling with empty beer bottles.

'Come on *okes*,' cried Kobie. 'Let's do the dance of the flaming arseholes! Get some newspaper. Down with your pants Andrew.'

'Bugger off Kobie.'

Kobie lumbered out of his shirt.

'What's Kobie up to?' said Annatjie suspiciously. '*Ag nee!*' she cried. 'Kobie, listen yere! Don't be childish! Stop showing off!'

'Go away Annatjie!' he retorted. 'You not invited to watch!'

Someone returned from the house with a newspaper tightly screwed into a stick.

The other drinkers round the fire guffawed and shouted encouragement as Kobie stripped slowly with large, insinuating gestures. At last, naked but for his socks and shoes, he lit the newspaper and clenched it between his buttocks. The paper burned down quickly. When the flame touched his skin Kobie leapt up and down, roaring and howling. He ran round the garden clutching his bum.

'Kobie must be so bladdy crude!' said Annatjie crossly. 'Whenever we have a party it's the same. He just can't keep his pants on!' She turned on her heel. 'Come and dance with me Jannie—you promised you would.'

Jan led her to the *stoep* where the others danced in the lamplight. Kobie, rather bellingerent at the rebuff, came up to Annatjie and Jan and said, 'This is my goose, Jan. It's my turn now.'

'Go away Kobie!' snapped Annatjie. 'I don't want to dance with you when you being so stupid.'

'Hey?' Kobie wiped his hand across his moustache. 'Did I hear you right?'

'Jan's not drunk Kobie, so I'd rather dance with him. He knows how to talk to a lady without breathing beer all over her.'

Kobie laughed and nudged Jan roughly. 'Shows how much she knows, hey Jan?' He waved his beer around and said, 'Annatjie, meet heavy-breathing de Villiers. He's a dark horse, this Jan. Only has to see a bit of *poes* and he's after it!'

'Shut up Kobie!' hissed Annatjie.

Deftly Andrew guided Elsa away, said something innocuous, rather loudly. Taking her cue from Andew, Joy Fraser took Kobie's arm. 'I don't mind beery men, Kobie.' She dragged him off, jollying him along as the tempo of the music quickened. She took his drink from him and tossed it into the garden.

Annatjie followed Jan inside. He was standing alone in the dining room by the table where the salads were laid out among the candles.

'I'm sorry about what happened out there, Jan,' she said.

'It's all right Annatjie.'

'Jan?'

'Ja?' He was abrupt.

'Hang on Jan.' She took his arm. 'I'm really sorry.' She hesitated. 'We won't tell Elsa, I promise.'

'Tell what?'

Annatjie let her hand fall. 'About you.' She faltered. 'At the dam.'

He looked at her, his eyes angry and distant.

'It's OK, Jan. I'm sorry,' she said, retreating. She walked away then, back to the verandah and turned up the music.

Elsa came in search of Jan. 'What's going on Jan?'

'Nothing, why?' He picked up a roll and bit into it.

'Why won't you dance with me?'

'Don't feel like it.' He chewed the roll and said, with his mouth full, 'Want something to eat?'

'What's the matter Jan? You seemed to be having a good time earlier?'

He stared out of the window at the darkness, the glow of the fire beyond. 'Come,' he said, 'let's go. It's late.'

'We can't go now,' she protested.
'Why not?'
'No one else has left.'
'Someone has to be first.'
Before she could stop him he had gone in search of Nella and carried her out to the car.

# ❦ 12 ❦

Petrus Ngubane's case claiming damages from the police was to be heard in the Grahamstown Court on the tenth of October. Nick Chase had phoned to give Elsa the details. 'Isn't it going to be a bit awkward for you?' he'd asked. 'Adrian de Villiers is acting for the cops.'

'I know,' Elsa had replied.

'It's pretty unusual for things to work out this way—the family and all that. How come he's appearing for them?'

'It's a long story. I won't bore you with it now.'

'I'll do my best then,' Nick Chase had said cheerfully, enquiring no further. A calm, thoughtful voice, there had been no need to reassure her. Adrian with all his posturing would be hard-pressed to match him, she knew.

Word got around that Jan and Elsa were taking the police to court and that Adrian was Counsel for the Minister of Police. The de Villiers had never been controversial before; they had kept their disputes to themselves. The new situation was disturbing.

Adrian was held in awe. The community felt proud to have nurtured Dick de Villiers' brilliant son in their midst, despite his arrogance. It could be overlooked in someone with so much talent. But Jan was different. He was one of them. He was respected as a farmer, even by the older men. He had captained the cricket team, he was always good company at the Club. He was someone to rely on, someone who belonged. His new stand was so uncharacteristic it bordered on betrayal. Speculation was rife.

'It's Elsa of course,' said Flo Harcourt. 'Norman Southey was definitely very liberal. He had some extraordinary ideas about the natives. I'm not at all surprised really. I always said Elsa was just like her father.'

'Jan's gone *bossies*, I tell you,' remarked Kobie. 'It's since the time at the dam. He let Elsa get out of hand and he can't control her now. Of course, you know what she needs, don't you . . .?' he grinned meaningfully.

'Listen Kobie, it's a bad business, but you know, Jan was very upset about Freek Koen's death. That's why all this has happened. And Jan was right about Koen's land. I agreed with him from the start,' interrupted Andrew loyally.

'It's got bugger-all to do with Koen's land, man! It's mad to take the police to court over a cheeky coon. I always said that boy Petrus was bad news.'

'It's that bitch Elsa,' Elizabeth said to Adrian. 'She's very peculiar—I always said she was and you wouldn't listen. She's thick as thieves with Helen Chase these days and you know what *she's* like about blacks!'

'Don't come whispering to me Petra,' said Joy Fraser. 'I'll stick by Jan and Elsa no matter what.'

'I'm telling you,' said Annatjie. 'It's because of that bladdy girl from the bank!'

'I'll have to teach Jan a lesson once and for all,' Adrian to Cedric. 'This nonsense has gone far enough! It's a flagrant disregard for the rest of the family. Get them to court I say. We won't have any more trouble after that. It's a pity, Uncle Ced, and I know you don't approve'—condescending Adrian—'but it can't be helped. Jan never knows when to leave well alone.'

Andrew arrived at Blackheath one day. He came to give his friendship if not his full support and to try and persuade Jan to settle the matter out of court. 'We can't afford to antagonize the local police Jan, let's face it. We need them too much and relations have always been good with Captain Olivier. Anyway, how can you fight a case with your own brother on the other side?'

'Adrian's told me what to do all my life, Andrew. I'm stuffed if I'm going to settle this one just to suit him. Petrus can't work with his arm as it is.'

'You can replace him, Jan. Give him an easier job. You don't have to get rid of him.'

'Why the hell should he be satisfied with an "easier job"? What happens if I'm not around one day and he has to find another place? Who'd take him on—you tell me?'

'He can still work at something.'

'That's not the issue! I've known him since I was a kid. Why should I let him down just because Adrian owes the police a favour? It's a matter of principle.'

'Blood's thicker than water.'

'Oh crap, man.'

Andrew went away despondently.

Petrus had said little since his operation. He had returned from the hospital in Grahamstown and gone back to work but Jan was aware of the frustration that he felt at the lack of deftness of his right hand. One morning as they stood together at the workbench in the shed and Petrus held a length of damaged pipe for Jan to realign, he let it slip, unable to keep it steady with his weakened hand. The pipe rolled heavily. It caught Jan's thumb. He recoiled in pain, cursing.

'I'm sorry.' Petrus was resigned. 'It is no use, this arm of mine.'

'It'll improve,' mumbled Jan, nursing his thumb.

But Petrus shook his head. 'It is finished,' he said. He took out his pipe and filled it methodically. Jan kept down his impatience to continue with the task. He folded his arms and leant against the workbench, waiting for Petrus to speak.

'This case,' said Petrus slowly. 'The lawyer said that if I win I will get some money.'

'That's if you win,' said Jan. 'Maybe the police are too clever.'

'Yes,' said Petrus. 'He is clever, that man who broke my arm. It is he—the one with the white hair, the one who walks like a dog looking for bitches.'

Jan laughed. 'Smit,' he said. 'Who else could it be?'

'I do not know his name.'

'They can give any story they like,' warned Jan. 'It is difficult to tell a policeman he is lying.'

'I will speak the truth,' said Petrus. 'Why should the Judge not believe me? That is what the lawyer in Grahamstown has said.'

'The law is a funny thing,' said Jan. 'It does not always respect the truth.'

'True,' said Petrus, remembering the child Sipho, but saying nothing. He sucked on his pipe for a moment and then he said, 'I wish to use the money that the Judge will give me to start a business there at my own place.'

Jan looked up sharply. 'What do you mean?'

'Just so,' said Petrus. 'I can still drive a tractor, even with this hand. I can plough. I will buy an old tractor, a small one. I will plough the fields for the people. I will charge them, there on Gcashe and Mpumalanga.'

'You want to leave Blackheath?'

'Ploughing, it is something I can do. We have saved money —even Chrissie, she has saved.'

'Aren't you happy here?' Jan was defensive. He could feel the blood beating slowly in his ears, through his head. It was unthinkable that Petrus should want to go. 'Is it the money?'

'It is not the money,' said Petrus, a little impatiently. 'But this is your land.'

'It's your home too, Petrus. You know that. This thing with your arm makes no difference.'

'It is your land, *Nkosan'*.'

Jan heard the word, the subservience that it implied. He understood Petrus's purpose in using it. He looked across at him steadily and said, 'And Mpumalanga is yours.'

'It is mine.'

They stood a moment in the silence of the big workshop, the sounds of the yard far outside.

'Your father and your grandfather were here until they died. We have grown up on Blackheath like two bulls, you and I,' said Jan. 'I understand, Petrus, but I am sorry.'

'Like two bulls,' Petrus echoed. 'Like two bulls, it is so.'

They continued with their task, adapting their method to accommodate Petrus's weak arm. They worked quietly in the dimness of the old shed, the sunlight coming in through the open door. The sheepdog, haloed with dust motes, was stretched across the threshold in the warmth, watching patiently as it had over many years, shadowing Jan or Petrus wherever they went.

And Jan knew, working at the bench with Petrus—no words were needed to direct their hands—that the Blackheath he had always known and loved had gone. Inexorably, it had gone. The daily work remained the same, timeless in its seasonal routine: the rising of the sun, its long passage across the sky, its sinking down below Mpumalanga Mountain, the movement of the stock, the turning of the windmills, the trickle of water down the outlet pipe of the reservoir into the furrow, the carefully constructed jigsaw of the orchard wall. These would never change. It was only they, the people—Jan, Elsa, Petrus, Chrissie—who had changed, moved on, leaving Blackheath strangely empty.

Jan went back to the house for lunch, the sheepdog walking at his side. He opened the gate, feeling the familiar sting of the sun-hot metal on his fingers. Unquestioning, he had always had a faith, born of childhood, in the constancy of Blackheath and its people. And yet, the time had come for Petrus Ngubane and for Chrissie to make another life. Perhaps, like himself, when he had left the dam, they would go with some relief, with some regret, some half-acknowledged sadness. He walked on down towards the house, the sound of his boots heavy in the quiet of the early afternoon.

Jan took Elsa into the lands with him again. She said little, not wishing him to change his mind and send her back to the house, to the baking and the gardening. Unconsciously he had turned to her, needing her support, to share the business of the farming with someone, a defence against the time when Petrus would be gone.

They rode often as they had when they were first married. They took the horses up to the top camps in the hills where the wind blew and the helichrysums bloomed in the grass. They discussed the stock, the yield, Jan's plans for improving the workers' houses. They searched the pastures together, looking for the wiry rosettes of nasella grass, pulling them out and tossing them in a heap for burning.

The drought had gone, the rains had come and the pasture was recovering. Nella and Tombizodwa played again in their small house making food for their ragged dolls. Jan and Elsa sat in the lamplight on the *stoep* at night. They went to bed early for the days were long and busy. In the dark they held each other very close, sensing somehow that the hours should not be brushed aside.

Jan decided to go and see Cedric de Villiers. All his life Uncle Cedric had been irascible, eccentric even, but for Jan, predictable and therefore oddly consoling. Despite what had happened at their last visit to Melvynside, Jan could not leave matters unresolved.

'I'll go alone,' he said to Elsa. 'I'd like to speak to Uncle Cedric and explain. I don't want ill-feeling with him if I can avoid it.'

'He's not going to understand, Jannie. He's furious with me.'

'I'll sort it out,' said Jan. 'Uncle Cedric's quite amenable when he feels like it. It'll be OK.'

Jan rode across to Melvynside. He jumped the grids and cantered across the home camps where the sheep looked up to watch him curiously. He tethered the gelding to a tree in the garden and went in search of Cedric.

The old man was dozing over the morning newspaper on the side *stoep*. He was startled when Jan came up the steps. 'Just checking the stock market,' he said defensively.

Jan repressed a smile. Uncle Cedric always claimed that he was out in his lands ten, twelve, fourteen hours a day and never had time for visitors.

'Got to get back to the top camp in a moment, my boy,' he said peremptorily. 'Thought I'd nip down and get the weather report. It's going to rain in the next few days, you mark my words, no matter what those silly buggers say on the radio.'

He seemed to have forgotten, in his confusion at being found asleep, that the last time he had seen Jan he'd ordered him out of the house.

'Tea?' said Cedric. 'Beer?'

'Beer,' said Jan, knowing what Cedric's preference would be. Cedric had never felt himself endeared to tea drinkers. He kept a lamentably course brand in a blue and white tin above the stove and his maid never bothered to allow the kettle to boil before filling the pot.

Cedric fetched the beers. He handed Jan a bottle, cold from the crate in the dark pantry. He brought neither mugs nor glasses. He reached for his cigarettes, lit one and seemed to recall as he inhaled that Jan had done something of which he disapproved.

He squinted at him through the smoke. 'Jan,' he barked, 'what's this bloody stupid nonsense I hear about Elsa taking the police to court over that native? The bastard stole my sheep! I always said that those *kwedinis* who're allowed in the house when they're small get too big for their boots when they grow up. It happens every time, you mark my words! I told your father often enough—Dick, I said, you watch that boy, he'll start thinking he's a white man.'

Jan did not contradict him. He had heard it all before. 'Still,' he said easily, 'Petrus's arm is useless since the police assaulted him. If he'd broken it in an accident on the farm I'd have applied for Workman's Compensation. Same sort of thing.'

'Workman's Compensation, fair enough. This is different, quite different.'

'Uncle Cedric,' said Jan, choosing his words carefully. 'I don't blame you for getting up-tight about stock thieves. I'd feel the same. But assault is another matter. Petrus would have been tried—it wasn't for the police to beat him up.'

'You know the police, Jan,' Cedric waved a hand dismissively. 'They get so tired of the lying bastards! Breaking an arm's a bit much but still, I was so bloody wild myself I can't pretend I didn't lay into him too. I let him off lightly —I could have gladly broken the cheeky bugger's neck!' Uncle Cedric looked satisfied at this. He tossed his cigarette butt into the garden. 'The whole thing, my boy,' he continued, 'is that Captain Olivier is a friend and furthermore he did us all a great favour when that child was shot. This you must consider.'

'Uncle Cedric,' Jan said, 'I understand all that, but...'

'No, no my boy, you're being idealistic. It's because of Elsa I know, but look at Norman Southey! I don't want to cast aspersions, but really, he had a very lax policy regarding discipline. His *munts* used to walk around as though they owned the place. I wouldn't want to say anything against a young chap's lovely wife'—man to man, making allowances (fondly) for the inconsistencies of women—'but girls tend to be sentimental about the underdog—a softness I admire, mark my words, but still, hopeless my boy, in a case like this. We're men of the world, Jan. You can humour her by all means, but allowing her to sue the police leaves a bad taste in the mouth, especially in a small community like this.'

Jan was patient, Uncle Cedric could have his say. 'Besides Jan,' continued Cedric, 'it's all very embarrassing you know, with you and Adrian on either side. I think the police went a bit overboard but I can't pretend—on balance, you understand—that I approve of what you've done either although—I know it's very difficult with Elsa. She's not in the family way, is she? Women get very emotional when they are—it just crossed my mind . . .'

'Uncle Cedric,' said Jan. 'I appreciate how you feel and I don't want to put you in a difficult position but Elsa and I have thought it through carefully together. You'll understand that it's a matter of honour with us'—appealing to the old soldier in his uncle. 'We're not out to get at you or Adrian. Our concern is the police and their assault. It's unfortunate that you're involved. Despite that we had to make a choice. We have. I hope you'll accept that.'

Cedric de Villiers looked across his lands. He wiped his mouth with the back of his hand and set his empty beer bottle on the verandah railing. 'It'll make an outsider of you Jan.'

'I know.'

'It's hard to be an outsider in a place like this. People don't forget.' He turned and looked into Jan's face, knowing. He too had been an outsider in his way: unconventional in his lifestyle, his religion, his women. He had not escaped the censure of his neighbours.

'I'll take that chance,' said Jan.

'All right, my boy. You must do what you must. I hope I'm not called to give evidence in court. I don't want to be part of this or take sides against either you or Adrian. I know I set the ball rolling, but as far as I'm concerned it's not my business any more.'

He picked up his hat, set it on his head. 'Can't dilly-dally here all day,' he said gruffly, dismissing Jan. 'Don't know how you young fellows can bugger about drinking beer mid-morning! Farming goats is a sure way to complacency, you mark my words!'

Jan grinned to himself as he mounted his horse. Uncle Cedric had reacted the way he had expected. It was reassuring. ''Bye Uncle Ced!' he called.

'At least you haven't forgotten how to sit a horse!' returned Uncle Cedric shortly. He stamped off across the yard without looking back. 'Useless bloody goats!' he muttered unreasonably. 'Move your arse Bheki!' he shouted at his stockman who had been waiting patiently for him at the gate. 'This isn't a holiday camp, damn it!'

Langa Stores had been burgled despite precautions. The shopkeeper, hearing a disturbance, had gone out to investigate. He had been threatened at gunpoint. He had not seen his assailant's face for he wore a balaclava pulled down over the eyes. He had been roughed around while another man emptied the shelves. The police were investigating but there was always a shortage of men and vehicles. There had been faction fights at Gcashe at the weekends so their hands were full. The storekeepers had to make out as best they could.

The proprietor at Langa boarded up the windows with blue-painted wooden slats. He bought a vicious dog which he left unchained at night so that no one dared walk in the road after dark for fear of being bitten. The banditry on Mpumalanga was not of particular concern to the farmers. It was only a store used by workers for buying tobacco, paraffin, cold drinks and cloth, the meeting place of women and school children.

Even Elsa did not think about it until a few days later when she went into the garden to direct Nontinti as she weeded the circular bed below the tall palm.

Nontinti said suddenly, '*Nkosazan*' there is someone who took the things from Langa Stores.'

'I have heard,' said Elsa absently. 'Here—these are weeds too, Mama. They must come out please.' She stooped and pried some small shoots from the soil.

'It is he who has been there.'

'What?'

'At Langa Stores.'

'Who?'

'It is he—Abedingo.'

Elsa looked at her, frowning. 'Why do you think that?'

'I know it. If he did not have a bad thing in his heart, he would have come home. He does not want to come home and it is because his heart is black from all the lies that have been told. It is because of fear and because of these lies that his heart is black.' She looked up at Elsa. 'A child that has gone with the *dlakadlaka*, the people of the road, will not come home. This is a truth that I know.' And she touched her ribbed chest, indicating her own heart, seat of thought and knowledge.

'That doesn't mean he robbed Langa Stores,' said Elsa, lamely.

Nontinti looked away, a little impatiently. 'I do not like this thing,' she said. 'I do not like this thing at all.'

A hamerkop had settled on the thatch of a worker's house. Chrissie saw it—just as she had seen the first on the homestead roof before the time when her baby was born. She had gone out in the early evening to give scraps to her pig. No one was about. As she turned, the bucket in her arms, she saw it hunched against the sky. A bird with small black eyes, anvil-headed, feathers brown as wasted leaves. It croaked once, a voice from the dead. It took off on ungainly wings —a slow flight that was lost at last in shadow.

Chrissie hurried towards her hut where the fire was lit and her children were gathered round eating their porridge and beans. She drew her shawl tightly about her for she could feel the trembling of her fingers. She looked back at the sky but it was empty and only the evening star was out, pale and limpid, shining up above the *bult*.

Early on the morning of the tenth Elsa and Jan left for Grahamstown with Petrus and Chrissie. The pre-dawn glow edged the hills in the east. They drove past Kleinfontein where the old white house stood among the poplars. The windows were still dark. No one had stirred. Nella had been left there the previous evening, excited at the prospect of staying with Grandma. Only the man with the milk cans was walking in the road. He raised his hat in greeting. Sheep rested under the trees in the camp near the dam. In the dimness of the sunrise Elsa could see the silhouettes of yellowbills and shovelers on the water. They creased the quiet surface as they drabbled. Hadidahs, shouting in alarm, flew overhead— humped within their wings. Elsa slipped her hand into Jan's.

'Are you nervous Els?'

'A bit.'

'You'd better put on your fighting boots! It's going to be a tough day.'

Jan spoke to Petrus as they drove, recapping on the court procedure. Elsa glanced at Petrus. He listened with attention but his face was still and inscrutable. Chrissie dabbed at her forehead with the edges of her shawl. She did not look at Elsa. Her thoughts were her own.

They reached Grahamstown, passing the outskirts, Jan's old school. Boys were on their way to the first lessons of the day, their breaths wisping white in the cold air. In High Street the spire of the cathedral spiked the early morning sky.

'Let's get breakfast,' said Jan. 'Where shall we go?'

'To the café by the garage,' said Elsa. 'It's early but it should be open.'

They turned into Beaufort Street and parked by the cloakrooms near the filling station. Elsa went into the café and ordered pies and coffee for Petrus and Chrissie.

Jan bought a newspaper and sat at a bleak formica table in the corner of the room. Elsa stood at the counter waiting to take Petrus and Chrissie their food. She scanned the display case of cheap curios, rubber snakes, plastic toys and shop-soiled greetings cards. The girl behind the counter listened to the request programme and picked at her chin with a chipped fingernail.

'Coffee's here Els,' said Jan from his corner.

'Won't be long.'

Jan turned to the sports page. He read through the columns idly. The pies arrived and Elsa took them out to the car. She returned for the plastic cups of coffee.

Jan flipped through the pages, waiting for Elsa. He stopped, startled. Among the group of photographs entitled 'recent weddings' was a picture of Yvonne. She sat, pen in hand, at the church register. Fanie stood beside her—a big man with a thick neck, a drooping moustache and arched black brows. His hair was receding prematurely. He looked rather astonished at being there in his light suit and wide floral tie. Yvonne smiled for the camera. The small diamante crown that held her veil was slightly crooked. Her hair was done in a knot at the top of her head. There were stiff Edwardian curls at her ears. Her dress was high-collared and demure, tucked with slim embroidered ribbon across her big bosom.

Jan stared at the picture, at Yvonne looking out in white, at Fanie with his Mexican-style moustache, his hand on her shoulder. The caption read, 'Pictured at their marriage in the Dutch Reformed Church in Colesberg were Mr and Mrs Fanie Prinsloo.'

—I'm getting married at Christmas after Fanie qualifies, she had said. —I'm glad.

It was only October.

Elsa came in and sat down opposite. 'What have you ordered Jannie?'

'Toasted cheese for you and Cornish pastie and gravy for me.'

She looked at him. 'Is something wrong?'

'No.' He took up the pot. 'Have some.'

'Thanks.'

He glanced at the picture again, at the face, the long tapered fingers holding the pen. As he set the pot down he knocked it with his hand. It tipped and the coffee spilled across the page. The print and pictures stained, disfigured. Fanie blurred. Yvonne. 'Shit' he muttered.

'Now you've spoiled the brides!' said Elsa, mopping at the mess with a napkin.

'Yes I know,' he said. He swept the newspaper from the table and crumpled it. It was soggy and wet between his fingers. He took it away to the bins arranged by the cloak-rooms outside. He threw the papers in among the empty oilcans, the cold drink tins and sweet wrappings. He clanged the lid shut and stood a moment to recover himself.

October. She was married already. He went back into the café to his breakfast. He did not wish to think of why she might have married Fanie so soon.

Captain Olivier, Sergeant Smit and Corporal Djantjes stood at the door of the court talking together with Adrian and the State attorney, a fat man with a short neck who looked about like a mole who had dug its way up into the light. Elsa watched them from her seat in the passage where Nick Chase had told her to wait until she was called as a witness.

Adrian appeared to be confident and brisk. He glanced at her every now and then. Predatory Adrian—she knew he was trying to intimidate her.

Elizabeth had come to court as well. Elegant in red and white, she had passed by without a greeting. She sent Adrian a small, fluttering wave and gazed about her, self-aware. She touched her hair and inspected her lipstick in a pocket mirror before she made her entrance to the gallery.

Nick Chase and Petrus Ngubane came down the passage together, followed by their attorney. Petrus stared at his feet, turned his hat nervously in his hands. Elsa smiled. It was so characteristic of him. Nick Chase greeted her, shook hands with Jan and Chrissie, said to them, 'Come and find a seat near the front.' He turned to Petrus. 'You and Mrs de Villiers will have to wait out here until you've given evidence. Then you can watch the fun from inside.'

Jan bent to Elsa, squeezed her arm. 'See you,' he said softly. 'Good luck.' He laid his hand briefly on Petrus's shoulder and then he followed Nick Chase and Chrissie into the court.

Elsa could see Sergeant Smit through the doorway. He sat next to Captain Olivier, his legs crossed, his arms folded.

He pulled the ends of his moustache, scratched at his neck. Dark rings of sweat showed at his armpits. He chewed no gum today. He was watching Nick Chase and the attorney. As they moved, so his head moved, his eyes following. Like a blue-headed *koggelmander* turning with the passage of flies, so Sergeant Smit sat watching. Then he leant back, slouched a little in his chair and stared at the ceiling. After a while he began to finger his nose surreptitiously.

The Judge came in. The court rose. There was silence. The doors to the room were closed quietly and Elsa, Petrus and Corporal Djantjes were left alone outside. Elsa could hear the people settle, clear their throats, shuffle and subside. She looked over at Petrus. He wiped his face with his handkerchief for the sweat was creeping down the thick lesion on his cheek.

Here they sat, on the long benches outside the courtroom, she and Petrus, opposite each other. He smiled at her, as though a recollection had crossed his mind and she said, more to reassure herself than him, 'It will be all right. As Mama Nontinti says—I can feel it in my heart and in my bones.'

She glanced at Corporal Djantjes to see if he was listening, but he stared ahead. He did not acknowledge they were there.

Inside the court the Advocates rose and faced the Judge. Nick Chase said, 'I appear on behalf of the plaintiff, m'lord.'

Adrian's voice was resonant. It reached all the watchers in the gallery. 'I appear on behalf of the defendants, m'lord.'

There was a pause and then Nick Chase, settling his papers before him began to speak, outlining Petrus Ngubane's case. 'Damages have been agreed between the two parties, m'lord, in the sum of two thousand rands. I hand in the Rule thirty-seven minute which reflects the agreement. The only issue before the court is liability on the part of the first defendant, the Minister of Police, and the second defendant, Sergeant Hendrik Smit.' He handed a paper to the usher. 'I call my first witness, the plaintiff, Mr Petrus Ngubane.'

Petrus was summoned. He laid his hat on the bench and followed the usher into the court. He went to the witness box accompanied by the interpreter. He stood, his head slightly cocked, waiting.

After taking him briefly through the introductory preliminaries, Nick Chase looked directly at Petrus and said, 'Mr Ngubane, can you tell his lordship what happened on the day you said the police took you into custody?'

Petrus licked his lips, glanced at the interpreter and back at Nick Chase. He kept his eyes on him as he spoke, as if to draw from him both confidence and wisdom. 'The policeman—the sergeant—was asking me questions about the sheep. He kept asking. Then he said I was lying. I said no —that sheep was not mine. I did not take it. Again he said I was lying. He came then, he took my arm like this'— Petrus gripped his right wrist with his left hand '—and then he pulled it round. Hard, very hard so that I shouted and the pain was very bad, like an axe that is chopping wood. The sergeant pulled it round, round. It broke. I could feel that thing. He is saying all the time—you are lying. After that I fell down.'

'Excuse me, Mr Ngubane,' interrupted Nick Chase. The interpreter stopped speaking, arrested mid-sentence. 'Just to clarify, could you tell his lordship exactly when you believe your arm broke—when Sergeant Smit was twisting it, or when you fell down?'

Petrus touched his temple with a surreptitious finger to divert a drop of sweat forming there. The interpreter translated. Petrus said, 'He took my arm. He pulled it round until it broke. The pain was great.' Again, he held out his wrist. 'I fell then, just there by the table.'

'Did you fall against the table?'

'Yes. It got me here, by the back.'

'Thank you.'

'After that they took me to the hospital,' said Petrus. 'They fixed my arm. Still,' he said, 'I cannot do my work any more. Not properly.' He flexed his hand, dropped it slowly.

When he had been through the evidence, taking Petrus over every aspect of the incident, Nick Chase sat down and turned expectantly to Adrian.

Adrian got to his feet, held the edges of his gown. His small lace bib thrust out at his throat. He rose on the balls of his feet, rocked down again. Petrus gazed back at him, dabbed ineffectually at his temples.

213

Moment by moment, reconstructing the minutes in the police station in the smallest detail, Adrian cross-examined Petrus, trying to draw from him more information than it was possible to recollect with the accuracy Adrian seemed determined to exact. Petrus stood as though mesmerized.

There was a pause and then, with a change in tone, his voice pitched low and rising with an edge of accusation, Adrian said, 'The court has heard your evidence, Mr Ngubane. However, I put it to you that you are mistaken, that in fact, according to the evidence that my client Sergeant Hendrik Smit will be giving before this court shortly, you lost your temper during routine questioning, started towards the sergeant with your fists up. It appeared that it was your intention to strike him. Sergeant Smit stated that he grabbed your right arm in self-defence to stop the blow, and that you twisted round into a position in which your arm was behind your back. You pulled away to be free—pulled with considerable force. Sergeant Smit states that at that moment you slipped and fell against the table. That was when, according to him, you broke your arm. Sergeant Smit's evidence is corroborated by Corporal Djantjes who was present in the room.'

Before the interpreter had finished translating Petrus objected. 'That is not true,' he said. He turned to Nick Chase for support, glanced over at Smit. He sat impassive. 'It is not true. It is not I who would hit the policeman. The sergeant came to me, took my arm, twisted it!'

'And did you resist him?'

'Yes. How can he take a man's arm like that for nothing?'

'You resisted him. I put it to you that you twisted this way and that, trying to free your hands.'

'Yes.'

'You were struggling?'

'Yes.'

'So you could get free?'

'Yes.'

'You were angry with the sergeant?'

'Yes.'

'Angry enough to hit him?'

Petrus licked his lips again, turned nervously towards Nick Chase, but Nick was writing notes, his forehead resting on his hand, his hair flopping down across his fingers.

'Answer the question,' said Adrian.

'I did not hit the white man . . .'

'You were angry and struggling. Is it not possible that you slipped then on the polished linoleum floor—as I have been instructed it is—fell awkwardly and broke your arm, the cause of which was your own fault for resisting the normal process of interrogation and for threatening a police sergeant?' He paused. 'Thank you Mr Ngubane, that is all,' he said abruptly.

Elsa was called as a witness after tea. Her palms left small damp prints on the surface of the witness box. Jan smiled at her with the hint of a wink. Nick Chase addressed her, asking her name and for confirmation of the date and time of her visit to the police station. Then he said, 'Please could you tell the court what happened, Mrs de Villiers?'

Elsa began to speak. Her voice rose and broke. She cleared her throat and started again. The old fan circled slowly, stirring up the stale air. Elizabeth was bright and restless in her seat. Sergeant Smit regarded Elsa with a detached kind of amusement. She looked away, remembering his face lit by the flare of the match as he lighted a cigarette out on the dark road to Mpumalanga.

—I've never seen anyone to shit-scared in my life, he had said. It was there that Sergeant Smit had discovered her inconsistency. Somehow it seemed more than a coincidence. Confused, Elsa turned her eyes to Petrus sitting in Jan's old suit, gaunt, his head shaved, his hands quiet in his lap. She kept Petrus in focus. It was for him that she was standing in the witness box. And yet, she wondered fleetingly, if even that was true. Had he really wanted her to follow up his cause? She'd done what she thought best and he had simply been compliant. Perhaps she stood there only for herself and her bad conscience, the *ithinzi* that had troubled her: she didn't know. And yet, if it was so, Smit had found her out and he despised her for it—she felt sure—making her despise herself in turn, for double standards.

'I went to the police station to find out why Petrus Ngubane had been arrested,' she said. 'There was no one in the
charge office. I heard voices down the passage from behind
a closed door. I heard someone shouting inside and then I
heard footsteps and a scuffle and a cry—a loud cry as though
someone was in great pain. After that there was a crash. I
recognized Petrus Ngubane's voice. I tried to open the door
but it was locked. The station commander appeared just then
and told me that I could only apply for bail for Mr Ngubane
once he'd been brought before a Magistrate.'

'Why do you say it was Petrus Ngubane's voice?' asked
Nick Chase.

'I've known him since I was a child. I have no doubt.'

When it was Adrian's turn to cross-examine Elsa he stood
a long moment and regarded her. 'Mrs de Villiers,' he said.
Only Elsa, only Jan, could have sensed a sneer as he spoke
the name. 'Is it not true that you were running your farm
Blackheath without the assistance of your husband who was
away for several months, including the time in question?'

'Yes.'

'And do you not think, given the circumstances of your
husband's absence and the unfamiliarity of the task, that you
may have been somewhat unobjective about the quality, for
example, of your farm workers?'

'What do you mean?'

'Mrs de Villiers, I'm afraid I ask the questions and you
are required to answer them. If you do not understand the
question, please tell me and I shall try to rephrase it. To
clarify,' he said, 'Mr Ngubane was taken into custody for
stealing a sheep—an allegation you strenuously denied. Sub-
sequently he was convicted on irrefutable evidence . . .'

Nick Chase rose to object. 'With respect to my learned
colleague,' he said, 'the only issue before this court is whether
the defendants are liable for damages as a result of an assault,
not the reason for the plaintiff's arrest.'

'Quite so, m'lord,' said Adrian. 'However, I wish to
demonstrate that Mrs de Villiers' judgement of what she heard
in the room in the police station may have been clouded by

a well-meaning but unobjective emotional response to the arrest of her chief stockman and right-hand man.'

'Continue, Mr de Villiers,' said the Judge.

'What evidence have you, Mrs de Villiers, that the sounds you heard in the room were those arising from an assault?'

'I heard shouts, a cry and a crash. When I saw Mr Ngubane in court the next day he had a broken arm. He told me what had happened.'

'And you believed him?'

'Yes.'

'You also believed him when he told you he had not stolen your uncle's sheep?'

'Yes.'

'Yet he was convicted?'

Adrian used Elsa's pause to his own advantage and continued smoothly in a way that gave no appropriate chance for intervention. 'Did you see Sergeant Smit on the morning in question?'

'No.'

'How can you be sure he was in the room?'

'Petrus said . . .'

'Petrus said . . .' He looked over at her superciliously. 'What did *you* see? Did you know Sergeant Smit? Did you recognize his voice?'

'I did not know Sergeant Smit. I had never spoken to him.'

'Yet you allege he was in the room.'

'Corporal Djantjes came out of the room.'

'Corporal Djantjes is not a defendant in this case.'

Elsa said nothing.

'Who else did you encounter at the police station?'

'Captain Olivier.'

'Did you see the plaintiff, Petrus Ngubane?'

'No.'

'How can you be so sure then, that it was he in the room in question?'

'I heard him cry out.'

'What words did he say?'

'It was only a cry.'

'Only a cry?' Adrian raised an eyebrow. 'No words? No distinctive voice? Is it not possible that you could have been mistaken?'

'No.'

'In the records handed to me by Sergeant Smit, seven people were interrogated that day.'

'Were seven people assaulted? Were seven arms broken?' said Elsa defiantly.

'I have already pointed out to you,' said Adrian, 'that it is not for you to ask the questions. I am not denying that the plaintiff broke his arm while he was in custody but the manner in which it was broken and the time at which the incident occurred is what I am trying to establish.' Adrian turned from Elsa dismissively and sat down.

Shaken, Elsa walked to the seat that Jan had reserved for her. She could feel the eyes of the people in the gallery as they watched her cross the floor, the sound of her heels ringing loud in the quiet of the room.

'I messed that up completely,' she whispered to Jan. As he took her hand she could feel the tears rising.

The court adjourned for lunch. The Judge wiped his spectacles on the edge of his gown, gathered up his papers and went out. Adrian herded his contingent to the door and guided them down the passage into the street. 'Lunch!' he said to Captain Olivier and Sergeant Smit. 'I booked a table at the hotel. Mind if my wife joins us? She was in court today and she'd like to meet you.'

They crossed to the hotel and only Corporal Djantjes was left to sit on the wooden bench to wait for the resumption of the case.

'I'm sorry that I told it badly,' Elsa said to Nick Chase. 'If only I could do it over . . .'

Nick stretched and swallowed a yawn. He seemed unconcerned. 'No problem,' he said. 'The orthopaedic surgeon will be in the box this afternoon. I think his evidence will be our trump card.'

'Still.'

'Listen, why don't you get yourselves some lunch. Sorry

I can't be with you but Mr du Toit said he'd meet me at my chambers at one. He had a clinic at the hospital and couldn't get here any earlier. I need to have a few words with him before he stands up in court.'

'Do you think what he's got to say will work in our favour?' asked Jan.

'He might just button it up for us,' said Nick Chase. 'Be back at two.' He hurried away and Elsa and Jan went in search of a café and another round of pies for Petrus, Chrissie and themselves.

They drove up to the Botanic Gardens and sat under the trees. Petrus and Chrissie squatted down on the grass, their food divided between them. Chrissie spread her handkerchief on her knees and broke small pieces from her pie with delicate fingers.

'I told the truth,' said Petrus to Jan.

'I know, *mfo'wethu*. But like I said, it is not always the truth that wins.'

Petrus clicked his tongue. He pursed his lips and gazed off down the gravel path to the gates beyond.

Elizabeth de Villiers chattered brightly at lunch, played the good hostess to the two silent policemen and the State attorney. She cast a helpless glance at Adrian, willing him to assist her in her efforts.

The attorney unfolded his starched table napkin and inspected the cutlery for dirt.

'I don't like the look of that other Advocate,' said Captain Olivier suddenly. 'He's too sharp by far.'

'Relax, Captain,' said Adrian, waving the remark aside with far more conviction than he felt. 'I can handle him.'

'Who's paying for this, by the way?' said Elizabeth. 'Jan can't afford it, I'm sure.'

'Nick Chase? No one. *Pro Deo*.'

'Who'd work *Pro Deo* in this day and age?' said Captain Olivier.

'A few radicals,' remarked Adrian. 'He does it for love.'

'Commies, all of them, let me tell you,' said the Captain.

'Well,' said Elizabeth with an artful smile, 'I'd take on

Advocate Chase *Pro Deo* and for love. He's divine . . .'

Sergeant Smit laughed, shifted his eyes from their absorption in the breast pockets on her thin georgette blouse to her face and gave a conspiratorial grin, party to the reference. Captain Olivier did not smile. Nick Chase was not a laughing matter. The attorney paid no attention for he was suspiciously probing his flaked haddock in its blanket of white sauce.

Adrian said, 'People like Nick Chase don't go for Jo'burg socialites like you, my dear! You know quite well that his wife's the original earth mother.'

'Is that so?' said Elizabeth, raising an eyebrow archly and tilting her chin.

Sergeant Smit resumed his covert inspection of her blouse front.

'When's this orthopaedic surgeon giving evidence?' asked Captain Olivier. He dabbed at his moustache with his serviette and repressed a belch.

'Mr du Toit will be called straight after lunch,' said Adrian. 'He's the one we've got to watch. I've read his statement and it could be tricky. He seems very emphatic about how the injury was caused. I must warn you that his evidence could be damaging to us. I'll do my best but I can't promise anything more. Du Toit was rather annoyed about having to appear. He only comes up to Grahamstown to do clinics and he's very busy. I don't think he'll feel inclined to drag things out. No Captain, if it wasn't for du Toit, I'd say Ngubane's case was FBR,' said Adrian in an attempt to lift the spirits of his clients.

'FBR?' said the Captain.

'Elizabeth will excuse the language this once—it's an old joke—but in the words of a learned colleague of mine,' he shielded his mouth with his hand and whispered conspiratorily, 'their case if Fucked Beyond Redemption!'

Captain Olivier smiled politely but Sergeant Smit shouted with laughter, slapped the table so that the cutlery bounced and his coffee slopped into the saucer.

Nick Chase, his attorney and the doctor were already in the

courtroom when Adrian and his party returned from lunch. As Elizabeth swept to her seat she looked Nick Chase boldly in the face, aware that the sergeant was also watching. Nick Chase glanced back at her. The amusement in his smile was lost on Elizabeth. She turned triumphantly to Adrian but he was too busy talking to the Captain to notice.

Mr du Toit, the orthopaedic surgeon who Petrus had consulted had been subpoenaed as an expert medical witness. He was concise, detached and unemotional. Appearing in court was something with which he was quite familiar. A hazard of the profession he had once called it. He had given his opinion in numerous matters in the past related to injury and disability.

'Mr du Toit,' said Nick Chase, 'could you describe exactly the nature of Mr Ngubane's injury?'

'Mr Ngubane's arm was fractured at the upper end of the radius. A large part of the radial head was sheared off leaving the patient unable to extend his forearm fully.'

'Is this form of fracture unusual?'

'Yes.'

'Please explain.'

'It would take both considerable force and a degree of manipulation such as rotating the arm for this injury to occur.'

'In your opinion as an expert in the field of medicine can you comment on whether the injury suffered by the plaintiff is commensurate with an assault whereby the wrist was twisted and the arm forced up behind the back of the victim?'

'Yes.'

'Further, if you were given a hypothetical case in which a fracture was sustained because the arm had been gripped at the wrist and twisted quickly with considerable, even brutal force, what in your opinion would be the nature of the injuries be?'

'Most probably the same as those suffered by the plaintiff.'

'Are you satisfied that Mr Ngubane's arm was broken in the manner described?'

'Yes.'

'Would you like to comment on whether those injuries could have been caused in any other manner—for example, by a fall?'

'Extremely unlikely.'

'Are you quite sure?'

'Yes. It might be possible, I suppose, if the person took the weight of a fall on the fully-extended hand which rotated at the exact moment of impact, but that is highly improbable. I can state without doubt that the injury sustained by Mr Ngubane could not have been caused by a fall except under extremely unusual circumstances.'

Sergeant Smith was impassive. He sat leaning his forearms on his spread thighs. His left fist rested in the palm of his right hand. He seemed preoccupied with cracking his knuckles.

Adrian stood. He cleared his throat and adjusted his papers several times in front of him before he began to speak.

'Mr du Toit,' he said. 'I have listened to your evidence with some interest and with great respect. However, allow me to reconstruct the scene in Sergeant Smit's office in the police station when Mr Ngubane broke his arm and ask your comments when you know the facts as related to me by my client, Sergeant Smit.' With a small but practised touch of drama, Adrian retold the story of Petrus's alleged attack on Sergeant Smit, his struggle and his fall.

The doctor made no comment. He waited for Adrian to question him.

'Mr Ngubane claims that Sergeant Smit deliberately wrenched his arm round,' said Adrian. 'However, I am instructed that in his struggle to free himself, Mr Ngubane pulled away from the sergeant with considerable force, slipped and fell awkwardly against a large and heavy teak table. I suggest to you,' said Adrian, 'that Mr Ngubane, in his foolish attempt to free himself from the grip that Sergeant Smit had imposed on him in order to avoid the intended blow, slipped on the linoleum floor, causing his arm to rotate further. This situation would not have arisen if he had resisted the impulse to attack the policeman. What is your comment, Mr du Toit?'

'It is not altogether impossible.'

'It is not impossible? Therefore, to be less cautious' — Adrian smiled a little ingratiatingly—'it *is* possible.'

'To say it is possible is inaccurate. It is highly improbable. In the thirteen years in which I have had cause to examine X-rays of the radius—among other things—I cannot recall coming across this particular injury, the cause of which was a fall.'

'And have you come across this particular form of fracture having been caused by a similar assault as the one alleged by the plaintiff?'

The surgeon smiled: Adrian was sharp. 'No—not that I can recall. It is not a common fracture.'

Elsa was tired. Her head ached and she longed to go outside and breathe the warm afternoon air. Adrian and the doctor seemed to talk and talk. So many words for a story that was infinitely simple: a woman with a little child, a sheep stolen from a flock against the hunger of the winter days, Petrus gone to hear the truth and now, here they sat dissecting and comparing the degrees of possibility against degrees of probability while the Judge sat hunched and seemingly asleep except that his eyes darted back and forth from Advocate to witness.

Nick Chase closed the case for the plaintiff and the Judge, hoarse from the hours of silence as he listened to the pleadings, adjourned the court for the day. Everyone rose as he left the Bench. Even Elizabeth de Villiers, always so immaculate and glossy had wilted. Her farewells to the policemen were restrained. She waited while Adrian shook their hands. Without a glance at either Elsa or at Jan he followed Elizabeth through the doors.

As she walked from the room and into the passage Elsa noticed Corporal Djantjes still sitting on the benches waiting as he had for nearly seven hours. Feet together, cap at his side, he would not move without instructions.

It was strange to be in Grahamstown and not to stay in Adrian's big house in Durban Street in the blue and white guest room with the padded satin bedhead, the ruffled curtains and the porcelain posy of flowers on the dressing table where she and Jan had always been consumed with laughter because the bed creaked raucously and they seemed so out of place amongst the daintiness.

Instead they took a room at a cheap hotel after they had jolted their way through the labyrinth of roads of Fingo Village looking for the house where Petrus's cousin and his family lived as lodgers. They at least were greeted with delight. The family came out together to watch as Petrus and as Chrissie alighted from the car. They were guided to the house, a tiny unit, smoke-stained above the windows, and they disappeared inside, the adults first, the children nudging at each other from behind. The door closed and Jan and Elsa were left alone in the dusty roadway.

'God,' said Jan, looking around the hotel room. 'It's got as much atmosphere as the Cookhouse café on a Sunday night!'

Elsa laughed. 'Why complain? It's our first night in a hotel since our honeymoon!'

'And the last!' said Jan pulling off his tie and hooking his jacket over the corner of the cupboard door.

The bedspreads were orange candlewick. A Gideon Bible lay on the cubicle by a glass ashtray and a grubby doily. The hotel had been updated some years before. The floor had been fitted with a multicoloured acrylic carpet with a small, geometric design. At the windows hung the ubiquitous sun-filter curtains. Otherwise, the age of the room, its past interior, was represented by an ancient light fitting hanging on a twisted pair of woven brown flex cords and a bath with a hollow at the far end, where scores of bottoms had reposed.

'At least the towels are clean,' said Elsa. 'And there are lots of them.' She bounced on the bed. 'It might be quite fun after all, Jannie. Don't look so gloomy!'

But it was not easy to keep their spirits up. They shared the dining room with two commercial travellers. The tables were laid with white cloths and carefully starched napkins but they were empty. It seemed that no one ever came to dine. It was difficult to talk with a silent guest at the table beside them. The sound of him eating his soup and breaking his Melba toast was uncomfortably close.

'Let's get out of here and go for a walk,' said Jan. He

twitched his shoulders as though to shrug off something, pushed his chair back. 'Enough's enough.'

It had begun to rain. A soft misty drizzle danced gnat-like round the street lamps. The nine o'clock curfew sounded. Jan and Elsa stood and listened to its strident warning.

'Funny how I never really knew what that curfew implied when I was at school,' said Elsa. 'It only meant half an hour to lights-out.'

'Kaffirs-into-bed,' said Jan wryly, remembering the school-boy chant.

They walked up beside the cathedral, crossed to look in the window of a photographer's shop at the display of numbered dance photos from a recent University ball. Elsa gazed through the glass at the students: couple after couple, groups of four, arms around each other, entwined in paper streamers, dress suits all awry. She pressed her nose against the window to see better. Her breath misted the glass. She rubbed at it with her finger. Jan watched her as she tucked her hair behind her ear, tugged absently at the ends. 'D'you still wish you'd been there, Elsie?'

'Sometimes,' she said, a little wistfully.

'Pity about the boring old farmer, hey?'

'I wouldn't swop the boring old farmer, not even for that' —she pointed to a study of a dark bearded student with a pipe.

Jan rolled his eyes in mock despair. 'Oh my God!' he said. 'Don't say I have that for competition!'

Elsa laughed and took his arm. 'Let's go down New Street,' she said. 'Wasn't it out of bounds when you were at school? I used to have the idea that it was the original Primrose Way —the path to perdition.'

'It was said that a few interesting ladies hung out in New Street and that it was unsuitable for little boys to know about them,' said Jan. 'If only!'

But New Street was empty, flanked with trees whose roots pushed up the pavements. The small settler cottages seemed tucked in against the rain, the light soft behind closed shutters. Only when they passed the Victoria Hotel did they hear the sound of voices coming from the bar, the sporadic rise and fall of words and laughter. They kept on walking—up New Street, along Somerset and back down High Street towards the dark edifice of the cathedral, the rain drifting in.

Jan did not want to return to the hotel. At reception, when he had signed in, the morning papers that had been neatly stacked for guests still lay unclaimed on the desk. Inside would be Yvonne—five, six, seven versions of Yvonne in her wedding dress and her diamante crown.

When he lay in bed much later and Elsa was asleep, the Gideon Bible and the cubicle between them, he stared up at the flat patch of light from the streetlamp against the ceiling and he listened to a truck turning up from Bathurst Street, its bodywork jolting as it took the bend. There was something about the narrow single bed, the empty room, the sounds of the town outside, that was reminiscent of the damsite with its bleak staff quarters and its dusty roads. And Yvonne. He tried to visualize her face, her body. But she belonged to another lifetime. Another place.

Sergeant Hendrik Smit was called to the witness box. He strutted across the court, his buttons gleaming. He seemed to swing himself up the step to take the stand. His confidence was unassailable.

Adrian was abrupt. Elsa could sense that he was tired. His manner was irritable, his gestures less expansive than they had been the day before. 'I call my first witness, the second defendant, Sergeant Hendrik Smit,' he said.

Sergeant Smit was nonchalant. His hands rested loose and relaxed before him.

'Sergeant Smit,' said Adrian. 'Please could you describe what happened the morning you took Mr Petrus Ngubane into custody?'

'Ngubane,' said Smit, 'was booked for stock theft. Our information was that he had accomplices but he wouldn't tell us who were these people. We think they were some treks squatting . . .'

'Excuse me, Sergeant. These people are not relevant,' interrupted Adrian.

'OK, sorry m'lord,' said Smit with a small gesture of his

fingers as though dismissing them himself. 'So anyway, I was trying to find out who were his friends. He was telling me he didn't know them but I could see he was lying. And anyway the person who brought him in saw those people with him. Ngubane got very cross—maybe he'd been drinking, you never know, or smoking *dagga* maybe—but he got quite upset. He seems a stubborn kind of person, like some Bantus you get.'

'Stick to the facts, Sergeant,' said Adrian tiredly.

'O K, so then he got up-tight and suddenly—just suddenly, like he was really angry—he comes at me with his fist. So I caught it.' Smit demonstrated the action. His hand shot out, gripped the air.

Adrian described the action for the purposes of the court records. 'Continue, Sergeant,' he said when he had finished.

'I got his right wrist,' said Sergeant Smit. 'In the meantime he's kicking and shouting. He twisted round so his arm is at the back and now he's really wild—I'm telling you — and he pulls away. The floor's slippery in my office. It's covered with that stuff—you know—what's it called? Like they put in the kitchen?'

'Linoleum,' said Adrian.

'Ja, linoleum. And so he slips and his arm is jerked away and he falls. So,' Smit paused a moment as though to consider. 'So as he fell he put out his hand like this'—he extended his arm, splayed his fingers. 'But then he twists over and crashes against the table leg.'

'To clarify,' said Adrian, looking down at his papers momentarily to hide his irritation. He knew Smit had changed his story—slightly, but crucially—having heard the doctor's evidence. He had never mentioned an extended arm during consultations, only the heavy table. Adrian had no choice but to go along with him. 'He twisted away from you while his arm was still behind his back. He slipped and as he fell he extended his right arm to break his fall. Please describe how he contacted the floor?'

'He came down hard on his right hand. And then basically he kind of rolled over into the table, like that,' and Smit rotated his right arm in imitation.

Again Adrian described the action for the records. The sweat was forming on his upper lip. He wiped it away coolly, giving no sign he was disturbed.

Nick Chase leaned back in his seat and examined the pen he held balanced between his fingers. Then he stood, hitched up his gown at the shoulders and turned to Sergeant Smit. He began his cross-examination. 'Sergeant Smit,' he said, 'you have heard my client's evidence. His version of the incident in the police station differs significantly from yours.' Smit gave a wry smile and drummed his fingers lightly against the wood of the witness stand. 'You say the plaintiff started towards you, his fist up as if to strike you?'

'Yes.'

'And that he was kicking and shouting?'

Smit hesitated and looked at Adrian. 'Kicking, ja.'

'I believe you said "kicking and shouting".'

'Yes,' Smit would brazen it out.

'Yet the third witness, Mrs de Villiers, who was standing at the other side of the door only heard *one* cry and then a crash.'

'How does she know who was in the room?'

'Her evidence was that she recognized the plaintiff's cry. However, if it was not the plaintiff who was in the room with you, one must assume that the police in your particular station indulge in fisticuffs with every prisoner or that your area is remarkable for the number of pugnacious people you are required to take into custody.'

Adrian interrupted to object to Nick Chase's tone but the Judge waved him aside and said, 'Continue, Mr Chase.'

'Therefore, Sergeant, it seems reasonable to assume that the prisoner you were interrogating at the moment Mrs de Villiers arrived outside the door was indeed Mr Ngubane?'

Smit made no reply. Nick Chase continued. 'You stated further that Mr Ngubane pulled away from you with some force, slipped, fell, and as he fell he extended his right arm. As it touched the floor Mr Ngubane twisted away and crashed into the table leg.'

'Yes.'

'I put it to you, Sergeant Smit, that you initiated the scuffle,

228

that you advanced on Mr Ngubane because you believed that only physical force would extract the information you required, that you grabbed his wrist, brutally twisted it, then forced it behind his back and once you had done your deed you let him fall.'

'He attacked me. He was angry. You don't know these Bantus we get in the police station.'

'Sergeant!' said Nick Chase coldly. 'Are you seriously contending before this court that a small man such as the plaintiff who cannot weigh more than a hundred and thirty pounds would attack an interrogator considerably heavier than himself and at least eight inches taller—and in the presence of another policeman?'

Adrian took out his handkerchief and mopped his face. He stood. 'I call my last witness, Corporal Pius Djantjes,' he said.

Corporal Djantjes was ushered into the courtroom. He crossed to the witness box, his steps clipped. He held his cap between his fingers. He looked straight ahead but Elsa saw him swallow twice, in quick succession.

'Corporal Djantjes,' said Adrian when he had covered the preliminaries, 'please tell his lordship what happened in the police station the day the plaintiff was interrogated.'

'Ngubane did not like to answer the questions the sergeant was asking,' said Corporal Djantjes. 'The sergeant was asking who are those people who stole the sheep with him. Ngubane would not tell the sergeant and then he got cross.'

'Who got cross?'

'Ngubane.'

'And then?'

'And then he was going to hit Sergeant Smit so the sergeant takes his hand, very quickly, to stop him and Ngubane struggles and then he slips and falls.'

Adrian went over the incident again, avoiding questions about the actual manner of the fall.

Nick Chase shifted impatiently in his seat. He ran his hand through his hair, tapped at his notes with his pencil. At last, when Adrian turned from Djantjes and indicated that he was finished, Nick rose swiftly.

'Corporal Djantjes,' he said, 'let us consider your evidence afresh. You say that Sergeant Smit grabbed Mr Ngubane's arm to stop a blow and twisted it.'

'Yes,' Djantjes' eyes flicked to Smit. Smit was sitting back now, his arms folded.

'And then,' continued Nick Chase, 'he pulled away from the sergeant and slipped.'

'He slipped,' affirmed the corporal.

'Describe to his lordship *exactly* how Mr Ngubane fell.'

'He slipped and he fell into the table.'

'He fell into the table? He did not fall on the floor?'

'Into the table. Then he fell on the floor after.'

'He hit the table and then the floor?'

'That is right.' Djantjes swallowed again. Up down, up down—his windpipe seemed to tremble at the edge of his starched collar.

'And what was he doing with his arms?'

'I don't remember.'

'Were they like this,' Nick Chase drew his arms to his chest, 'or like this?' He extended them.

'I think,' Djantjes looked at the interpreter as if for guidance. Elsa held her breath. The courtroom was very silent. 'Like this. Yes,' said Djantjes. 'Like this.' And he raised his arms and clutched them to his chest.

'Thank you Corporal,' said Nick Chase. 'That is all.'

A little wearily and without his previous swagger, Adrian closed the case for the defendants. Elsa watching him, felt almost sorry. Jan, beside her, let out his breath slowly, like a sigh. 'That's it,' he said.

The Judge poured a glass of water and took a sip. He settled himself again and folded his hands before him. He looked over at Nick Chase as he rose from his seat to present his final argument for the plaintiff. 'M'lord,' Nick began.

'One moment,' said the Judge, waving his hand a little impatiently. Nick Chase stopped, taken aback. 'I don't need to hear you, Mr Chase. However I shall be interested in what Mr de Villiers has to say.'

Nick Chase stood poised a moment, then he dropped his head slightly and sat down. He knew the claim would succeed.

Adrian glanced at his opponent, acknowledged him briefly and rose, trying to muster some of the flair and sureness he had displayed the day before. If he was to lose, he'd lose with style. For the minutes he stood before the court, upright —and somehow beyond the credulous gaping of the audience in the galleries—Adrian, centre stage, seemed undaunted. It was a creditable performance.

'The court will take time,' said the Judge. 'I will deliver judgement at two fifteen this afternoon.' He rose to leave the room.

In the passage outside the court, Captain Olivier walked up and down with Smit and Adrian. Corporal Djantjes stood to the side, awkward and bewildered.

Elizabeth disappeared to the cloakroom. The small, womanly ritual of powdering her nose, renewing her lipstick and brushing her hair would keep away anxiety. She knew how angry and humiliated Adrian would be.

The judgement was short, delivered perfunctorily. The evidence of the second defendant and Corporal Djantjes was conflicting. On the balance of probabilities Petrus Ngubane's version was accepted by the court. The medical evidence supported his case.

Rain began to patter against the windows. The crisp swish of tyres on tar came from the street outside. Listening breathlessly, each sense alert, Elsa heard, somewhere beyond the window—in sharp contrast to the proceedings within and the Judge's drone—a voice raised in song, accompanied by a home-made guitar. There was a shout of laughter, the slap of bare feet on wet pavements. Like thumbing the nose at the pomposity within, Elsa knew it was a portent. She squeezed Jan's hand.

Petrus Ngubane was awarded two thousand rands damages. He was awarded costs. He had won the case. The Judge closed his folder. He walked down from his seat. It had been a long day.

Adrian left the room, his gown billowing. The door bounced back and forth behind him. Elizabeth stalked out. She did not glance at Nick Chase again.

Elsa felt euphoric as she left the court. She hurried towards Petrus and Chrissie waiting at the entrance. 'Petrus.' she said. But he did not hear her for Chrissie stood before him, speaking quietly. Elsa stopped, half-turned away. Somehow they did not need her any more.

Sergeant Smit sauntered past Elsa. He paused, his momentum arrested just a beat, to look into her face. She turned from the fleeting insolence of his smile.

Jan stood apart. Elsa went to him, took his arm. 'Aren't you glad Jan?' she said.

'Yes.'

'It worked out. I never dared hope it would.'

He was silent and Elsa said, a little exasperated, 'Why aren't you saying anything, Jan?'

'Adrian's my brother,' he replied quietly. 'That's all.'

# ❦ 13 ❦

Monday the twentieth. It was spring, early summer even. The goats had kidded. The air was warm. A *Piet-my-vrou* was calling somewhere in the *kloof.* The red dust of the track was fine, smelling of earth and pollen and wholesome dung. The new leaves were out on the thorn bushes. The *veld* was full of flowers—the pale mauve of the mint shrubs by the *spruit* mixed with the small white flowerets of the soap bushes. Bachelor buttons bent to the wind. The river was flowing, slow and smooth and the otters were back for there were wet marks in the sand where they had caught crabs and eaten them. Tortoises were about. Elsa had found an old fellow munching blossoms in the front garden. Nella had taken him to the orchard.

'Ride with me to the top camp, Els. I want to check the pipe from the reservoir. Petrus says there's a leak,' said Jan.
 They saddled the horses and rode out together, jumping the grids, cantering diagonally across the hillside. They took the path above the Rooikloof. The big trees of the ravine were budding leaves: orange, pink and lime. The shadows were misty in the heat haze and they could hear the cicadas shrieking down amongst the damp foliage.
 Higher and higher they rode, the creak of saddles, the clink of bridles, a hoof striking stone. They stopped on the crest, high above the Rooikloof, startling a pair of francolin from their hiding place.
 In patches the helichrysums bloomed—pink fading to white, yellow to cream. Elsa picked a few and stuck them in her buttonhole. Nontinti had always told her they were the flowers of the shades, that somewhere beneath the ground

where the helichrysums grew, the shades were present, silent witness for those that followed.

Jan tethered the horses. He walked down the pipeline with Elsa. 'Here's the leak,' he said. 'It's not too bad.' He squatted and inspected the joint where the lengths were socketed together. 'I'll send one of the chaps up later.'

Elsa perched on a rock, looking out across Blackheath. Jan sat beside her and put his arm around her shoulders. She nestled in, close to him, the wind at their backs.

'It won't be the same when Petrus goes,' said Elsa.

'It isn't the same any more, anyway.'

'Does that worry you?'

'It did when I came back from the dam. I didn't want changes.'

'And now?'

'I'm glad we've come through it.'

Elsa picked up a small stone and cupped it in her hand. Its underside was damp and cool against her palm. 'Do you think Adrian's ever going to forgive us?'

Jan was silent a moment. 'He didn't have much choice,' he said. 'He had to act for the police but he also knew he had very little chance of winning the case because of du Toit's evidence. It was hard for him. He doesn't like to be humiliated.'

'I know,' she said. 'But maybe it was even harder to lose his hold over you.'

'Perhaps.'

'Will you try and patch things up?'

'Why not? He's my brother.'

'On his terms?'

'On all of ours.'

'And Blackheath?'

'How do you mean?'

'Petrus and Chrissie were always here. Now they'll be gone.' She glanced off towards Rooikloof, remembering the child Sipho. 'It's since Sipho died and Abedingo ran away, Jan. It's as though since them—or because of them—the old order's changed and Blackheath's gone.'

'We'll start again.'

'How can we?'

He turned abruptly, searched her face. 'Do you know what you're saying?'

'It's funny how I feel displaced.'

'I said we'll start again.'

'Even though it can never be the same?' she persisted.

'I would never leave it.' He said it slowly so there could be no question of her doubting him.

She passed the stone from one hand to the other and back again. 'And I would never leave you,' she replied softly.

Way out towards Melkbos Siding they could see a train. Small as a toy it steamed, its breath drifting out above the thorn scrub growing all along the tracks.

'There's the train,' said Jan. 'Perhaps it's going to Doringbult.' Elsa drew closer. 'You really did believe in Doringbult, didn't you?'

'Yes.'

'What did you think it was like?'

'One of those oddly deserted places where people used to be.' She tossed the small stone away. It bounced and rolled into the grass. 'A nowhere. A place that's suddenly died but is somehow full of voices.' She laughed then and Jan touched her hair, slid his hand down to the nape of her neck with warm reassuring fingers.

'Look,' he said. 'It's leaving.'

The sound of the train reached them high on the hillside as it gathered up its strength from its iron heart and started out along the tracks, the cattle cars rocking behind it. It moved on and on until it disappeared within the thickets of euphorbia growing on the slopes of Mpumalanga Mountain.

The little station down at Melkbos Siding with its coal shed and its stock pens and its clumps of *gwarri*, stood quiet and empty by the rails.

Jan looked at the sky and frowned. 'The clouds are coming up,' he said. 'I didn't listen to the weather report. Did you?'

'I forgot. I'm sorry. I was reading to Nella.'

'We'd better get back then. I must send the stockmen out to bring in the goats and find someone to get up here and repair the pipe.'

They mounted their horses. Elsa cantered ahead, down to the road. She turned and waited for him.

'OK Elsa,' he shouted. 'Let's race.'

He urged his horse on. They tore down the track. He passed her, glanced over his shoulder and whooped.

'Wait for me Jannie,' she cried. Laughing, she shook back her hair and galloped after him.

At the gate Jan reined in his horse. It pranced a little, kicking up the dust.

Elsa clattered to a halt. 'You always beat me!' she said. 'That used to make me so cross!'

He helped her down and kissed her on the nose. 'Bad luck *kleintjie*.'

She put her hands on his shoulders, reached up and returned the kiss.

'It's cooler now, Uncle Cedric,' said Adrian, looking out of the dining room window at Melvynside. 'Let's walk across to Brakkloof. I need some exercise after that lunch. Are you coming Liz? I really want to inspect the house and see if anything can be done with it.'

'No thanks,' said Elizabeth. 'It's not every day that I'm on my own without the kids. I'd rather read my book on the verandah and have a snooze. Besides, I want that house knocked down and you'll only frustrate me with your Heath Robinson plans about how to renovate the old heap.'

'I should have left you at home,' said Adrian crossly.

'Darling Aidie,' she retorted. 'I needed a break as much as you did and there's no better place to rest than the farm where there's absolutely nothing to do but sleep and amble about. Run along,' she said as she searched for her sunglasses and book. 'It's getting cloudy and I want to tan in the last of the sunshine.'

Adrian selected a hat from Cedric's grubby assortment on the hall stand. He changed his shoes and pulled on an old pair of khaki shorts.

'You look divine Aidie!' said Elizabeth, giggling. 'Farmer Giles in all his glory! I wish your colleagues could see you now!'

'Come along Adrian,' said Uncle Cedric. 'It's quite a way. We'll see how you're puffing at the end of this.'

They went off down the road. Elizabeth sighed, lay back and opened her book.

The old shed at Brakkloof stood deserted by the sweet-thorn. The plaster was smeared with dirt where mud had washed along the walls. A sheet of corrugated iron, the black paint blistered grey by the sun, lay twisted on the grass.

'Storm hit this place hard,' said Adrian. He wiped the sweat from his face and glanced up at the gable.

'It's solid enough,' said Cedric. 'Shouldn't take too much to get it back in shape.' He pushed at the door, went in and dragged it open.

'Derelict old dump!' remarked Adrian, looking about.

'Perfectly functional,' said Cedric.

'How much would a new, properly equipped shearing shed cost these days?' asked Adrian.

'A bloody fortune! This is quite adequate for our purposes.'

A sloughed snake skin lay on the floor. Adrian picked it up.

'Cobra,' said Cedric. 'The place is probably crawling with them.'

'That'll make Liz happy!'

Something scuttered across the floor. There was a secret scratching in the pens. 'What was that?' said Adrian, startled.

'A rat, probably. No wonder there are snakes about.'

'I think we'll knock the place down,' said Adrian uncomfortably.

Below the shed, where the workers' houses stood in a row behind the tangled barrier of *garingbome*, a man stood in the shadow of a wall. He waited. He had heard the voices. He made no sound with his feet as he walked towards the *garingbome* and peered between the sword edges of their leaves at the shed above. He saw Cedric de Villiers framed momentarily in the doorway. He breathed quickly as he watched. At his heel the yellow dog whined. He cuffed it to be quiet.

The clouds had gathered up above the ridge. They had

grown, banking in, grey and purple. The wind had changed. It was beginning to get cold. The first drops of rain thudded down. Furtively the man returned to the hut.

The woman sat with her baby at her cooking fire. 'Put that out,' said the man. 'There are whites in the shed. They may see the smoke. Stay here and be quiet.'

He went out again, keeping close to the wall. He made his way hastily across the open ground towards the homestead. He took the back steps two at a time and pushed open the door.

Abedingo was asleep on the pantry floor, his balaclava pulled down over his eyes. Around him, piled up in the gloom, were the goods that he and the man had stolen from Langa Store. He sat up, startled. '*Yintoni?*' he breathed. 'What is it?'

'There are whites, Abedingo.'

'Which whites?'

'I think it is the old one. The one that hit Ngubane. There is also another.'

'They may come in here.'

'They may,' said the man.

Abedingo stood slowly—thin with privation. He reached up to the top shelf. His fingers searched it briefly. He drew down the rifle that had once belonged to Jan de Villiers and loaded it. The two men stood silently among the scattered blankets, bolts of cloth and meal sacks. Together they waited.

The rain sent up the smell of earth and leaves. Elsa turned from the window and sat down at the table. She opened the account books and searched for a pen. Nella sprawled on the floor, Tombizodwa beside her. They coloured in, quarrelling over who would have the pink crayon.

Jan was out in the camps bringing in the last of the angoras before the storm broke. Elsa could hear the shouts of the men, the bleating of goats carrying clearly in the still air.

'Come with me to the camp by the dam!' Jan yelled to Petrus, pointing towards the *vlei*. He strode down the slope, his boots

238

gathering damp earth. He did not mind the rain. It was invigorating, full of growing.

'These are the last, then home and dry,' he said to Petrus as they crossed the district road that led up through Blackheath towards Melvynside. Jan closed the gate across it so that the flock would not be diverted when they went over into the home camp at the other side. The sheepdog ran ahead.

Elizabeth awoke. It was cold. The sun had disappeared behind grey clouds. She sat up and shivered. She went inside and changed into slacks and a jersey and brushed her hair thoughtfully in front of the mirror. She stood at the window, drew back as lightning tore across a distant hill. The rain came suddenly—as it always did—plummeting from the sky. Within minutes runnels of mud were sluicing down the garden terraces and the drive.

Elizabeth searched for the car keys among the bottles and cosmetics on the dressing table. She found them, took Adrian's overcoat from the suitcase and Cedric's mackintosh from the hall stand. Throwing a scarf over her hair she ran across the driveway to their big grey car. She climbed in and shook the raindrops from the scarf.

She drove out of the gates and down the road towards Blackheath and Brakkloof. She switched on the car radio but it only crackled and faded with static, whining with the rhythm of the windscreen wipers. The wheels slid on the mud. The chassis banged and bumped as she drove over stones. She went on nervously, peering through the rain.

Jan saw the big Mercedes slither to a standstill at the closed gate. The goats jostled ahead of him, reluctant to move. Wiping the rain from his eyes he hurried towards the car. Elizabeth wound down the window.

'Hello Elizabeth,' he said cheerfully. 'Sorry I closed the gate on you but I must chase these goats across. It's almost impossible to drive them in the rain. I'll open it as soon as we get them into the other camp. I didn't realize you were down. Where are you going by yourself in this weather?'

'Adrian and Uncle Cedric walked over to Brakkloof just

after lunch,' she said coolly. 'Now that it's pouring I thought I'd better fetch them.'

'Don't try and cross the causeway at Koen's, Elizabeth,' said Jan. 'It's very low and the river's quite full anyway. It overflows with the smallest rain. You could wet your distributor.'

Elizabeth looked scared. 'I'm not even sure I know the way.' She hesitated. Her mouth puckered a little.

'No need to get upset,' he said. 'I'll come with you.'

'It's OK,' she said abruptly. 'I'll manage if you tell me where to go.'

'I'm getting bloody wet just standing here talking,' he replied. He grinned down at her. 'Move up, I'll drive you. I can't let you get stuck in the mud.'

She gave him a small, reluctant smile and slid over into the passenger seat.

'Petrus!' Jan yelled. 'Take the goats in and tell *Nkosazan*' to bring the truck and fetch me at the drift at Brakkloof.' Petrus put his hand to his ear. 'The drift at Brakkloof!' shouted Jan. 'I'll wait there.'

Petrus nodded. He whistled to the sheepdog and urged the goats on towards the shelter of the *kraal*.

Jan opened the gate. He went back to the car. 'I'm wet as hell, Elizabeth. Do you have something for me to sit on so I don't bugger up the seat?'

'Take this,' she said, handing him Adrian's coat. 'You must be freezing.'

Jan climbed in behind the wheel and started the engine.

'This rain is too bloody much!' said Adrian gloomily. 'All my life to be stuck in a shed with cobras and rats!'

'And most of all—me for company!' said Cedric jovially. He lit a cigarette and said, 'I'm sure your dear wife will come to the rescue.'

'She hasn't a clue how to get here.'

'Well, we'll just have to stay the night or walk up to Black-heath.'

'Rather stay the night!' said Adrian. 'Jan hasn't apologised yet.'

240

Cedric drew on his cigarette and said, 'That's asking a bit much, Adrian. It's not a matter of apologies. I told Jan what I thought before he took the police to court. We knew where we stood with each other. We agreed to differ. Life's too damned short for vendettas. Besides,' said Cedric grudgingly, 'when all's said and done he's got his principles—you can't blame a chap for that. Young fellows are impulsive, especially when their women push them into things. He'll learn the hard way. But, you mark my words, he's a good lad, one of the best.'

Adrian leaned against a goat pen and looked at Cedric sceptically, not wishing to consider the truth. He had decided long ago that it was Jan who must ask for a reconciliation. After that he would see. He gnawed at his lip and gazed at the rain.

Elsa pulled on her mackintosh and went outside. She leapt across a puddle, her keys jingling in her pocket. Nella waved from the kitchen door. 'Tombi and Chrissie and me will make tea for you and Daddy when you come back, Mama,' she cried.

'Thanks, love,' called Elsa. 'Won't be long.'

She clambered into the truck and backed it out of the shed. She turned into the road and drove towards Brakkloof.

'Here's Liz!' cried Adrian.

'There! I told you!' said Cedric. They could see the big car, squat as a toad, toiling down the track.

'I hope to God she doesn't try to get over the causeway,' said Cedric. 'I don't know why Jaap never built a decent crossing.'

'I'd better go and stop her,' said Adrian. 'It's the kind of damned-fool thing she'd do!'

'Just a minute!' said Cedric. 'Jan's with her!' He watched Jan climb out of the car and go down to the drift to check the level of the water. 'Thank God she had the sense to bring him.'

Adrian did not comment.

241

Abedingo Ngubane peered out of the small window of the pantry. He had heard the car, had seen it draw up. He knew that car. He knew it well. Many times he had washed it with a rag in the yard of Blackheath. He saw the big man get out, the man who'd shot his brother Sipho. He saw him walk towards the causeway, the collar of his coat turned up against the rain. Abedingo checked the rifle's breach.

Jan went back to Elizabeth and said, 'The river's not too high over the bridge but I'd rather walk across. Adrian and Uncle Cedric must be in the house. I'll go and see.'

'I'll come with you,' said Elizabeth. 'I've never been inside before.'

'Liz,' said Jan, as he led her over the causeway, the water dividing around their ankles, 'why don't you all come back to Blackheath and get dry and have something to eat. Elsa and I would like that.' He smiled reassuringly at her. 'We would, you know.'

'That would be nice, Jan,' she said, not looking at him. 'The only thing is—I don't know if Adrian would.'

Jan nodded. 'The invitation is open any time.'

The rain squalled in, in gusts. 'Run!' said Jan, putting out his hand to her.

'Jan!' Cedric shouted, his hands cupped round his mouth, as he stood at the door of the shed high above the river. But Jan did not hear his voice over the drumming of the rain.

'They've gone to the house,' said Adrian.

'We'll be as wet as hell by the end of this anyway,' said Cedric. 'Let's go.'

They pulled the shed door closed behind them and started down the slope, water streaming from the sodden brims of their hats.

From the bend beyond the farm gate, Elsa could see Jaap Koen's old house. The cypress trees hunched black as crows around it. She jolted on. Way below her Adrian's big car was parked in the *veld* by the drift. Jan and Elizabeth were trudging up the muddy path towards the front verandah.

Jan tried the front door. It was unlocked but the wind,

the dryness and then the damp of the August rains had jammed it tight within its frame. He put his shoulder to it, pushed, kicked with his boot. It flew open.

'God, what a gloomy old place!' said Elizabeth, following him in.

They went to the living room. The yellow wood floor gleamed honey pale despite the dust. Elizabeth turned round, staring up at the moulded ceiling. Jan did not hear what she was saying, for standing there in the entrance of the old house, where the Victorian fireplace, made from cast iron and surrounded by tiles decorated with delicate cream and butter water lilies, lay empty and dusted with soot, he remembered Freek—so long ago, another lifetime—caught an instant by a girder, high above the raging torrent of the gorge and the wind breaking up like surf against the grey curve of the dam wall. He turned away from Elizabeth and her exclamations and walked slowly down the passage.

Elsa climbed out of the bakkie and ran towards the causeway. At the other side of the house, splashing down among the thorn scrub past the workers' huts, she could see Adrian and Cedric. They disappeared behind the hedge that bordered the back *stoep*. She waded onto the bridge, arms held out to balance herself against the fierce tug of the current.

Abedingo Ngubane and the man crouched in the shadow of the pantry door. The rain beat at the corrugated iron of the roof, crept in through the joints of the ceiling, dripped down, drop by drop onto the floor. They heard the footsteps of a man walking slowly through the house. Abedingo Ngubane waited, the rifle ready in his hands.

Jan opened the door to the kitchen. The shutters were closed. It was dark but for the wedge of light that fell across the brickwork where the back door stood ajar. He could hear the flat splash of water dripping, dripping onto the linoleum. He stood at the threshold, accustoming his eyes to the gloom.

Abedingo was ready. The butt of the gun was cool against his cheek but as he slid his finger to the trigger Adrian clattered up the back steps and thrust open the door with his foot, seeing, in that moment, the dark figure hunched just within the pantry, the brief silhouette against the small pane of the window, the gleam of metal.

'*Boet,*' he said—a touch of anxiety—'is that you?'

But Abedingo did not hesitate. He held his aim.

At the sound of his brother's voice Jan turned and stepped into the kitchen.

The shot was sharp, explosive—but there was no answering echo, no reply from the *krantzes* of the Rooikloof or the sentinal stones above the *bult*. The report was drowned in mud and the rushing of the rain.

Elsa, scrambling up the path, hesitated, looked around, trying to define the sound. She saw two figures moving out across the hill. The doorway and the windows of the house were black and silent. And then, above the wind, she heard Elizabeth. Somewhere far away it seemed, Elizabeth was screaming.

Elsa ran into the house. Her footsteps echoed through the empty rooms. She reached the threshold of the kitchen, stopped bewildered. For an instant Elsa stood transfixed. Then she put her hands before her face and turned away.

She had no voice to say his name.

# GLOSSARY

**Afrikaans
Words:**

| | |
|---|---|
| *Baas* | boss, master |
| *Bakkie* | truck |
| *Bantu* | a one-time official word for a black person, now derogatory |
| *Berg-wind* | hot wind |
| *Besembos* | exotic shrub |
| *Biltong* | strip of dried meat |
| *Blesbok* | type of antelope |
| *Bliksem!* | bastard (slang, not always as strong) |
| *Boerewors* | local sausage, eaten at braais, or barbecues |
| *Boerboon* | farmer's bean |
| *Boet* | brother |
| *Bok-bok* | game, like leap-frog |
| *Boklam* | small one, little lamb (endearment) |
| *Bossies* | mad, off one's head |
| *Braai* | barbecue |
| *Bulbul* | common, small, fruit-eating bird |
| *Bult* | hill, ridge |
| *Dagga* | cannabis |
| *Dassie* | rock hyrax; small mammal found in veld |
| *Dikkop* | large plover-like ground bird |
| *Doek* | square scarf or cloth covering woman's head |
| *Dompas* | compulsory identity document carried by black people |
| *Donga* | gulley, ditch |
| *Duiker* | common, small antelope |
| *Fishmoth* | silverfish |
| *Garingboom (pl garingbome)* | plant of the sisal family |
| *Gwarri* | indigenous shrub or small tree |
| *Hadihah* | large ibis |

| | |
|---|---|
| *Hamerkop* | large brown wading bird, feared by traditional people as bird of evil omen |
| *Helanca* | synthetic fabric |
| *Hout* | derogatory word for black person |
| *Kannabos* | common species of indigenous tree |
| *Kapokbos* | common small shrub in Karoo, with cotton-like flowers |
| *Karee* | indigenous shrub or tree |
| *Kiepersol* | cabbage tree (Cussonia species) |
| *Kleinboet* | younger brother |
| *Kleintjie* | little one |
| *Kloof* | ravine |
| *Koggelmander* | large blue-headed lizard, dragon-like |
| *Kokerboom* (pl *kokerbome*) | quiver tree |
| *Koppie* | hill |
| *Koringkriek* | large insect |
| *Kraal* | enclosure for stock |
| *Krantz* | cliff |
| *Lekker bly* | stay well |
| *Munt* | derogatory word for black person |
| *Nasella grass* | exotic grass that spoils pasture |
| *Oke* | fellow |
| *Oom* | uncle |
| *Ouma* | grandmother. Also used as euphemism for menstruation |
| *Pencil-bait* | mollusc dug up in estuaries for bait |
| *Piet-my-Vrou* | red-chested cuckoo |
| *Poes is koning* | puss is king |
| *Pondok* | shack |
| *Poort* | entrance, pass |
| *Poppie* | dolly |
| *Rhebok* | type of antelope |
| *Rooikat* | caracal lynx |
| *Rusbank* | traditional wooden bench with hide-thonged seat |
| *Samoosa* | fried Indian pastry, popular in cafés |
| *Sneeze-wood* | species of hard-wooded indigenous tree |
| *Span* | team |
| *Sprew, spreeu* | common bird of the starling family |
| *Spruit* | stream, small river |
| *Stoep* | verandah |
| *Tecoma* | Cape honeysuckle |

| | |
|---|---|
| *Treks* | people who trek about the countryside with their belongings, doing odd jobs on farms |
| *Vasbyt* | Hang in there, keep going |
| *Veld* | the land, pasture |
| *Velskoen* | hide shoe, now refers more commonly to a commercially made rough suede ankle-boot or shoe |
| *Vlei* | marsh, swamp |
| *Witgat* | white-trunked indigenous tree |
| *Yellowbill* | species of duck |
| *Yirra!* | exclamation derived from 'Here, Lord' |

## Xhosa words:

| | |
|---|---|
| *Andazi* | I do not know |
| *Bayeza kusasa, bayeza* | they come tomorrow, they come |
| *Bhekile* | tin can for carrying food, billycan |
| *Dlakadlaka* | vagabond |
| *Ewe* | yes |
| *Godukani* | go home, all of you |
| *Hayi* | no |
| *Icashile* | it is hiding |
| *Induna* | tribal headman |
| *Ingqola* | toy car made of wire |
| *Ithinzi* | small grief or anxiety to trouble the spirit |
| *Kanti* | and even yet (typical, musing expression, showing there is another side to things) |
| *Kwedini* | boy |
| *Maas (amasi)* | Sour, curdled milk |
| *Makoti* | young wife |
| *Mama* | mother, respectful form of address |
| *Mazambane* | 'potato' farms, prison farms (Zulu word) |
| *Mazimuzimu* | mythical, one-legged cannibals |
| *Mfan'am* | my boy |
| *Mfo'wethu* | my friend |
| *Mlungu* | white man |
| *Molo* | hello, greetings |
| *Molo wethu* | hello all of you |
| *Mvelangqangi* | the great God, the Creator |
| *Nkonka* | bushbuck |

| | |
|---|---|
| *Nkosana* | young chief, respectful form of address |
| *Nkosazana* | young woman, respectful form of address |
| *Thekwane* | hammerhead bird, much feared by traditional people as bird of evil omen |
| *Tsiba!* | Jump! |
| *Ukutya* | food |
| *Xhosa* | a people of South Africa who speak Xhosa |
| *Yima!* | stop! |
| *Yintombazana* | it is a girl |
| *Yintoni?* | what is it? |
| *Yiza* | come |